Krysty's voice cried out, her blaster blazing steadily

More voices rang out, the smoke and the steel walls distorting their origins. The LeMat discharged five, six, seven times in a row, the last answered by an anguished scream. Slapping in a fresh clip, Ryan grunted his approval.

Suddenly he heard the sound of splintering wood, followed by the sound of two blasters firing together. Pocketing the gren, Ryan headed for the baron's home. As he jogged past a well, a spear stabbed out of the swirling fumes, the shaft coming so close it passed through his hair, ripping some out by the roots. Ignoring the pain, Ryan spun and fired from the hip. There was a meaty thump of a slug striking flesh, but no cry of pain.

A flintlock discharged, a revolver answered; then there was silence. Barely breathing, Ryan stood stock-still, straining to hear anything. But the eerie silence continued, seeming thicker than the clouds of gray smoke.

**Other titles in the
Deathlands saga:**

JAMES AXLER

DEATH LANDS®

Judas Strike

THE
SKYDARK
CHRONICLES
Book II

A GOLD EAGLE BOOK FROM
WORLDWIDE®

TORONTO • NEW YORK • LONDON
AMSTERDAM • PARIS • SYDNEY • HAMBURG
STOCKHOLM • ATHENS • TOKYO • MILAN
MADRID • WARSAW • BUDAPEST • AUCKLAND

To Abduhl Benny Hassan,
gone but not forgotten

First edition June 2001

ISBN 0-373-62564-2

JUDAS STRIKE

Copyright © 2001 by Worldwide Library.

Printed in U.S.A.

Beware of smiles. A heart-bound oath spoken with ease often means duplicity. Betrayal is a two-edged sword that can mortally strike your enemy while only wounding you— if you are wise, if you are ruthless, and if you know exactly when the betrayal will take place, and more importantly, by whom. Then the spiteful traitors will die in their own trap.

—Li Quan,
Warrior/philosopher
China, 700 B.C.

THE DEATHLANDS SAGA

This world is their legacy, a world born in the violent nuclear spasm of 2001 that was the bitter outcome of a struggle for global dominance.

There is no real escape from this shockscape where life always hangs in the balance, vulnerable to newly demonic nature, barbarism, lawlessness.

But they are the warrior survivalists, and they endure—in the way of the lion, the hawk and the tiger, true to nature's heart despite its ruination.

Ryan Cawdor: The privileged son of an East Coast baron. Acquainted with betrayal from a tender age, he is a master of the hard realities.

Krysty Wroth: Harmony ville's own Titian-haired beauty, a woman with the strength of tempered steel. Her premonitions and Gaia powers have been fostered by her Mother Sonja.

J. B. Dix, the Armorer: Weapons master and Ryan's close ally, he, too, honed his skills traversing the Deathlands with the legendary Trader.

Doctor Theophilus Tanner: Torn from his family and a gentler life in 1896, Doc has been thrown into a future he couldn't have imagined.

Dr. Mildred Wyeth: Her father was killed by the Ku Klux Klan, but her fate is not much lighter. Restored from predark cryogenic suspension, she brings twentieth-century healing skills to a nightmare.

Jak Lauren: A true child of the wastelands, reared on adversity, loss and danger, the albino teenager is a fierce fighter and loyal friend.

Dean Cawdor: Ryan's young son by Sharona accepts the only world he knows, and yet he is the seedling bearing the promise of tomorrow.

In a world where all was lost, they are humanity's last hope....

Prologue

On a brisk January afternoon, the United States of America disappeared in a thundering microsecond of nuclear fire.

Within a heartbeat, the governments of the world were gone, scattered to the searing radioactive winds. Every major city was reduced to glowing ruins under rumbling mushroom clouds, while tidal waves of boiling water swept along the coastlines of the continents. Mountains rose and fell, lakes were burned dry, volcanoes erupted at random and titanic earthquakes racked the landscape, shattering bridges and dams and changing the shape of the planet forever. In New York, London, Paris, Tokyo, millions perished in screaming agony before most people even realized what was happening. It was the end of civilization.

When the firestorms finally ceased, and the quakes calmed to gentle rumblings beneath the broken streets, the few survivors stumbled from the ruins of their homes only to discover that the telephones, radios, computers, automobiles and trucks that they depended upon were now useless lumps of plastic and steel. Advanced technology was gone. Glowing craters dotted the landscape, creating deadly deserts where once proudly stood thick forests, cool lakes and rich green fields.

The sky was dark for decades, the endless thunder and lightning heralding the deadly storms of acid rain, torrents of pollution that stripped the flesh off a body in only minutes. Humanity learned to hide from the lethal downpours, but then hordes of mutants rose from the radioactive craters, shambling creatures in every shape imaginable.

Dressed in rags, thousands fled the blackened ruins of the cities, hoping for a better life in the wilds. But the rad-blasted earth would not grow crops, and the scattered clean areas were viciously fought over. Crude cities—often surrounded by high walls—were built from the twisted scrap of the predark world to protect the patches of clean earth and to keep out the slavering muties. Safe behind the ramshackle walls, a primitive form of civilization started to evolve. However, these barbarous enclaves were brutally ruled by self-proclaimed barons and their private armies of sec men who walked the thick defensive walls. In any ville, to disobey a command from a baron meant instant death.

Hideous new diseases, savage cannibals, muties, slavers, acid rain, rad pits, that was America in the twenty-second century.

Welcome to the Deathlands.

Yet amid the madness and death, a handful of
fighters roamed the cursed earth of North America.
These companions were led by Ryan Cawdor, the
son of a baron.

Endlessly searching for some section of the world
where they could live in peace, the companions traveled incredible distances in relative safety because
they had access to the greatest scientific secret of
the predark world. Buried deep underground were
huge military bases called redoubts. Nuke-proof,
these fortified bunkers were powered by fusion generators and were safe havens of fresh air, electric
lights and clean water, their vanadium-steel doors
resistant to any conceivable attack. Designed to
house hundreds of soldiers, the secret bases had
originally been stocked with megatons of food, medical supplies, clothing and weapons. But sometime
soon after skydark, the troops disappeared, taking
almost all of the supplies with them, leaving only
the occasional MRE food pack or stray box of ammo
for the companions to salvage. A pair of boots here,
a can of oil there, yet these precious items gave them
the necessary edge to stay alive in the Deathlands.

Even more amazing than the redoubts themselves
were the mat-trans units. These incredible machines
were somehow able to shift objects from one redoubt to another in only seconds, no matter how
distant the second redoubt. Unfortunately, the
knowledge of how to precisely control a mat-trans

"jump" had been lost, so the friends had to make a blind jump into the unknown. Usually, it was only to an empty redoubt, once to an Alaskan redoubt full of weapons and food, and sometimes to a bunker full of muties that had forcibly penetrated the defensives of the underground base.

Arriving at a hand-built gateway, Ryan and the others found themselves trapped in the Marshall Islands of the South Pacific, one of which was the infamous Bikini Atoll, ground zero for dozens of nuclear bomb tests. The companions also arrived in the middle of a revolt against Lord Baron Kinnison, a disease-ridden drug addict who ruled the tiny villes of the rad-blasted islands with an iron fist.

With muties everywhere, the companions raced to regain the damaged gateway and escape, but were ambushed and blown off the side of a mountain to plummet helplessly into the cold sea....

Chapter One

Slowly, Ryan Cawdor awoke to the feeling of being dragged.

Rough grass moved along the back of his head, and as he tried to brush it away, he discovered that he couldn't move his arms. In a sudden rush of icy adrenaline, the one-eyed warrior fully awakened to see a giant three-foot-wide crab dragging him by the boots over a flat expanse of warm sand, its shiny black mandibles closed around his combat boots like a serrated vise. Somewhere nearby came the sound of waves breaking on a shore, and the tangy smell of salt was thick in the air.

What was going on? Where were the sec men from the PT boat? For a brief moment he had a flashback to the previous night and the fight on the bridge with the giant spider. Rockets came from the blackness of the ocean, explosions filled the world and he plummeted into the briny depths of the Cific Ocean along with the rest of the companions. Vague memories of fighting to stay afloat filled his mind, brutal currents pulling them into the night, away from the gunboat and the burning wreckage. Wher-

ever the hell he was now, it wasn't on any of the
islands he knew about. There were no mountains on
the horizon, no sounds of the jungle or the bitter
smell of a partially dormant volcano. He had to have
washed ashore someplace new. Which meant the sec
men could arrive at any moment. Those PT boats
were fast, and way too well armed, even if only with
black-powder blasters.

The weeds scratching at his bare skin, Ryan muttered a curse as he tried again to reach the 9 mm
SIG-Sauer pistol at his hip, but his right arm was
pinned down by mounds of sticky white goo covering most of his shirt. He was cocooned for dinner.

Fumbling with his left arm, Ryan found his belt
knife and clumsily drew the deadly curved length of
the panga. Awkwardly, he started sawing at the flex-
ible goop holding him prisoner, trying to be as subtle as possible. He had to get the blaster before the
crab noticed he was alive. Trapped like this, he
would be an easy chill for the big blue mutie. Those
pincers holding his boots looked as sharp as broken
glass.

But small as his movements were, the crab swiv-
eled the eyeballs at the end of slim stalks toward
him and abruptly released Ryan's boots to scuttle
over the man, drooling more wet goo from its segmented mouth onto his knife. The stuff was warm
and felt heavy, thicker than old honey. Almost instantly his movements were slowed.

The body of the mutie was out of his reach, so Ryan flipped the blade over and slashed sideways at the closest leg. The colorful chitin armor cracked and hot green blood pumped from the jagged wound. The crab retreated, squealing in agony, then turned in a circle and snapped its mandibles for the one-eyed man's vulnerable face. Ryan quickly jerked back, and only a snippet of his long black hair fell to the ground.

Too close! Thrusting his legs upward, the Deathlands warrior pinned the creature to his chest and started to stab wildly, more hot blood spraying from the savage cuts. Its legs thrashing about, the wiggling mutie squealed in pain, its mandibles snapping constantly, but it was unable to reach the flesh of its tormentor from the awkward angle. Ramming the blade into the back of the crab, Ryan moved the panga about inside, trying to cause as much internal damage as possible. A river of green blood began to pour out, and the knife slipped from his grasp. Ryan scrambled to reclaim the blade without releasing the mutie. His clothes were soaked with warm gore, and he knew the creature was dying. The battle would soon be over. Then from out of nowhere, two louvered tails arched into view from behind the crab and thrust for his face.

Throwing the mutie off, Ryan saw it land on its back, legs and twin scorpion tails thrashing madly about in the air as the creature fought to get upright again. This close, Ryan could see that the hooked barbs at the tips of the tails glistened with some sort of oily residue. Most likely poison.

Rolling to his feet, Ryan staggered a moment, trying to get his balance, and was surprised to find himself feeling so weak. How long had he been unconscious? It might have been days since he'd last eaten. Now that he was awake, his stomach felt like a rad crater, hot and empty. Swallowing saliva, he ignored the stomach cramps and started hacking at the sticky bonds once more. More than once Ryan slipped and cut himself, but he didn't care. Reaching the blaster was all that mattered.

Glancing around, Ryan saw he was in a vast field of low weeds, a warm breeze from the sea ruffling his long hair and clothing. Gulls circled high in the polluted sky, waiting to feed upon the loser of the battle. He wondered where the rest of his friends were. Could it be that he was only survivor of the bridge explosion? If so, then he had a major score to settle with Kinnison and his pretty-boy lieutenant. But first he had to reach his blaster.

Catching a root in its mandibles, the crab managed to flip itself over and immediately started to circle its prey. Still working on the goop, Ryan turned slowly to keep the creature directly in front. Warily, the huge crab moved forward only to retreat as Ryan clumsily brandished the blade. It knew what the knife could do, and it respected the danger, but there was no fear in its movements. Constantly bobbing behind the crab, the two barbed tails poised expectantly in the air, occasionally thrusting at Ryan in a feint. No dumb brute this.

The panga was making progress, but not fast enough. The goo on his chest was still tacky, and Ryan had to cut carefully to keep the blade from becoming stuck. The crab darted forward, and Ryan kicked sand in its face. It retreated, but not very far. As he strained against his bonds, a section of the material parted with a ripping sound and his right arm came free from the elbow down. Grimly, the one-eyed man clawed for the blaster at his side, a fingertip brushing against the checkered grip of the predark weapon and the crab charged again.

Waiting until the last moment, Ryan dived forward, going over the mutie, landing painfully on his shoulder and rolling to his feet. But now the panga was gone, dropped in the desperate maneuver.

Stingers waving, mandibles snapping, the crab tried to get behind the man, but Ryan spun on his heel and put his combat boot into its face with all of his strength. The impact jarred him to the bone, and the mutie scuttled away, its left eye completely gone, the orb crushed into fibrous pulp.

As the crab scurried back, on the offensive, Ryan kicked dirt into its face and shouted. It darted away in surprise, but came right back even faster than before. Ryan dodged, and they circled each other again. He tried for the blaster again, but simply couldn't get a satisfactory grip. Clear fluid dribbling from the ruin of its face, the crab shuffled around trying for a snap, always darting out of the way of the steel-toed boot.

Then Ryan spotted the panga in the muddled weeds and threw himself on the knife, fumbling in the sand for the handle. Sensing weakness, the crab rushed forward. Ryan reared back both boots and launched a double kick to its body. But the crab dodged, and the boots only struck one of its many legs. With a crack, the limb broke clean off and fresh blood flowed from the yawning pit in its shell.

Galvanized with the pain, the crab whipped both stingers around in a defensive pattern just as Ryan found the knife. Struggling to his knees, he hacked at the weakened goop on his right arm. Come on, almost there…

Suddenly, the crab charged and slashed out with both tails. Twisting out of the way, Ryan avoided one, but the other hit his thigh and searing pain exploded like electric fire. Gasping for breath, he sliced down with the panga and cut off the tip of the tail embedded in his thigh. Oily fluid pumped from the sheared stump, and the crab darted into the weeds.

Gritting his teeth, Ryan dropped the knife and recklessly plucked the slippery barb from his skin, throwing it away. But a numbness was starting to spread in the limb, and the one-eyed man knew he had only seconds before he was on the last train west. He was barely able to hold off the mutie; with a wound he wouldn't stand a chance.

Grimly, the Deathlands warrior put everything he had into forcing his right arm downward. A fingertip brushed cool metal, but that was all. Ryan ignored the growing lack of feeling in his left leg and raged against the cloying bonds. Tendons swelled and the remaining goo stretched a little. Gritting his teeth, he redoubled the effort, the predark shirt ripping slightly from the strain. Ryan gained an inch, his fingers almost going around the grip of the blaster. Minutes passed in the silent struggle, but the numbness in his leg was getting worse, and his breathing was labored, his physical resources depleted from starvation. Sweat was stinging the old cut on his palm, and it made his fingers slippery. Refusing to quit, Ryan snarled in defiance and rammed his arm down one last time, gaining another inch, but the blaster still eluded his grasp. Then the cuff button of his shirt snapped off, his arm came free and he had the weapon.

Only Ryan found that he still couldn't get it out of the holster. There still wasn't enough room to pull the blaster free. The crab scuttled from the weeds, and he turned to keep it in view. The creature was going to attack again, and Ryan couldn't chance another strike from its tail.

Having no choice, Ryan fell on his back and started to pull the trigger of the blaster, shooting through the bottom of the old leather holster. Caught in the open, the crab paused at the gentle cough of the silenced weapon, then jumped as it was hit by a 9 mm Parabellum round. The soft lead slug punched completely through the shell, shattering the chitin and exposing the pulsating organs inside. But instead of running, the mutie actually charged, the undamaged stinger lashing about insanely.

Firing nonstop, Ryan swung his legs after the side walker, tracking as best he could. The first couple of shots only scored furrows in its hard shell, but then a round slammed into the gaping shoulder wound. Organs burst apart as the slug plowed through the mutie. The barbed tail went instantly limp, the crab shuddered violently, then toppled over and went very still.

Keeping a close watch on the creature, a grunting Ryan reclaimed his knife and without any further interruptions was soon free from the imprisoning white goo.

"Tough bastard," he growled, pocketing the spent clip and sliding in one of his few remaining reloads. There was more ammo in his backpack, wherever the hell that was. It had to have fallen into the sea along with everybody else. He could only hope the others had also washed up on the same shore that he had. But he knew the backpack and the extra ammo were long gone. He had to save every round he could.

Then his oddly numb knee buckled, and the man got busy cutting away a section of his pants until the stab wound was exposed. The skin was white and puckered at the center, a bright red all around and very tender to the touch. Not good.

Wiping the blade clean on his shirt, Ryan played the flame of a predark butane lighter along the blade to sterilize it. Then he carefully sliced open the skin and a clear oily fluid oozed out. Good, the poison was still in the wound, not in his blood yet. He had a chance. Squeezing the area hard, Ryan kneaded the numb flesh until more transparent fluid came out, then some yellow pus and finally red blood.

Some feeling was returning, and the man braced himself for the next part. This was going to be bad, but without anybody to suck out any remaining poison he had no choice. Jacking the slide on his blaster, Ryan ejected a few rounds, cut off the wads of lead and poured the silvery powder directly into the raw wound. The nitro stung slightly, then he flicked the butane lighter into life and ignited the powder.

There was a sharp flash without smoke, and Ryan heard or saw nothing for several minutes as he rode out the explosion of pain. Slowly, the throbbing waves of hot torture ebbed, leaving his leg wrapped in throbbing anguish. Wiping the sweat off his face,

Ryan inspected the wound. All of the hair was burned off his thigh, and the flesh around the puncture was puckered with white ridges. Gently touching it, he found the area hurt like hell, but that only meant he had moved fast enough. The poison appeared to be gone.

Reaching for his canteen, Ryan cursed to find it missing, and made do with sucking a smooth pebble to curb his thirst. Using a clean handkerchief to bind the cauterized wound, he tried to stand and found that normal walking was impossible. The best he could do was a slow step and drag. He'd have to find a stick or something to use as a crutch if he was going to do much traveling. His longblaster would have been perfect, but that was with his backpack.

Shuffling over to the corpse of the mutie crab, Ryan saw its remaining legs were faintly twitching. A hunter since childhood, Ryan knew that lots of things moved slightly after they were chilled, but he had no intention of taking a chance on this bastard. Ruthlessly, he stomped the corpse, grinding the thing under the heel of his combat boot until there was no chance it could regenerate.

Satisfied for the moment, Ryan stood tall and glanced around. His next move was to find the others, and hopefully his backpack. But only low swells of sand with some patches of dry weeds were visible in every direction. Nothing else. Rubbing his chin,

Ryan wondered how long he had been unconscious. Could the crab have eaten six other people, and he was simply the last? But checking his beard, Ryan decided it had only been a day or two. Nowhere near long enough, unless there were a hell of a lot more of these crabs.

The sounds of the ocean came from several directions, and Ryan headed for the loudest waves. That should be the closest, and the beach was a logical place to start a recce. At first, the going was slow, his wounded leg stiff and unable to carry his full weight, but the pain diminished and strength returned after only a few dozen yards.

Reaching the crest of a dune, Ryan paused as his stomach loudly announced its emptiness with a long sustained rumble. Yeah, it had to have been a while since that big meal at Cold Harbor ville. Ryan searched his pockets for anything edible and found only sand. Turning, he glanced at the dead crab and saw that it was already covered with a flock of seagulls tearing the corpse apart with their needle-sharp beaks. The man touched his blaster, then decided against it. Raw gull tasted like he imagined used underwear would. He wasn't quite that hungry yet. Besides, he was down to the last full clip for the SIG-Sauer. Best to save every round until absolutely necessary. If he didn't find his backpack, there might not be any more.

Hobbling down the far side of the dune, Ryan

found the tracks where he had been dragged into the weeds and followed the marks with his blaster firmly in hand. The dune was cut with a rain gully that ended in a fan of small rocks, which extended across a pristine white beach. A hundred or so feet away lay a lone figure sprawled on the sand. Long flame-red hair covered the features, but the woman was wearing Khaki coveralls, a bearskin coat and blue Western boots decorated with the outline of a spread-winged falcon. There was no question it was Krysty Wroth, and her chest rose and fell in a regular pattern. She was alive.

As Ryan worked his way across the beach, a fat blue crab crawled into view from the other side of the supine woman and started dribbling white goo from its segmented mouth onto her right arm. In one smooth move, Ryan aimed and fired. The distance was fifty yards, but the soft-lead slug slammed the crab off the top of her breast and sent it tumbling into the ocean. The mutie hit with a splash and sank out of sight, leaving a trail of green blood in its descending wake.

Reaching the woman, Ryan checked her over quickly and was relieved when there were no signs of damage. "Krysty, it's me," he said softly, shaking her shoulder.

Her eyelids fluttered, then opened wide. "Ryan?" she croaked, her long hair flexing and moving around her lovely face as if the red filaments were endowed with a life of their own.

"Alive and well, lover," he answered gently.

Coughing hard, she tried to sit up and became instantly wide-awake. "Gaia! What's wrong with my arm?"

Drawing his knife, Ryan brought her up to date while cutting away the tacky goop. When he was finished, Krysty pulled her arm free from the white residue smeared on her coveralls. The material stretched but didn't rip. Rising carefully, she swayed for a moment, then stood easily, her animated hair a wild corona in the breeze.

"Any sign of the others?" Krysty asked, drawing her blaster and checking the weapon. Safe in its leather holster, the S&W .38 revolver was undamaged, the stainless-steel piece still shiny with oil. Cracking the cylinder, she ejected four spent shells and tucked them into a pocket of her bearskin coat before thumbing in fresh rounds. Without her pack, the woman was down to only five spare rounds for the revolver.

"Not yet," Ryan answered truthfully. "But we can search for them later. Gotta find some shelter for the night. It's getting dark, and those crabs will be a triple bitch to ace in the dark."

"Could use some food, too," Krysty said over the growling of her stomach. Briefly, her hands checked pockets and came up empty. Not even a used piece of gum. "Got your canteen? Mine was in my backpack."

He shook his head. "Same here."

"Gaia! Hopefully those washed onto the same island as us," Krysty said, remembering only a few days ago when the precious supplies had sunk into a shark-filled harbor. They had gotten them back, but at a terrible cost.

"Hell, I'm surprised any of us survived that rocket attack from the PT boat," he stated. "Got no idea how we stayed afloat in the water for so long."

Grunting in agreement, Krysty looked along the beach in both directions. The clean white sand was perfectly flat where the waves reached. Not a footprint was in sight.

"We could split up," Krysty suggested. "Go both ways and save time."

"Trader always said never to divide your forces in unknown territory," Ryan said, quoting his old teacher. "We'll go a hundred yards toward that dune, and if we don't find anything, we'll try the other way. Folks almost always turn to the right, do it automatically if they're hurt or confused."

Brushing some loose sand from her shaggy coat, Krysty studied Ryan for a moment, then smiled.

"Sounds good, lover," she agreed, putting some feeling into the words. "Lead the way."

The compact sand of the beach made for easy walking in spite of Ryan's bad leg, and the couple reached the turnback point in only a short time. After glancing around, Ryan started back when a motion in the sky caught Krysty's attention.

"Gulls," she said, pointing. "Might be circling a kill."

"Probably only some dead fish, but we better check," he agreed, rubbing the wound on his thigh. It was throbbing now, but nothing he couldn't handle.

Continuing onward, the man and woman went past a stinking pile of rotting seaweed. Just beyond that, the beach started to rise in irregular mounds of what they could tell were pieces of predark buildings and broken sidewalks. Wreckage from skydark. A fallen collection of marble and bricks blocked the way, and the pair was forced to wade waist deep into the surf to get past. Both kept a sharp watch for crabs, but none was in sight below the foamy waves.

Once back on the shore, Krysty stopped in her tracks and Ryan scowled as they saw the corpse of a gigantic spider sprawled in the wet sand farther down the beach. The mound of flesh rose more than six feet high, the splayed legs dangling loosely in the shallows. Its head was completely gone, the yellow-and-black body fur charred as if by fire, loose strips of flesh hanging off the gleaming white bones of an internal skeleton. And its entire length was covered with dozens of the blue crabs. Sharp pincers ripped away strips of the rotting flesh as the shelled scavengers steadily tore the spider apart. The skin writhed from endless motion inside the body, and a crab wiggled into view from the neck stump to pass out a glistening length of entrails. Some small crabs danced around the crowd of larger blues, occasionally darting forward to grab a morsel of food for themselves. The rest of the meat was being carried into the shoals by the bigger crabs. They disappeared beneath the waves, only to return moments later with empty pincers.

Frowning deeply, Ryan saw that he had fought one of the small crabs. These new ones were huge, and looked brutishly strong, their legs as thick as soup cans. He wondered if the companions had ridden the dead insect like a raft. Made sense.

In a flash of white, a gull dived from the sky toward the ripe corpse and a crab perched on the spider's back leaped into the air, slashing with both stingers. A spray of feathers went swirling, but the undamaged gull winged once more into the sky, crying loudly in frustration.

They fought in teams, Ryan realized, and with assigned tasks. Just how smart were the creatures?

"Too damn smart," Krysty said aloud, as if reading his thoughts.

"No sign of the others," Ryan said, studying the area for strips of cloth or human bones. "Best we check the other side. Just to be sure."

Thumbing back the hammer on her blaster, Krysty started to walk inland to go around the feeding ground. Ryan limped along as best he could, but a couple of the smaller crabs scuttled over to investigate. Once they were in the weeds and out of sight of their brethren, Ryan dispatched the muties with his silenced pistol, then Krysty crushed their heads under her boots to make sure the crabs stayed dead.

The muffled crunches of splintering chitin caught the attention of the large blue patrolling on top of the spider, and its eye stalks extended fully to watch as the two-legs traveled around the precious lump of food. Since they kept their distance and didn't threaten the horde, the big male saw no reason to attack them and continued its vigil against the winged predators in the sky.

Stopping on the crest of the dune, Ryan and Krysty could see there was nothing on the lee side of the huge corpse to indicate that any human had been slain by the crabs. But the lack of physical remains didn't raise any false hopes. It didn't mean the others were alive; it simply showed that their friends hadn't been chilled and eaten here.

"Back we go," Krysty said listlessly, holstering her piece.

"Later," Ryan countered, walking along the top of the dune heading toward a ragged cliff. "First, we eat."

Shielding her face with a cupped hand against the

setting sun, Krysty soon spied what he was referring to. Food, and lots of it.

Working their way back to the shore along a rocky arroyo, Krysty and Ryan splashed into an irregular bay dotted with hundreds of small tide pools. Basins of seawater had been trapped in depressions in the hard ground as the tide withdrew, accidentally leaving behind some of the bounty of the sea. Most of the puddles contained only water and colorful shells, but several were impromptu aquariums housing an assortment of small marine life, tiny fish, sea horses or waving kelp.

Kneeling in a pool, Ryan reached into the inches of water and came up with a fat oyster. "Dinner," he announced, tossing over the mollusk.

Krysty made the catch and eagerly pulled out a knife to open the hard shell. The oyster resisted and failed. "There must be hundreds of them," she stated, chewing steadily. "Enough food for months!" The raw meat was slimy but delicious. However, her stomach rumbled unabated, the tiny morsel barely denting her ravenous appetite.

Tossing her another, Ryan readily agreed. He took the third oyster himself, splitting the shell and slurping down the creature intact. Chewing would have only wasted time. Casting the empty shell aside, he started to pass Krysty another when he saw the woman was already splitting an oyster she had located.

Together, the couple waded across the basin raiding every tide pool, devouring the oysters equally. They almost feasted on a small squid, but the nimble creature squirted out oily black ink when captured and squirmed from Ryan's grasp to escape back into the rising sea.

"Too bad," Ryan said, washing his hands clean in a puddle. "They taste like chicken."

Spitting out a flawless pearl, Krysty started to make a comment when she was interrupted by the crackle of distant gunfire, closely followed by the dull thud of a black-powder gren.

"Sounds like us," she stated, sheathing the blade.

"Could be. Let's go see," Ryan said, and they began to splash toward the sounds of combat.

Chapter Two

Not far away, a group of armed people strode around the base of a predark lighthouse. Located at the far end of a sandbar that jutted into the ocean, the hundred-year-old structure was intact and undamaged from war or weather. The sloping walls of granite blocks were as strong as the day it was built, and the resilient Plexiglas panels unbroken around the crystal-and-glass beacon atop the tower.

The roof was covered with bird droppings, and piles of seaweed and driftwood partially buried under windblown sand were banked against the base of the tower. The white paint had been removed by sheer passage of time to expose the blue-veined granite blocks composing the building. Unfortunately, there was no door in sight, and fat blue crabs were underfoot everywhere. It seemed as if the more the companions shot, the more crawled out of the water. It was as if the damn creatures were attracted to explosions.

Swinging his shotgun off his shoulder, J. B. Dix rammed the stock of the weapon against the side of the lighthouse. The resulting thud gave no indication of weakness, or even of empty space beyond the adamantine material. The lighthouse was a fortress.

Adjusting his glasses, the wiry man returned the shotgun to its usual position over his shoulder slung opposite the Uzi machine pistol.

"Nothing," he said, rubbing his unshaved chin. "Anybody got some ideas?"

"Well, the balcony is too high to reach," Dr. Mildred Wyeth stated, her hand resting on a canvas bag slung over one shoulder. The faded lettering M*A*S*H was almost unreadable, but the bag was neatly patched and contained a meagre store of medical supplies.

Held at her side was a sleek Czech ZKR target pistol, a state trooper gun belt with attached holster strapped over her regular belt. Loops for extra ammo ringed the gun belt, but most of them were empty. The vacant sheath of a small knife peeked from her left boot, and a long thin dagger bearing the logo of the Navy SEALs hung from her belt.

Just then, something blue scuttled around the side of the lighthouse, closely followed by three men armed with blasters, their faces grim and unsmiling. As the crab came close, J.B. crushed it underfoot. The shell burst apart, and the hideously mangled mutie started thrashing about.

"Bastard things are everywhere," Dean Cawdor complained, kicking the bleeding creature into the waves. It disappeared with a splash. "I killed six more on the other side."

"Good," J.B. snorted. "The more aced the better."

The young boy nodded in agreement. Almost twelve years of age, Dean was beginning to resemble his father in frightening detail and already carried himself with the calm assurance of a seasoned combat veteran. A Browning semiautomatic pistol was in his hand, jacked and ready for trouble. There was a slash across his denim shirt, showing some badly bruised ribs, minor damage incurred from the exploding bridge at Spider Island. A fat leather pouch hung from his belt distended with ammo clips, but the pack rode high, telling of scant ammo in the precious collection of magazines. An oversize bowie knife rode at the small of his back with easy access for either hand.

The nearby waves gently crested on the rough shoreline, foaming and breaking endlessly. A seagull winged silently overhead, something small and wiggling held tight in its deadly beak.

"Normally, a lighthouse would be placed on a cliff or jetty to maximize visibility," Mildred said thoughtfully, gazing at the railing that encircled the walkway around the beacon on the top level. "Must have been some major earthquakes to move it to sea level."

"Built to withstand the worst weather possible,"

J.B. said. "Only reason it's still standing after sky-dark."

"It doesn't matter," Dean said. "There's no door, so I say we keep walking along the beach." He hitched up his belt. "We haven't even covered half of the island yet."

"Very true, my young friend," Dr. Theophilus Algernon Tanner rumbled. In a frock coat and frilly shirt, the silver-haired gentleman appeared to be from another era, which, in fact, he was. "Yet the panoramic view offered by the sheer height of this construct should be invaluable in helping to locate your father and Krysty."

Doc's clothes were of the finest material and patched in a dozen places. He was leaning on an ebony swordstick, the silver lion's head peeking out between his fingers, and a mammoth revolver was hung at his waist. The LeMat was a Civil War weapon holding nine .44 rounds, with a single shot-gun round under the main barrel. The blaster used black powder, not cordite, but the solid lead mini-balls did more damage than a sledgehammer at short range.

"Besides, with the tide comes those damn crabs," Mildred added grumpily, watching the shoreline for any sign of the nasty muties.

"Indeed, madam. Our local cornucopia of ante-diluvian crustace is merely another reason why shelter for the night is mandatory," Doc espoused, baring his astonishingly white teeth.

"Still gotta get inside," Dean stated stubbornly.

"Tower short," Jak Lauren said, crossing his lean, muscular white arms.

A true albino, the teenager was dressed in camou fatigues with a bulky Colt Python .357 Magnum hung from his belt. An ammo pouch lay flat at his opposite hip. His camouflage leather jacket was decorated with bits of shiny metal and feathers, and more than one sec man had seized the teenager by the lapels only to have his fingers cut off by the razor blades sewn into the lining. At present, the arms of his jacket were tied around his waist, showing a lot of his pale skin. His hair was shoulder length and bone-white, his red eyes peering out of his scarred face like ruby lasers. More than a dozen leaf-bladed throwing knives were hidden on his person, with two more tucked into his belt. The handle of a gravity knife was visible in his left combat boot.

"Is it?" Dean asked suspiciously. "Looks okay to me."

Doc walked closer to the structure as if seeing it for the first time. "By the Three Kennedys, it *is* too short," he stated in agreement. "By necessity, lighthouses are always tall, sixty to eighty feet high. This is only, say, thirty."

The man glanced at the ground. "The lower half

must be buried beneath the sand. The front door must be buried, twenty, thirty feet underground."

"It'll take days to dig that deep by hand," Mildred said, scowling. There was already traces of purple on the horizon. Night was coming fast.

"Try a gren," Dean suggested.

"Only got one," J.B. answered, titling back his fedora. "I'm saving that for an emergency."

"If we could reach the balcony," Mildred continued thoughtfully, "then getting inside would be no problem. Even if the door is locked, we could go through the lens itself. Those were made of glass to withstand the searing heat of the beacon."

J.B. removed his hat, smoothed down his hair, then replaced it. "Sounds good. But how do we get up there?"

"Mayhap there is another way in," Doc rumbled.

Going to the lighthouse, Doc put his back to the building and gazed out over the field. He appeared to be counting under his breath.

"There!" Doc said, and walked briskly to the end of the sandbar where there was a short stack of rocks covered with seaweed. Removing handfuls of the soggy greenery, Doc exposed not jumbled rocks, but broken bricks. Tossing them aside, he soon exposed a perfectly square hole that went straight down and out of sight.

"It's a chimney," J.B. said with a grin, slapping

the man on the back. "Good work, Doc. I didn't know a lighthouse would have a house attached."

"A cottage, actually," Doc replied primly. "But yes, many do."

Cupping his hands as protection from the sea breeze, Jak lit a match and dropped it down the opening. The tiny flame fluttered away and was gone. The teenager then lit another and stuck his entire head into the passage.

"Too small me," his voice echoed, and he stepped away from the chimney. "Mebbe Dean, too."

Dubiously, the boy eyed the flue, then used a stick to measure the opening, then himself. "Tight," he agreed, and slid his backpack to the ground. He removed his canteen and belt knife, then unbuckled his gun belt and took off the ammo pouch.

"I'm going to need every inch to get down that," Dean stated, shucking his Army jacket.

"What if filled with crabs?" Jak asked point-blank. "Trapped where no help, no light. Candles iffy."

"Here, this will help," Mildred said, rummaging in her med kit to extract a small flashlight. She squeezed the handle on the side of the device several times to charge the ancient batteries, and flicked the switch. The light was weak, but still serviceable.

Dean accepted the flashlight and tucked it into his shirt for safekeeping. Then he double-checked his blaster, making sure there was a round under the hammer for instant use.

"You see or hear any of the blues, get out of there fast," J.B. said sternly. "Just cut and run."

The boy nodded in agreement, his thoughts private.

"Now, lad, there should be plenty of ropes and tackle near the base of the tower," Doc said, the wind blowing his hair across his face like silver rain. "Along with torches and cork jackets to rescue people from drowning. Just toss a line over the balcony and we shall climb up."

"Gotcha." Dean climbed onto the pile of rubble and carefully slid his legs into the brick-lined darkness. He wiggled back and forth a bit, going lower with each move, until his hips passed the top of the flue and he unexpectedly dropped. J.B. and Jak both snatched a wrist, but Dean had already stopped himself by grabbing the top layer of bricks.

"Thanks," he panted, shifting his stance in the flue until his boots were more solidly braced on the rough surface. "I'm okay now."

The adults released the boy, and he started into the darkness once more. The rest of the companions backed away from the hole to allow the greatest amount of the dying sunlight to illuminate his way. In only a few moments he was gone from sight.

"How you doing?" J.B. called after a while.

"Busy," the boy's voice echoed back upward, closely followed by a muffled curse.

Long minutes passed with only the sound of the surf and the breeze disturbing the peaceful ocean front peninsula. Overhead, the always present storm clouds began to darken as the setting sun drained all color from the world, the shadows growing long and thick. Doc and Jak began to gather driftwood into a pile for a campfire.

"How much longer do we give him?" Mildred asked, brushing back her tangled mass of beaded locks.

Rubbing his chin to the sound of sandpaper, J.B. scowled. "Long as it takes. We don't have a way to go down there and check on him."

"Good thing there is no sign of those accursed PT boats," Doc rumbled, looking out over the sea. "At present, we are prepared neither to wage war nor to retreat."

"Got that right." Mildred sighed. "I'm down to ten rounds."

Feeling uneasy, J.B. unfolded the wire stock on the Uzi. "What had Jones called the baron again?"

"Kinnison," Jak answered, whittling on a piece of wood with a knife. The pile of tinder grew steadily under his adroit ministrations. "Called him Lord Bastard, too."

Suddenly, a sharp whistle sounded twice from the weeds and stunted brush growing inland, and the companions dropped into combat positions, taking cover behind the bricks. Working the bolt on his machine pistol, J.B. replied to the call with one long whistle. It was answered by the same, and everybody relaxed as Ryan and Krysty rose into view, holstering their blasters.

"You're hurt," Mildred said, rushing forward and kneeling to probe Ryan's wounded leg.

The Deathlands warrior inhaled sharply at the contact of her fingers. "Just a scratch," he grunted. "I got the poison out and cauterized the hole."

"Maybe. Better let me be the judge of that," the physician said, untying the torn pieces of cloth. Closely, she looked over the puckered scar, shiny and new among many older ones.

"Well?" he said in controlled impatience.

"It's clean enough," Mildred reported, tying the strips of cloth closed again. "And thankfully not infected. But it must hurt like hell."

"Pain means you're still alive," Ryan muttered, then glanced around. "Where's Dean, on patrol?"

"Down chimney," Jak replied, jerking a thumb. "Finding door for lighthouse."

His face a stone mask, Ryan limped to the pile of bricks and looked down the hole. He whistled sharply and waited, but there was no response.

"Any other way inside?" Ryan asked.

J.B. snorted. "Not that we could find. Lighthouse

has got solid granite walls. Need a C-4 satchel charge to even dent the place.''

As Ryan limped over to the lighthouse, Doc started to offer the man his ebony stick, then thought better of the gesture. Ryan would never take it. Not from foolish macho pride, but with one of them possibly in danger the man wouldn't have the time to spare thinking about his own pain. In the *New York Herald* of his day, Doc sometimes read of officers whose troopers claimed they would charge with them straight into hell. The scholar had never met such a person until Ryan freed him from a slave pit so very long ago.

Another crab scuttled by, and Jak caught the mutie in his hand, keeping well clear of the scorpion tails. ''Wonder if good eat?'' the teenager asked. The eye stalks of the creature extended fully, and it stared at the albino as if in open hatred. It unnerved him slightly how much intelligence there seemed to be in its steady expression.

With a gentle laugh, Krysty pointed to the east. ''There's an oyster bed in a tide pool some hundred yards that way with enough to feed an army.''

''Excellent, madam. Exemplary!'' Doc stated, lifting an imaginary hat to the redheaded woman. ''Once more you are the source of our succor.''

Jak tossed the crab away, uncaring where it landed. The mutie hit the beach on its back just in time for a wave to flip it over, and it hastily disappeared into the briny foam.

"I fill sack," the teenager stated, and took off at a run.

"Speaking of which," J.B. said, walking over to a slab of bare rock and lifting up a canvas bag. "Here are your backpacks. They washed ashore near us couple of miles down the beach."

Krysty took them both and passed one to Ryan. The packs were torn in spots, probably from coral reefs, and still damp from the ocean, but were still okay.

Easing the longblaster free from the tangled straps, Ryan briefly checked the Steyr SSG-70 sniper rifle for damage. He worked the bolt a few times to make sure sand and salt hadn't gummed the works. The carriage moved smoothly, chambering a 7.62 mm brass round from the transparent plastic clip.

"Some sand in the barrel," Ryan announced, sliding the weapon over a shoulder, "but no blockage." He had actually felt off balance with the longblaster gone.

Going through the backpack, he used his big hands to squeeze excess moisture from the stiff canvas. Everything inside smelled dank, especially the dog-hair socks, but nothing seemed seriously damaged. Satisfied for the moment, Ryan stuffed some more rotary clips for the Steyr into his jacket pocket and filled the ammo pouch on his belt with clips for the SIG-Sauer. He was still very low on ammo, but better armed now then he was before.

Closing her backpack, Krysty tossed away a handful of soggy mush that had once been dried fish wrapped carefully in banana leaves. The sagging glob of food smelled rancid, and she heaved it into the weeds. Immediately, insects began to converge on the unexpected bounty.

"Any idea where we might be?" Krysty asked, sliding her pack onto her back. "Got no idea which island this is," J.B. answered, touching the minisextant hanging around his neck. "The sun has been behind clouds since I woke up. Never once got a chance to fix our position. This doesn't look like Spider Island, though. Too barren. No mountains."

But the woman barely heard the man's reply. Her hair wildly flexing, Krysty was listening to the wind. What was that odd sound? It was like hard rain hitting a tin roof, only lower, softer. How odd.

"Well, we can't be too far away," Mildred said. "Without a raft of some kind, we couldn't have stayed afloat in the water for very long, even if the currents were with us."

Ryan started to explain about the dead spider when a pistol shot rang out and Jak burst into view over the low sand dune. He paused at the crest to fire two more rounds, then raced toward the companions.

"Crabs!" the teenager shouted in warning just as a horrible blanket of blues swarmed over the dune, their armored bodies covering the ground for yards.

"Chill them all!" Ryan shouted, sliding the Steyr SSG-70 off his shoulder and working the bolt. It was the big crabs from the spider carcass. They had to have been following him and Krysty to see if they could find more people. And he led them right here.

Snarling in fury, Ryan fired and a blue exploded, spraying its guts over a dozen others. But the rest of the pack kept coming, and even as Ryan fired again, chilling another, he already knew there were a hell of a lot more crabs than they had ammo.

"Bastards are enormous!" J.B. muttered, firing short bursts from the Uzi. The 9 mm rounds wreaked havoc along the front ranks, but even as they fell the others scuttled callously over their fallen brethren.

As the rest of the companions opened fire with their blasters, spent brass flying everywhere, Doc slid the ebony stick into his belt, drew the LeMat and set the selector pin from the shotgun round to the .44 cylinder. Cocking the huge hammer, Doc began firing point-blank at the nearest crabs. A lance of flame stabbed through the billowing black cloud that thundered from the maw of the huge weapon. A three-foot-wide crab literally exploded under the trip-hammer arrival of the .44 miniball, then there came the musical twang of a ricochet from an outcropping near the chimney. Doc savagely grinned and dropped flat the ground to fire again. The solid lead miniball plowed through the first crab, blowing the shell off its body, and continued on to chill two more. Then one of the small pale blue crabs darted for his face, and Doc scrambled to his feet. Only to find the tiny mutie was clinging to his silvery locks with its pincers, while its scorpion tails probed for his eyes. He slapped the weapon at the crab, and there was a sharp tink as a barbed tail bounced off the steel barrel.

"Damn it!" the scholar cursed, cocking back the hammer.

"Hold still!" Mildred ordered, and with lightning speed she sliced off a chunk of the man's hair with a knife. The crab landed among the boots of the companions and was stomped in a second.

Glancing at the crushed crab, Mildred spied the war over the rancid fish, the beetles covered with ants, being eaten alive. The symbolism rattled her nerves, and the physician dropped a round while frantically shoving ammo into her empty blaster. Her hands hadn't shaken this bad since her first autopsy as a med student. Then the woman forced herself calm and began to eliminate the muties with surgical precision. It was them or her. End of discussion.

Through the fading light of the setting sun, the friends could see that the tide was steadily rising, the waves crashing high on the peninsula, spraying them with salt water. How high it would go they had no idea. To their knees, waist, more? Plus, every gunshot seemed to attract more of the muties, the scattered array quickly becoming a solid mass of the squat invaders.

"Put your back to the wall!" Krysty shouted, throwing herself backward.

The companions followed her lead, and safe from one direction, they tried to coordinate their firepower. Only now, tiny crabs raced over their boots, and one managed to climb inside the torn leg of Ryan's fatigues. He swung the wounded leg against the lighthouse, crushing the mutie. The noise made the rest arch their stingers in shocked reply, and the horde advanced, their barbed tails stabbing forward constantly.

Stomping on another crab, Jak dropped the spent brass from his weapon and slid his last four rounds into the cylinders of the Colt Magnum pistol. That was it for ammo. Thirty feet away, a large adult crab snapped its pincers in the air at the teen, and Jak flicked his arm. A second later, a leaf-bladed knife slammed into the mutie's face, and it went stock-still, paralyzed or dead from the attack.

The SIG-Sauer coughing hot lead death, Ryan cursed under his breath. If he didn't know better, the man would swear the crabs were sending their old and young to attack the companions, keeping their big adults in reserve, so the companions would waste ammo on the weakest members of the horde. Was that possible?

"Ignore the little ones!" Ryan shouted, holstering his blaster and unslinging the Steyr SSG-70. "Chill the adults!"

J.B. passed the Uzi to Mildred and swung around the S&W M-4000 shotgun. Pumping the action, he frowned at how stiff the slide was. It had to be choked by salt residue. It still worked, but not very well. Aiming at the biggest group of crabs, J.B. fired and the deafening spray of fléchettes from the shotgun blew away the sea creatures by the score, chunks and pieces flying everywhere. J.B. fired three more times, destroying the front line of the clattering muties, then reloaded as fast as possible. The rest of the adult muties hastily retreated, the old and young scuttling about in total confusion.

"How many you got left?" Ryan demanded, working the bolt on the Steyr to clear a jammed round from the breech.

"Ten more shells," J.B. reported, thumbing a fat cartridge into the belly of his weapon. There were loops sewn into the shoulder strap used for carrying the scattergun, most of them empty now. "And there's gotta be fifty or sixty more of these things."

A crab was on the wall beside him, and Ryan crushed it flat with the heavy wooden stock of his longblaster. They could try to blow a path through the gathering creatures and escape off the peninsula, but it was too close for a gren. Besides, the crabs would only follow until the companions dropped from exhaustion and were overrun. Hundreds to six were bad odds in any fight. And even with the fresh ammo, he was down to thirty rounds for the SIG-Sauer, and even less for the Steyr.

Jak shot a crab off Mildred's leg, then holstered his piece. Krysty placed three .38 shells in his hand, and the teen nodded in thanks as he hastily reloaded. The main reason he carried the Colt Magnum blaster was the fact it could use both .357 rounds and regular .38 ammo. More than once that had kept him off the last train west.

"Dean, hurry!" Krysty shouted at the top of her lungs, blowing away an old blue with deep scars in its chitin armor. There was no reply from the lighthouse or chimney, and she sent a silent prayer to Gaia to watch over the boy. He was alone in the dark; at least they were in a group.

"Here they come again," J.B. shouted, readying his weapon. The crabs were advancing once more, but slower this time, as if testing the deadly firepower of the two-legs. They had seen what the shotgun could do and were afraid now.

The cylinder of his blaster empty, Doc slid the selector pin to his one shotgun round. After that, he'd be down to hammering the creatures with the gun butt. The sword hidden inside his ebony stick would be useless against these armored muties.

Conserving ammo, Krysty and Mildred both waited until the last moment to fire. Crabs died, but the horde kept advancing as steadily as the rising tide.

"We could try for the ocean," Doc suggested above the clacking of the creatures. "Crabs do not swim well, and we could easily outdistance them in deep water."

"We gotta get some distance first," Ryan stated, firing a fast three times. Two more crabs died; the third was only wounded, green blood seeping from the gash in its thick shell.

"Got any plas or grens?" he asked, brushing black hair off his face with the hot baffle silencer.

The Armorer reached into his munitions bag and passed over the last. Ryan ripped off the safety tape, twisted loose the firing pin, dropped the handle and dropped the charge on the ground directly at their feet. Instantly, the companions broke ranks and raced around opposite sides of the lighthouse while the crabs poured after them, sensing victory.

Counting to eight, the companions stopped and covered their ears as thunder shook the tiny peninsula. A minute later a couple of bleeding crabs crawled into view from around the building. Those were easily stomped to death by Jak and Doc, while Ryan chanced a quick recce around the building.

The rest of the crabs were still retreating from the smoking crater of the blast, the old and young actually going over the other adults in their haste to leave.

Then Ryan spotted the large blue sitting away from the others on top of a tree stump. It sat there like a general surveying his troops in battle. Ryan swung his blaster in that direction, and the big blue dropped out of sight behind the rocks. Holstering his piece, Ryan felt a cold shiver run through his body. A mutie with intelligence. Unbidden, a memory of Kaa and his terrible army filled the man's mind, and Ryan shook off the thoughts. These were just crabs, nothing more.

"Did it work?" Mildred asked hopefully as he returned.

"No. Only bought us some time," Ryan stated grimly.

"But not for swimming," Krysty said, glancing at the jagged rocks filling the shoals below them.

"More grens?" Jak asked, pulling back the hammer of his revolver and firing repeatedly. In his other hand, the teen held a knife by its blade, ready for a fast throw.

Scowling, J.B. thumbed in his last shotgun round. "That's it."

Shading his good eye, Ryan glanced upward, then unexpectedly shouldered his longblaster. "Krysty, guard the right. Mildred, the left. We're gonna form a pyramid and get to that balcony. J.B. on my back!''

"But your leg," Mildred stated in concern.

"Fuck it. Move!" he bellowed.

Watching the ground, the women assumed firing positions as Ryan placed his hands flat on the rough granite blocks. The Deathlands warrior grunted in pain as J.B. climbed onto his back, bracing his boots against Ryan's hip bones and gun belt. Doc went up next and finally Jak. Balanced precariously atop the tall scholar, the teenager stretched out a hand as far as he could and just barely managed to brush his fingertips against the rust-streaked bottom of the steel posts supporting the railing.

"Not enough!" he cried. "Gonna jump!"

On the ground, a small crab scuttled into view, then another.

The lower men braced themselves and the youth lunged upward, his hands grabbing the lowest pipe. But the thick layer of rust crumbled under his grip, and one hand slipped completely off the railing. Supported by only one arm, Jak dangled helpless for a moment as he fought to reach the railing once more. Then a pair of hands reached over the balcony and helped the teenager up and out of sight. More crabs arched around the lighthouse, and the women opened fire as a bundle of rope sailed over the balcony, uncoiling as it fell. It hit the rocks, landing partially in the surf, and the muties immediately attacked the new invader with their sharp pincers.

The men climbed to the ground and stomped the old crabs to death, rescuing the rope. There was a large loop at the end for no discernible reason.

Shouting a warning, J.B. cut loose with the M-4000 as the first of the big crabs appeared around the lighthouse, and the others started to scramble up the length of rope. One by one, as they reached the top, each companion gave cover fire to the remaining people below until only Ryan was left. Working as a team, the people hauled up the big man, his wounded leg hanging limply behind. As he ascended, a crab jumped after him, but it missed and fell to its death amid the other bloody corpses.

Reaching the top, Ryan stiffly stood and shot a half smile at his son. The boy was bleeding from a scratch on his cheek, and had the beginning of a black eye, but otherwise seemed fine.

"Good job," Ryan grunted.

"Thank God you found some rope in time," Mildred panted, holstering her piece after two tries. Exhaustion draped over her like a shroud. "But why is it knotted at the end?"

"It came that way," Dean replied.

"What mean?" Jak asked suspiciously.

"I got it off a dead guy. Come on, I'll show you," Dean said, and started to walk into the bowels of the old lighthouse.

Chapter Three

"Hold it a sec," Ryan said, going to the edge of the balcony.

Looking out over the island, he could see only sand and weeds, the crumbling ruins of some predark skyscrapers jutting from the earth like the bones of a colossus. Then he studied the ruins more closely and realized those were the skeletons of warships, not houses. Carriers, battleships, destroyers, the maritime might of the predark world lay embedded in the dunes, their vaunted armor peeled away to reveal the bare inner layers of struts, and rusting keels. Those were useless. Anything valuable on board had been long ago destroyed by the wind and the surf.

Out to sea, there was empty water to their left and right, the calm expanse broken only by the occasional splash of a fish jumping at the reflected light of the setting sun. However, to the east were neat rows of thin islands, each slightly higher than the one before, steadily rising toward the north. Their island was about in the middle of the formation.

"Looks like the sea bed buckled upward from

nuke quakes,'' he said, waiting for the throbbing in his leg to subside.

Krysty shielded her vision from the setting sun. ''Some sort of a ville three, no, four islands over,'' she said, gesturing with her chin. ''I see a big wall, and smoke.''

Extracting a device from his munitions bag, J.B. extended the antique Navy telescope to its full length. The device compacted to smaller than a soup can, but had much better range than even the best predark binocs.

''Yeah, it's a ville,'' he said. ''Big one, too, with one hell of a good wall.''

''Cold Harbor?'' Dean asked anxiously, his young face fiercely stern.

''Nope, someplace new.''

''Good,'' the boy grunted. ''Any place better than there.''

Leaning against the railing to support himself, Ryan took a turn at the telescope. ''These nearby islands are only a hundred or so yards away from each other. Be an easy swim.''

''Except for the crabs,'' Krysty said, pausing so they could hear the endless scraping from below.

''Let's go inside,'' Mildred suggested, heading for the open door of the beacon room. ''Get away from those things.''

Trundling inside the framed structure on top of the granite tower, the companions found it stifling hot behind the glass walls. But as the heavy glass door closed, the sounds of the fighting crabs and crashing waves completely vanished. Silence reigned supreme.

"Perhaps it would be wise to leave the door open," Doc suggested. "We shall be needing cross ventilation from the chimney to breathe downstairs."

"Right," Dean said with a nod, and propped the door ajar with a pile of the rope.

The central area of the beacon room was small, the huge lens assembly taking up most of the space. The walls were thick glass with massive support columns every few feet. The floor was only three feet wide and circled the beacon until reaching a steep set of wrought-iron stairs with no railing. Support was offered by grabbing hold of the steel column the stairs wound around.

Ryan looked at his son. "Any problems downstairs?"

"The place is empty," Dean replied, scrunching one side of his face. "Except for the dead guy."

"Hey, what if the crabs get inside through the chimney flue!"

"I closed the flue," Dean replied. "No way they're getting through plate steel."

"Good. Smart move."

"Mighty hot," Jak said, loosening his collar.

"Greenhouse effect," Mildred muttered, a bead

of sweat trickling down her cheek. "Sunlight comes in and the heat gets trapped."

"Like a magnifying glass?"

"Sort of, yes."

Screwing the cap back on his canteen, Ryan wiped his mouth on a sleeve. He knew that explanation wasn't quite right, but let it pass.

Taking a sip from his canteen, Doc wandered closer to the huge prism and lens assembly that dominated the middle of the room. The intricately carved glass lens stood six feet high, with concentric circles cut in short arcs on the thick glass, the reflective prisms spaced evenly around a central bull's-eye-style magnifying glass. Behind the lens was some sort of a mechanism with a silvery reflecting dish.

"A first-order Fresnel lens," Doc said, sounding impressed. "This must have been some very bad water. These are extremely powerful."

"Yeah? How far?" Dean asked, fingering the pattern on the thick glass.

"Twenty miles, or so I have been told," Doc replied. "And since the horizon is only seven miles away, that gives it quite a decent range."

Jak scowled at the information. After night fell, they could see far, but the beam itself would broadcast their presence to the world. No good. He had no wish to face another of the baron's PT boats until they had more blasters. Maybe even some of those Firebird rockets, too.

"Fresnel?" Mildred asked curiously, rubbing her neck with a damp cloth.

Leaning on his ebony swordstick, Doc pursed his lips. "A Frenchman, I believe. I have a cousin who retired from the Navy and became a lighthouse keeper. He used to regale my dear Emily and I at every opportunity with stories about the new types of lenses, and such. Poor man was always afraid the Confederate Army would smash his beacon to make Union Army supply ships crash on the shore. Odd fellow."

His smile fading, Doc blinked several times. "Why, even after the Civil War was over..." The gentleman paused, his voice taking on a soft quality. "Is the war over? Only last week, we heard about Lee crossing the Potomac. Or was it last month?"

As he wandered off, the others paid the man no attention. Doc often slipped into the past, but always returned if there was trouble. Privately, Mildred envied the man slightly. At least for a few brief minutes, he was back among his family and friends, a land without radiation or muties. As time passed, she found it ever harder to recall her life before awakening in the cryo unit and joining Ryan. Sometimes, she even imagined that this had always been her life and the past was but a dream from childhood. On impulse, she reached out and took J.B. by

the hand, giving it a gentle squeeze. The man turned
and smiled at her, maintaining the intimate contact.

"Something wrong, Millie?" J.B. asked softly.

Only he called her that. She had always been Mil-
dred to her family and associates. The past had many
pleasures: clean sheets, pizza, air-conditioning, cable
TV, but there had never been a man in her life like
John. He was worth the violence and horrors of the
Deathlands. To be with him was worth any price.

"Not a thing, John," she said with a smile. "Just
thinking."

Giving her a hug, J.B. released her hand and continued his examination of the huge lens.

"What's the light source for the beacon?" Ryan
asked, grabbing hold of a ceiling to rest his leg.

"Electric," J.B. replied, then grinned. "Which
means generators and juice in the basement."

"Emergency jenny, if nothing else," Ryan agreed.
The generator was old, but still serviceable. "If the
baron's sec men haven't located the gateway, we
might find enough juice here to operate the generators and still leave these islands. Dean, show us the
way."

"Yes, sir!" The boy started down the steep stairs
with the immortal assurance of youth.

Taking Doc by the elbow, Krysty guided the
mumbling old man down the stairs along with the
others. The wealth of light reflecting off the lenses
and prisms of the beacon cast bizarre shadows down

the circular staircase, and the companions had to light candles before even reaching halfway down.

"This is the spot," Dean said, playing the beam of the flashlight over a bare section of the stairs. "The rope was tied here, and he was hanging over there."

"Suicide," Jak said, frowning. "Easier throw somebody off top. Let grav chill."

Ryan looked down and could see nothing below. "Better check the corpse," he said, drawing his blaster. He could get a lot of info from the corpse, suicide or not.

The yellowish cone of the flashlight bobbing about, the companions proceeded carefully down the angled steps and spread out when they reached the bottom level of the tower. Mildred took the flashlight from Dean and pumped the charging handle several times, but the beam stayed as dim as before. The battery was dying again. Turning it off, she pocketed the device to save for medical emergencies.

Now in the flickering light of the candles, the companions did a quick recce of the tower. This area was twice as wide as the beacon room, and it was much cooler, probably because they were now twenty feet under the sand. There were several large wooden lockers full of tackle, and assorted equipment for rescuing drowning people and maintaining the beacon. A heavy-gauge power switch was set on the granite block wall between a couple of windows, each showing only a smooth expanse of compacted sand against the other side of the glass.

A tangle of bones and cloth stood in the middle of the floor. Ryan and Mildred knelt alongside the mess to pull out a human skeleton. There was a terrible crack yawning wide in the skull, but the breakage was fresh, obviously caused by the fall and not from a blow to the temple while the man was alive.

"I found him hanging halfway down the circular stairs," Dean reported, setting the candle on a wall shelf. "The rope was in fine shape, so I cut him loose and took it."

As Ryan started to go through the pockets of the ragged clothing, Mildred lifted the skull and turned it.

"Well, he's definitely from the predark days," she stated, opening the jaw wide as it could reach. "Look at those ceramic fillings! That's prime dentistry."

"How die?" Jak asked bluntly.

"Tell you in a minute," Mildred replied. Carefully, she laid out the bones, placing them in order. Then she ran her trained hands over the skeleton, checking for damage, and found nothing.

"Okay, he died of strangulation," Mildred announced, rocking back on her heels. "Damn fool must have tied the noose wrong and it didn't snap his neck when he jumped off the stairs. Poor bastard just hung there until his air ran out. Might have been a couple of minutes, or a whole day if he was particularly strong.''

''A bad way to die,'' Krysty stated.

''There's no good way to get aced,'' J.B. said with conviction. ''Some are just worse than others.''

For some reason, that made Mildred feel incredibly sad. Maybe it was because, while they often found dead folks, few were from predark. It made her feel a sort of kinship with the nameless man. ''Ashes to ashes,'' she whispered, making the sign of the cross, ''dust to dust. And may God have mercy on your soul.''

''Soul,'' Jak snorted in disdain. ''Right.''

Holding a small leather journal in his hand, Ryan stood and tried to force open the lock, but the ancient mechanism was strong. He stopped when the leather cover started to give instead of the lock. Shit, he'd have to open this later or risk tearing it apart.

''Okay, let's finish our sweep,'' Ryan said, tucking the journal into a shirt pocket.

A big door closed with heavy bolts seemed to lead outside from the trickles of sand that rained down along the jamb every time they touched the handle. A second door led to a hallway that opened directly to the cottage, and the third was locked tight.

''This should be the basement,'' Ryan decided. ''Mebbe storage area, or even a bomb shelter, if we're lucky. Could be useful stuff down there.''

"On it," J.B. said, removing tools from his shoulder bag.

But just then, a clang sounded from the second doorway, the noise echoing slightly in the darkness.

Quickly leading the way, Ryan found a set of double doors standing open, and strode into the kitchen of the subterranean cottage. Nothing seemed amiss there, and he waited for the sound to ring out again.

Ryan stood guard while the others swept the kitchen. The range and refrigerator were both electric, there was a dishwasher under the counter and a full assortment of fancy cooking machines, each totally useless without electric power. The cabinets yielded some herbal tea, which Mildred appropriated, and a small amount of exotic spices, but no real food. Checking under the sink, J.B. took some of the cleaning solutions to tuck into his munitions bag, and left the others.

Moving on, they found a small laundry room behind a pantry, the shelves starkly empty. Past the kitchen was the main room of the cottage. It was a big place. The living room had a small eating table with some chairs. In the far corner was a big-screen television and DVD player, stacks of rainbow disks piled high. Near the sand-filled windows was a large desk with a complex military radio and stacks of nautical charts showing the tides, deep currents and shipping schedules. Two side doors led to small bedrooms, one disheveled, the other neat. Everything was coated with a thin layer of dust, but otherwise seemed in good condition.

Holding their candles high, the companions stood in the flickering blackness, straining to hear anything. Then Doc shook off Krysty's arm and walked over to a sideboard, where he lifted a lantern from amid the items on the table. There was still a small residue of oil in the reservoir, and soon he had the wick going, bright white light filling the subterranean cottage.

Now they could see the recliners and sofa placed before the television, and a gun rack on the wall with several longblasters and several sagging cardboard boxes of ammunition. On the far wall was a large bookcases full of paperbacks that crumbled into dust as they approached, producing an amazingly large acrid cloud. The fresh air from the open door in the lighthouse was seeping into the cottage, finishing the job of destruction started by the sheer passage of time.

Then everybody froze as a soft metallic patter sounded. It came again as a faint spot of light appeared on the bricks of the hearth and with a loud clang the flue moved aside and a blue crab dropped into view.

"Hot pipe, they pried it open!" Dean shouted, and stomped on the mutie before it could scuttle away, grinding it underfoot until the thing was paste on the flagstone floor.

Grabbing a fireplace poker, Ryan hooked the catch on the flue and forcibly pulled it closed, cutting off the pincer of a crab halfway through the vent. The limb fell onto the andirons, and a frantic scratching could be heard as something moved wildly about on the sheet iron.

"Now what?"

"Build fire," Jak suggested, lifting a wooden chair.

"Have to open the flue or we choke to death on the smoke."

Ryan pulled the poker tighter to hold the flue closed. "Find something to jam it in place!"

Breaking a chair apart, Jak forced a piece of wood into the fireplace. The chair leg splintered as it scraped across the rough brick, and the teenager had to use the butt of his Colt Python to pound it into position. There was a lot of scampering about on top of the flue from the noise, but he sat back to inspect the work and nodded.

"Not come through this," he stated as a fact.

Nervously, Mildred glanced at the windows. "Some species of crabs can tunnel," she said. "We better nail those bookshelves over the glass just in case."

"Tools in the laundry room," Ryan said, moving his head. "Jak, Dean, give her a hand."

"I'll check the blaster rack," J.B. said, already moving in that direction.

With the Steyr cradled in his arms, Ryan rested his aching leg on the dining table and watched the open doorway and the fireplace for any sign of movement. The situation wasn't good. They were still alive, but trapped down there, low on candles, almost out of ammo and food. Eventually, they would have to leave, and then the waiting muties would swarm once more. They might be able to swim to the next island, but that would require a diversion to get rid of the crabs, and they had no more explosives of any kind. Hopefully, the rounds in the blaster rack were still live.

The work of closing off the windows went very slowly, the panes of glass vibrating with every fall of the hammer. Krysty solved that problem by sliding the sofa cushions between the glass and the wood slats. After that, the job progressed much faster.

Shifting to another position, Ryan felt the journal in his pocket. Pulling it out, he used the panga to slice off the lock and flipped through the book to see if there was a diagram of the cottage, or any useful info inside. The handwriting was faded, but still legible in the dancing illumination of the candles.

"Good enough," Mildred finally announced, and placed aside the hammer. Walking around the cottage, the woman surveyed the work. The planks were double thick over every window, almost four inches. No way could the crabs get through that. "Good idea about those nails, Dean."

The boy shrugged. Driving some nails through the wood before they attached them over the windows seemed an obvious thing to do. Anything coming through the glass would impale itself on the sharp steel points. Crude but effective.

"Looks pretty solid," J.B. stated, returning a rifle to the blaster rack. All of the weapon were useless, rusted solid, and the ammo was even worse.

Fortunately, he spotted some silverware in the kitchen. If it was real silver, and not just silver plate, then with some clean sheets and sunshine he could start producing high-explosive guncotton by the pound. Then disassemble the plumbing and they'd soon have some pipe bombs. Fuses were the problem. Maybe he could use the merc primer in the dead ammo to bleed a crude flash-fuse. Yeah, that just might work.

"Hey," Jak said, going to the dining table and emptying his pants pockets of oysters. "Forgot had. Got before crabs came."

Knowing the mollusks wouldn't stay fresh long once out of the water, the companions took seats and started dividing up the seafood. Having eaten only a short while ago, Krysty let the others have the oysters and took some small sips from her canteen to control her hunger. Even if they found edible food down here, there was no chance of clean water. That they would have to distill from the sea. A long and slow process.

Screwing the cap back on, Krysty noticed Ryan was still engrossed in the little journal.

"What is it, lover?" she asked, going closer. The man wouldn't be spending this much time reading some suicide note.

"Good news, or good luck for us, whatever you want to call it," Ryan said, thumbing deeper into the book until coming to blank pages. The last few pages were written in a different color ink than the rest, which made it easy to find the pertinent parts.

J.B. glanced up. "What do you mean?" he asked around a mouthful of oyster.

"The dead guy we found is from predark days, all right. He talks about how this lighthouse has a bomb shelter in the basement. If the seals held, there should be ammo, food, everything we need. And lots of it."

"Hot pipe!" Dean cried, jumping from his chair. "Let's go!"

"Slow down, son," Ryan said, rubbing his chin. "The door is booby-trapped. Gonna be a triple tough to get through. Plas mines in the floor and ceiling—we miss one, and the whole place goes up."

"Read in journal?" Jak asked frowning.

"Yeah, he rambled on about skydark for a while, then got to the important stuff."

"He saw the war." Mildred said the words as if each one were alone and independent of the others.

Ryan tossed over the journal. "Read for yourself. J.B., let's start on that door."

As the men walked off, Mildred snatched up the journal and started to turn the pages. The personal journal of somebody who actually saw the world end. Incredible.

In the background, Doc snored softly in a chair, and the mutie crabs clawed and scratched at the iron plate blocking their way into the underground cottage. Placing her blaster on the table for easy access, Mildred moved a candle closer for better light.

She began to read aloud:

"My name was Ronald Keifer, and in this journal I will confess everything. But I cannot be judged, because there is no law anymore. Not since this afternoon when the bombs began to fall and the whole world caught fire while David and I watched from the imagined safety of our island...."

PLACING ASIDE his fountain pen, Ron reached up to close the window above the tiny desk. For a moment, he listened to the thick silence, the ticking of

the windup clock on the shelf blessedly silent now
that he had smashed it with a hammer.

A trickle of sweat formed in his hair and flowed
down the side of his unshaved face to dangle from
his badly healing chin for a second before plum-
meting onto the clean white page of the pocket journal. He stared at the tiny stain as it spread across
the paper and blurred the words. His sister had given
him this book to jot down his thoughts, and to re-
mind him to write while he was stationed here in
the Marshall Islands. The goddamn middle of nowhere. The edge of the world. The words made the
man shake, and he concentrated on breathing to stay
in control. But it was so quiet here. So very quiet.

He had been watering the garden when the horizon strobed with brilliant light flashes. At first he
thought it was a ship at the Navy base exploding,
or maybe lightning, but then he felt the powerful
vibrations in the ground and realized those were
nukes going off. A lot of them.

Holding a bucket of paint and a brush, David
stopped painting the side of the cottage and stared
directly at the growing fireballs in disbelief until
suddenly he started clawing at his face, screaming.
Ron was already hugging the ground, his face buried
under both arms while he prayed to God this was
just some a horrible dream. But the terrible rumblings of the nuclear detonations grew in volume
until quakes shook the island, then came the hot

wind that stole the breath from their lungs, boiling atmosphere pushed out of the way of the expanding mushroom clouds. Even as he crawled for the door, every window on that side of the lighthouse shattered. Only the lighthouse beacon itself survived the atomic concussions.

Dragging the weeping David through the howling winds, debris from the annihilated naval base peppering the island, Ron somehow managed to get inside and to bolt the heavy door closed. Designed to withstand the worst tropical storm, the lighthouse saved their lives that day, the granite walls holding back the unimaginable hurricane of the sky bombs.

Bandaging David's eyes, Ron put his partner to bed and tried to summon medical help. But the telephone was dead, the static and hash so thick on the landline it was impossible to even know if it was working. And the radio didn't function at all, even though the internal parts hadn't been damaged from the glass shards of the windows. Then Ron recalled a lecture that the electronic pulse of a nuke would fry civilian computer chips, and such things as radios and computers would be permanently dead. The sudden realization that they were alone hit the man hard, and he forced it from his mind, clinging to the belief that the U.S. Navy or the local coast patrol would soon arrive to take them to safety.

Carrying the now unconscious David into the cellar, he fumbled with the military lock to open the lead-lined door of the bomb shelter and closed it tight, using all four bolts. It was a pointless act. They were alone on the island; besides, the gamma wave from the blasts had already come and gone. If he was dying of radiation, there was nothing he could do about it now. However, it made Ron feel better, safer. Without turning on the chemical lights, he slumped to the cold concrete floor and raged at the fool politicians who had ordered the death of the human race. What the hell had they been thinking, that humanity could somehow survive a nukestorm? Were they mad? Of course they were.

Outside, the hellstorm of cobalt fire raged louder than any possible hurricane, and days passed before the vibrations in the air and the ground slowly ebbed. While the winds battered the building above them, David wept insanely when he wasn't asleep, the rationed shots of morphine all that Ron could do for his friend. And every time he regained consciousness, the man began to scream, raking cracked nails across his sunburned face to rip away the dressings. Blisters had formed on every inch of exposed skin, and Ron didn't know if his friend would live. And he was certainly blind. The medical supplies were only the basic materials, field-surgery kits for fast repairs to keep a wounded sailor alive until the corpsman arrived.

But there would never be any more corpsman or doctors. No relief ship, no helicopter, no cops. The two men were on their own until further notice. Forever. The journal was his only solace, and Ron wrote in detail about a tidal wave that swept across the nearby islands, broken aircraft carriers and battleships mixed into the churning brown silt from the bottom of the sea. A radioactive tidal wave. Every ship in the archipelago had to have been destroyed. The Geiger counter built into the wall was still registering high, but no longer spiking the deadly red line. The bombs used had to have been the so-called clean nukes that the Pentagon was so proud of developing. Bombs with ultrashort half-life isotopes in the warheads. In ten or so years, any island still in existence would be livable again. That was, if there was anybody left alive.

Trying to pass the time, Ron did a detailed inventory of everything the Navy engineers had stashed in their little bolt-hole. Emergency supplies for the base personnel. It was a criminal offense for him to even open a box to peek inside. But there was no law anymore, and he felt no remorse as he went through the government property. It all belonged to him now.

Ripping open a wooden crate full of bottles, Ron used his teeth to work out the cork of a whiskey bottle and drank directly from the neck, ignoring the rows of clean plastic glasses lining the shelf. Food wasn't a problem; there was enough for twenty years, and quite a decent stash of weapons and ammunition. Enough to start a small war. But war was gone from the world for a while. Everybody would be simply trying to stay alive, way too busy to argue religion or political beliefs. Personal survival would be the only rule for those still in the world, and it would be the same here. Survival at any cost.

Standing, Ron took another deep swig from the bottle and walked over to where David sprawled in the bunk.

"Hey," the wounded man whispered, a pained smile twisting his feature. "It's not a dream is it? They dropped the Big One."

"Looks like," Ron said, placing the bottle aside. He felt cold. So very cold.

David sniffed. "You drinking booze?"

"Yeah."

"Morphine is doing me fine, but you go right ahead and have one for me. Hell, have one for everybody!"

"There's lots of food," Ron found himself saying. He had no idea why. It was as if somebody else were speaking through him. God, what was he doing? Dave was his best friend. Pulling the 10 mm U.S. Navy pistol from his belt, Ron clicked off the safety, the tiny noise incredibly loud in the locked bunker.

"Trouble?" David asked, struggling to sit upright. He reached out a hand for Ron, and the man stepped out of the way. "Somebody at the bunker door?"

Ron felt a hysterical laugh bubble up from inside. "I wish to God there was somebody at the door," he said softly, "but there isn't, and there never will be. We knew the risks when we took this assignment. World War III, pal. We're all alone and nobody is ever coming to rescue us."

"Nonsense," David began gently, a shaking hand rubbing his bandages. "Why, over on Kwalein Island they have an underground base the size of—"

"Shut up!" Ron screamed, his hand shaking so badly he almost dropped the weapon. "Shut the fuck up! There's only enough food for twenty years! Twenty, that's all!"

"So?" David asked, puzzled, leaning back in his bunk. "Hell, that's plenty. A lifetime!"

Ron fired again and again at the blind man until the corpse fell off the blood-soaked bunk.

"Now it's forty years," Ron whispered, watching the body twitch and then go terribly still.

That was ten years ago. Long lonely years. Taking up the fountain pen once more, Ron shook his head to banish the memory of that insane day. But it had been a decade since he heard a human voice. The TV and radio never worked again, the phone only static. The CD player and VCR were junk, the computer useless. The hundred thousand Web sites of the Internet vanished in the first microsecond pulse of the nuclear detonations. His new URL was now www.gonetohell.com.

There were still ten thousand gallons of diesel fuel in the storage tanks for the generator that powered the lighthouse. But he hadn't turned on the beam in years, first to save fuel, then out of fear others would arrive and discover his crime. Murder. That was the word. He was a murderer. Assassin. Coward.

Thousands of people were probably raping and killing one another across the world, but this had been while the ground was still shaking from the bombs. While the taste of civilization was still in his mouth. There had been enough food for forty men for one year, or two men for twenty years, or one man for forty years. The math was easy, the results unacceptable. He had wanted a full long life, but now Ron was paying the price for his bloody crime.

Sometimes in the dark, Ron could hear the dead sailors from the Navy base whispering, asking why he did it, calling him a traitor. He woke screaming, drenched in sweat and used up all of the whiskey to force dreamless sleep. When it was gone, he switched to the morphine, but now that was depleted, and the nightmares were tearing apart his mind, until he wasn't sure when he was awake or asleep. David stood behind him a lot these days, never visible, but always there, reminding him that he had something to do. One last act before he could finally sleep.

Putting aside the pen, Ron slowly walked to the middle of the stairwell, checked the rope he had tied there yesterday, slipped the noose around his neck and jumped. It was that easy.

The shock of the noose tightening filled him with cold adrenaline when Ron realized in horror that he hadn't tied the noose correctly. It was supposed to break his neck and kill him instantly. This was slow strangulation! Standing at the foot of the stairs, David watched him thrash about with those pure white eyes and did nothing to help. Clawing madly at the rope slowly crushing his windpipe, Ron managed to suck a sip of air into his burning lungs. Then another, and another. He was going to live. Live! With excruciating slowness, Ron started to climb the rope, going hand over hand back to the stairs.

That was last week.

He was ready to try again. David had told him what he had done wrong, so he wouldn't fail next time. *Knot the rope more, that'll do the trick.* Soon, he'd be asleep forever. Absolved of his crimes.

Oh God, please let me die this time.

"THAT'S IT, the rest is blank," Mildred said, closing the journal and placing it flat on the table. "Guess he finally made it."

Dean chewed a lip. "So he went mad from loneliness?"

She smiled sadly. "It's called cabin fever. Almost got it myself once."

"His mental failure was completely understandable," Doc rumbled, joining the conversation. "Most crimes merely mutter their presence. Only murder shouts." He had awakened in the middle of the reading and stood quietly by until she was done.

Out of breath, Krysty appeared at the hallway door. "We're in," she said urgently. "Lend a hand, we need some help moving the door."

Leaving the table, Mildred, Dean and Doc joined the others and put their backs into forcing aside the massive portal to the bomb shelter. Digging in his heels, Dean was surprised at the weight of the door, until he saw it was only wood on the outside, the thin veneer covering a mammoth slab of steel and lead. Good camou.

As the portal swung aside, air billowed out, smelling stale and dry.

"Been closed tight for a long time," J.B. observed, covering his face until the dead air dissipated. There was a cool breeze coming down from the open door atop the lighthouse, carrying the tangy smell of the sea.

While Jak jammed a knife under the door to make sure it didn't swing shut, Ryan jacked the action on his SIG-Sauer pistol and started down a short flight of brick stairs. In the enclosed space, the old lantern gave off a wealth of light, and the man could see the deactivated palm lock and keypad mounted on the wall normally used to seal off the shelter from intruders. A grille at the bottom of the stairs was ajar, and Ryan followed the path of a zigzagging tunnel very similar to the ones used in the redoubts. Rads could only travel in a straight line, and with a dogleg junction, once you stepped past the corner you were safe.

The tunnel opened onto a small room filled with stacks of crates and machines. The walls were lined with shelving packed with boxes and mysterious objects wrapped in vacuum-form plastic. Closed blaster racks were filled with military weapons, and tarpaulins covered large piles that could be anything.

"Jackpot," J.B. said, almost smiling.

The silenced muzzle of the SIG-Sauer sweeping the room ahead of him, Ryan strode through the maze of boxes, looking at everything but touching nothing. Doc stayed near the grille, a hand resting on the lion's head of his swordstick. Sometimes they found others waiting for them in a military supply dump—sec men, muties that had sneaked in through the ventilation system, wild animals and on a couple of occasions a sec droid, almost unstoppable machines designed to kill unauthorized intruders.

Warily, the companions spread out and started to hunt through the piles of supplies for specific items. Later on, they would do an inventory and decided

what to take, but first and foremost it was ammo and
food. Everything else was secondary.

"MRE packs." Dean grinned in delight, going to
a nearby shelf and pawing through a plastic box
marked with the military designation for the long-
storage food packs. Prying off the lid, he felt another
rush of trapped gas and started running his fingertips
carefully over the assortment of foil envelopes
searching for even the tiniest pinprick or corrosion.

"Perfect condition," the boy announced happily,
filling the pockets of his jacket until they bulged.

Snapping the pressure locks on a large plastic
box, J.B. flipped off the lid and grinned at the
M-16 automatic rifles nestled in a bed of thick
black-green grease. Another crate yielded an M-60
machine gun, but upon closer inspection there was
a crack in the case and the weapon was heavily corroded, especially its main recoil spring. As careful
as if handling a bomb, J.B. closed the case and set
it aside. The only way the M-60 could handle its
incredible recoil was to house an eighteen-foot-long
spring. Once long ago, the Armorer had been
trapped without ammo, and let the spring fly loose
just as a stickie was crawling in through a window.
The coiled length went straight through the mutie
and kept going for another fifty yards. A damaged
M-60 was a dangerous thing.

"Ammo over here," Krysty reported, opening a
sealed cabinet. The interior shelves were neatly

filled with a wide collection of different caliber ammunition. A lot of it was in 10 mm, which they couldn't use. They often found the ammo, but never a 10 mm blaster. However, there were a few boxes of the older 9 mm rounds, and some civilian grades. Probably stored here to trade with any survivors outside. Pushing aside the .44 and .45 packs, Krysty discovered quite a lot of plastic-wrapped 5 mm ammo blocks for a Heckler & Koch G-12 caseless rifle. Ryan used to carry one, and gave it up because ammo was so hard to find.

On a lower shelf behind some cleaning kits, she finally found some boxes of .357 ammo, whistled sharply and threw one to Jak. The teenager made the catch and nodded in thanks. Going to another locker, Krysty uncovered a staggering cache of .38 rounds and took every box, stuffing her coat pockets full. Never had enough of this caliber. It was used by herself, Mildred and Dean. Jak, too, sometimes.

Clearing some space on a workbench, Jak opened the cardboard box and reloaded his blaster on the spot, then he tucked a few extra rounds in his pockets and put the rest in his backpack. Armed once more, Jak continued his search for clothing. Their pants and shirts were in tatters, underwear and socks always in short supply, and his left boot had a spot worn thin as a baron's promise. Unfortunately, he was only finding things like flak jacks, scuba suits, rain gear and a lot of those computerized helmets that attached to the telescope mounted on a MR-1 rapid-fire blaster. J.B. had told him you could stick the blaster around a corner and see what was on the other side on a tiny vid screen suspended from your helmet. Then flip a switch and see in pitch darkness, or track an enemy by his body heat. Amazing stuff. When it worked. But that tech required heavy batteries, and all sorts of computer software. None of which they had ever found in any redoubt. Now where the hell were the boots?

Heading directly for a large red cross on the far wall, Mildred found a small medical section, most of the chem in the bottles only dust now. The latex gloves for surgery cracked apart from sheer age when she tried to put one on, and the rubber on a stethoscope was as brittle as glass. The frustrated physician located the M*A*S*H field-surgery kit mentioned in the journal stuffed in the fridge. She had hoped it would be in there. The refrigerator would make the morphine last longer, and even with the power off, the fridge should keep out most of the moisture and air. The med kit was almost identical to her own, except in much better shape, and Mildred immediately began transferring the contents of her old med kit into the new bag.

Reaching a clear area situated before a steel desk, Ryan saw a complex radio wired to a nuke battery from a Hummer. Checking the dials, he found the batteries had been left on, and were totally drained.

Even those amazing devices had limits. It was a sobering thought. The radio would have been worthless anyway, but they might have been able to use the nuke battery to power some electric lights. Too bad. They often found wags, or at least parts of vehicles in the redoubts. No chance of that in a bomb shelter.

He found a chem bathroom in the corner, next to a row of shower stalls carpeted with mildew, and a line of bunk beds attached to the wall, the pallets reaching from the ferroconcrete floor to the ceiling. Accommodations for a full company of soldiers. Only a single bed was disheveled, but another was stripped, the mattress gone leaving only the bare metal springs and frame. The scene of the crime, as Mildred would say.

Following the power cables attached to the bare wall, Ryan soon located the generator, or rather, what was left of it. A tiny drip from a water pipe in the ceiling had slowly reduced the huge machine into a pile of rust over the long decades.

"Never get those going again," J.B. stated, joining the man. He pushed back his fedora. "This isn't the prize we thought. Half this stuff is useless."

"But half isn't," Ryan stated. He gestured. "Any fuel in those tanks?"

The Armorer rapped on the side of the tank with a knuckle and got a dull answering thump. "Sure, lots," J.B. answered, puzzled. "But it's diesel.

Turned to jelly decades ago. Even if we got some to the gateway, it would be too thick to run the turbines. Need to cut it with something."

"Shine?"

"Anything that burns would be okay."

"Good, save a gallon to take with us," Ryan said, then paused to let the throbbing in his leg ease. They had been on the run, fighting every step of the way for too damn long. The half-healed cut on his gun hand was starting to stiffen, seriously slowing his speed. Not good. Across the shelter, Krysty was rubbing her bad shoulder, and the others looked as if they had been run over a couple of times by a war wag. Everybody was scratching at the itchy dried salt on their clothes, and down here in the close confines of the shelter house, the rank smell of unwashed bodies was starting to leave an oily taste in his mouth. Mildred was always touting cleanliness for health, but more importantly, when they went outside the stink would reveal their presence to anybody in the vicinity, and leave a hell of a fine trail for dogs to follow. And those triple-blasted crabs.

"We'll start on the juice tomorrow," Ryan said, sitting on a wall bunk. The mattress was a hell of a lot softer than the sand dune he awakened on that morning. "I think we'd better stay here for a while, get clean, catch some sleep. We have to cross three waterways to reach the island with a ville. Got the blasters to try now, but we're never going to make it if we're dragging ass every step of the way."

"Wouldn't mind a hot shower myself," J.B. said, glancing at the rusty stalls. "We could probably get those running in short order."

"How long?" Jak asked, padding over in his bare feet. The teenager was sliding laces through the holes of a brand-new pair of combat boots.

Ryan dropped his backpack and flexed his shoulders. "A week," he decided, laying the Steyr nearby. The blaster desperately needed to be completely disassembled and oiled. "We'll have to guard the fireplace for crabs, and have somebody in the lighthouse to watch for the baron's men. Place a few C-4 charges along the stairwell in case of trouble. But we should be safe enough down here. For a while, at least."

Dropping their backpacks with sighs of relief, the companions got busy rearranging the crates to make more space and started settling in for the night. After establishing a firing line for defense, food was gobbled straight from the MRE packs, and the exhausted friends took turns sleeping and standing guard. Soon, the soft breathing of exhausted sleep filled the bomb shelter.

But all through the starry tropical night, the army of crabs crawled around the peninsula outside like flies on a corpse, endlessly searching for some way inside.

Chapter Four

A hundred nautical miles away on another island, Lord Baron Maxwell Kinnison was driving a pre-dark Hummer along the edge of a steep cliff at breakneck speed. Slowly, dawn began to tint the east sky, the polluted storms clouds overhead rumbling with thunder.

Revving the powerful engine on the Hummer, Kinnison banked sharply around a small avalanche of rocks and cut away from the slide to go deeper into the thick jungle of Maturo Island. There was little terrain on his island ville he didn't know in detail, having crawled and run and fought pirates on every hill. His path to the throne as baron of all barons had been steeped in blood, not one single drop of it his. At least, none in combat.

Arcing through a dense copse of thorny bushes, Kinnison headed back toward the seaside cliffs, his two passengers holding on for dear life against the wag's wild rocking.

A growth of bamboo was smashed aside, and their goal popped into sight. The cottage stood on the swell of a cliff overlooking the calm sea. The roof was solid, glass filled the windows and the thick door was bolted on the inside. A clear stream flowed past the cottage and over the cliff, bringing fresh drinking water and carrying away each day's bucket of waste. The trees were heavy with fruit, the vines rich with flowers whose scent repelled most of the insects. A fence of thorny bushes cut off the cottage and its garden from the rest of the island, and at the gate was a hand-painted sign bearing the symbol of the lord baron, followed by a death's-head skull. The meaning was plain and clear. Cross the fence and die.

With the engine roaring, the Hummer smashed aside the sign and rolled over the gate as if the posts were no more than leaves on the road. The predark machine raced directly to the front door, and the three occupants stepped out, two much more quickly than the third.

Lord Baron Kinnison, ruler of the Thousand Islands, hoisted his tremendous bulk from the vehicle, grunting constantly. He was becoming weaker every day and knew that the end was near. He was wrapped in thick layers of protective cloth, the material spotted with dried blood and moist yellow patches from fresh skin eruptions. The ends had been cut off his boots to allow his toes to breathe. Circulation was very bad in his feet, and he feared gangrene daily. His face a mass of open sores, and the fingers of both hands were wrapped in strips of cloth stained black and yellow from the dried blood and pus.

Some half-mutie slut from one of the western islands had given him the Red Death during sex. The disease was incurable, and the baron had tortured the girl for a moon before allowing her to finally die.

The leprosy was eating him alive, faster all the time; the flash was no longer working. His end was near. But the baron had already prepared for that eventuality.

The slim driver and the young slave girl waited patiently as the gigantic man squeezed his bulk from the military vehicle and finally stood. Briefly, Kinnison checked the array of predark blasters hidden about his bulk. Impatiently, the driver started to speak and Kinnison silenced him with a raised hand. The soft cry of a newborn child could be heard from within the cottage.

"Boy or girl?" he demanded, staring at the slave.

She bowed her head and said, "A boy, master. A healthy boy."

"No mutations at all?" Kinnison insisted, brandishing a fist. "Are you absolutely sure?"

"Yes, my lord. He is a norm. Big, but a gene-pure norm."

"And you can smell them, little one," he rumbled, scratching inside his rags. "That's why I keep you alive, for that one special trait. You can smell the mutie on a man or woman as if it was the stink from a swamp.''

She bowed. "Yes, master."

Kinnison grunted. "You have served me well this day. But I cannot allow any to know of the child's real parents. Goodbye."

The girl stared in astonishment as the baron drew a silenced pistol from inside his clothing and fired. The blaster only coughed, but the slave violently staggered backward and sat down, blood trickling from the black hole in her face. In slow stages she toppled over, as if only laying herself down for a long nap.

Holstering the piece, Baron Kinnison stared at the house. The baron had given it to a faithful servant who saved his life from an assassin's blade. He had even given the man the most beautiful wife he could find, and made sure all of the food delivered to the couple was as clean as his own meals. Everything had been done to make the idiots breed him an heir, and two years later the bitch finally whelped. Two years! He wanted to tear them apart for that, but the man had saved his life once. The reward would be a clean chill.

"Here," Kinnison said, passing the silenced weapon to the doctor. "Ace the parents as painlessly as possible, and get the child. Do not let it touch me! If it gets my disease, your punishment will last for years after my own death."

Dr. Glassman nodded, holding the weapon awkwardly as if unfamiliar with how to use it.

Kinnison continued. "Then take the newborn to my rooms and kill the pregnant woman in my bed. Burn the unborn girl, and rub the boy with the woman's blood so they smell alike. Then send the news that I have a son."

"Of course, my lord, only..."

"What?" the baron raged, his piggy eyes glaring with fury.

"Afterward you'll have to chill me to keep the secret," Glassman said bluntly. "This I know. So I refuse to do as you command."

Kinnison stared at the man in disbelief.

"Unless you set my family free," the doctor continued quickly. Already he was afraid he had gone too far, asked for too much, but it was too late to turn back now. "Give them a boat and food and black powder enough for four blasters. When the boat is out of the harbor, I will announce the news of your son."

"You dare," Baron Kinnison grated low and dangerous, drawing another weapon from his clothing. It was a bigger blaster, trimmed with gold filigree and sporting a barrel wider than a grown man's thumb.

"You would do anything to make your son a blood heir to the Iron Throne of the Thousand Islands," Glassman replied, oddly calm. "Why do you think I would do less for my son to be free?"

Without speaking, Lord Baron Kinnison raised the blaster and thumbed back the hammer. Dr. Glassman stood there with the blaster in his hand, knowing that he could never use it. The punishment for attacking the baron would bring bloody horror to his family forever. He had played his card, father to father. The gambit would be accepted, or he would be chilled. That was all there was to it.

A long minute passed with only the sounds of the ocean breeze and the soft cries of the newborn child.

"Accepted," Kinnison said, easing down the hammer with his gore-streaked thumb. "They go free and you die."

"Agreed," Glassman said, and entered the tiny cottage. There were raised voices, a woman's scream, the soft chug of a silenced weapon firing again and again, and then the man walked out carrying a tiny wiggling bundle of life.

Glassman and the infant took the front seats, and Kinnison squeezed his bulk into the rear cargo area to stay as far away from his son as possible. Kinnison opened a canvas satchel and started to toss cylindrical grens through the open doorway of the cottage.

Gunning the engine to life, the doctor drove away from the cottage and passed the fence just as there was a brilliant flash of light and the first of the white

phosphorous charges ignited. Chem flame shot out
the door and windows, and soon the entire clearing
was a roaring inferno, flames licking into the sky for
a hundred feet. Kinnison watched the destruction
with some degree of satisfaction. Willy Peter didn't
burn as hot as thermite, but it made much less
smoke. Let people think what they wanted, but nobody would know the source of the child but himself
and the healer. And when Glassman was aced by his
hand, Kinnison would order one of the steam-
powered PT boats to find and destroy the runaway
slaves in the stolen ship. Setting the man's family
free, and letting them stay free were two entirely
different matters.

As they drove over the plains of grass, the jungle
rapidly approaching, a sea breeze carried the smell
of the burning cottage to the Hummer and the child
began to cry.

Every jounce of the wag bringing pain to his
sores, Kinnison bristled at the noise. "We'll never
smuggle him into the fortress this way. Silence the
thing!"

Slowing carefully, Glassman offered the newborn
a clean rag dipped in coconut milk, and it started
sucking happily, kicking tiny legs.

"All hail Corbet Kinnison," Glassman said,
"heir to the Iron Throne of the Thousand Islands,
admiral of the fleet, general of the army, master of
the black powder."

"Not yet," Kinnison said, glancing across the island to the imposing fortress on top of the main mountain of his island ville. "But very soon."

Avoiding the farms with their slaves and overseers, Glassman drove the Hummer through an arid stretch of land yet to be reclaimed from the last acid rainfall until reaching a rough culvert, actually a cooled river of lava from the island's active volcano. Here the baron painfully stepped from the wag and watched it drive off before starting his long journey toward the fortress on the hill.

Walking was difficult for the overweight man, and he was drenched in sweat by the time he reached the end of the culvert and emerged onto a great grassy plain.

Pausing on a low hill to catch his breath, the baron looked out upon the world he ruled. Tendrils of dark smoke rose from the mines, which delivered the basic ingredients for black powder, and a good mile away were the mills that mixed and rolled the explosive into usable form. More farms spread into the jungle hills, tiny plows pulled by slaves harvesting the grain and fruit for his table. Nearby stood the slave pens and the execution yard. Keep the dead in sight and the living will obey, his father had always said, and he had been correct.

Scattered among the hills and forest were the blockhouses filled with Firebirds, the real source of his power. Most of the fools believed he ruled the

Thousand Islands by controlling the secret of how to make the black powder. It wasn't true. The unstoppable missiles could blow the gate off any ville and sink the largest ship in minutes. None dared to stand against him as long as the Firebirds were his to command.

Once, a rogue sec man had turned one of the rockets on the young baron, and the would-be killer couldn't believe the sight when the weapon curved away from the baron in midflight and headed straight for the traitor, exploding his body into bloody smoke. Black powder brought Kinnison sec men, beautiful women to bed and lots of slaves, but his word was obeyed because of the Firebirds. If that secret ever fell from his hands, then nothing could save the man from a terrible retribution.

A stone castle stood on a distant mountaintop, its imposing array of Firebirds undetectable in the manicured gardens and trimmed hedges. Armed sec men patrolled the grounds day and night. A monumental flight of stairs, carved from the living rock of the mountainside, led down to the walled ville on the beach where his people lived in constant fear of his wrath. In the water were countless fishing canoes trawling the rich waters, and several large sailing ships called windjammers that used sails instead of steam engines. Prizes won in battle with the renegades to the south, they now served both as items to be sold to villes that needed to increase their fleets and as physical protection for the vulnerable dock-yards.

On the beach were the great docks that housed his fleet of PT boats, salvaged from a predark museum and repaired over many long years. Armed with Firebirds, those vessels were his iron fist to rob the weak villes, threaten the strong ones and beat back the growing menace of the pirates.

Feeling better, Kinnison started forward once more, mopping his face with a clean handkerchief. As he neared the estate, a bell began to ring and suddenly sec men came running from every direction with drawn blasters. Baron Kinnison stopped and watched as the guards spread out in a protective circle around him.

"Sir, you were walking the grounds alone?" a sergeant queried, sounding puzzled. "Is that wise, my lord?"

"Should I fear an attack on my own island?" Kinnison asked, sneering in reply.

The man blanched. "Ah, no, my lord! Of course not. I mean, that is…"

"Shut up, ass," Kinnison snapped, brushing past the guard. Competent sec men were so difficult to find. They either obeyed every command blindly and without thought, or else tried to ace the baron and take over. Nobody could be trusted, and traitors abounded.

Trying to pretend he enjoyed arduous walking,

the baron gave no sign of his fatigue as he crossed a decorative bridge arching over a burbling moat of clear mountain water. Tall hedges blocked a clear view of the mansion now, making it doubly hard for snipers to find a target. As Kinnison maneuvered through the maze, the gardeners and passing slave girls dropped to their knees in homage. Exiting the hedges, he encountered a group of visiting barons talking with one another, discussing some nonsense. Probably how to cheat him on the price of the next shipment of black powder. Bastards. As required, the visitors touched their chests and bowed their heads as a sign of respect.

Lord Baron Kinnison sneered. Respect, his ass. They feared his Firebirds, nothing more. Past a splashing fountain, he turned and headed for the side door of the massive structure. The mansion used to be some sort of government building, but the thick walls and lack of windows made it a perfect fortress. Every door was fronted by a low sandbag with armed sec men behind, and more guards walked the rooftop, equipped with bamboo tubes packed with black powder and sharp pieces of coral. The grisly results of detonating these bombs near living flesh were most interesting to see, from a great distance.

"Morning, Lord Baron!" a young sec man called out, and snapped a salute.

The older sec man snarled and cuffed the other to

the ground. "Idiot!" he roared. "Never salute with your gun hand! Do it again, and I'll see you in chains!"

Kinnison nodded at the exchange. At least some of his guards knew their job. Before entering the fortress, the baron glanced down the great stairs and out in the harbor. The view was magnificent, the rising sun filling the sea with crimson fire. Then the baron noticed a lone PT boat steaming into the dockyard. Badly battered, the craft was riddled with holes, white smoke spurting from damage to its aft steam engine, and it was listing badly as if taking on water. For a brief moment, Kinnison thought the craft was Lieutenant Craig Brandon's ship, PT 264, but that was impossible. Baron Kinnison had sent his chief sec man off with ten of the stout fighting craft, armed to the gunwales with Firebirds, to handle the problem of getting more flash from Cold Harbor ville. It was unthinkable that only a single vessel would return from such a simple task. Nothing less than a full fleet of pirate vessels could even challenge such an armada. He turned for the door and went inside. Just a trick of the light reflected off the dancing waters of the ocean. Nothing more.

But as he waddled along the cool corridor of the predark post office, the lord baron felt an unfamiliar shiver run down his spine. Odd, it almost felt like fear.

AFTER A HUGE breakfast, Kinnison went to the throne room to listen to petitioners from the lesser islands try to bargain for more black powder at lower prices. He really should have been walking through the mills, making sure the overseers were storing the powder properly. The last accident removed a chunk of the hillside larger than most villes. But the lord baron wanted the lesser barons to be present when he received the good news, not grubby techs and sec men.

The room was packed with visiting barons from other island villes and their attendants. Nobody was armed, not even with eating knives. Only his sec men standing guard in the corners were allowed to carry weapons in the presence of the lord baron. The huge room was lit by smoky torches even though it was morning, as there were no windows for an assassin to shoot through. The doors were double thick and banded with iron, and the walls of the throne room were covered with carpeting stolen from the ruins of a skyscraper on Forbidden Island. It cut down on the echoes of raised voices, which often hurt his ears these days.

A raised wooden platform supported his specially built throne with blasters hidden in both armrests, and steel plating under the seat was protection against bombs. Female servants stood attendant on either side holding trays of wine and small fried birds. More servants walked through the crowd offering brass mugs of tree-bark tea or warm coconut milk to the dignitaries. All accepted, but few drank. Hours passed as barons and sons of barons placed their cases before Kinnison. To some he said yes; to most it was no. It all depended on whether they looked him in the face when they spoke. Those that did were dangerous and got nothing, but the ones who averted their eyes out of fear received at least a portion of what they needed. But never all—nobody ever got everything they wanted. Keep them hungry and off balance. Ruling a ville was simply a matter of blasters, but controlling a hundred villes was a different matter entirely.

Accepting a mug from a full-breasted serving girl, Kinnison reached into a pocket and extracted a small purple capsule of predark design. He broke it apart between his strong fingers and sprinkled the powdery contents into the brew. He drank deeply and soon felt the telltale rush of warmth through his body. Jolt was the only thing keeping him alive these days. It cut his pain by half and gave the man back some small measure of his once formidable strength. Flash helped the open sores on his skin, but only jolt eased his pain. Unfortunately, he was needing larger and larger doses to achieve the same results and knew that one day he would cross the line and overdose, hopefully to die before wakening chained in his own dungeon. Anything but that.

"But these girls are not norms," the brother of a

baron from a southern island declared once more. "They are muties, and rarely speak because they're afraid of showing their forked tongues."

"Forked?" Kinnison repeated, trying not to get too impatient. The jolt had him wide awake now, and he tried not to glance at the main doors. Where the hell was Glassman? His family was already far to sea in their boat. Could the healer be holding his son hostage? Unthinkable!

The young man nodded. "Yes, my lord. Gods, they are beautiful and can pleasure a man in ways no gaudy slut would dare. But death follows the muties, and I have found that several have been seen in other villes." He paused. "And they all look alike."

"Sisters," Kinnison declared, bored with the subject. If the girls were trouble, fuck them, then chill them. Or do it the other way around; he really didn't care.

"No, my lord, they are identical. Absolutely identical in every way."

The crowd murmured unhappily at this news.

"Clones?" Griffin asked softly.

As always, the bony man was scrubbed painfully clean, from his pointed beard to his soft leather moccasins. His clothing was plain, almost nondescript, and if he was armed, no blaster or blade was in sight. The lack of a visible weapon frightened most people, although they couldn't quite say why.

Kinnison glowered at the high chancellor. "Crap," he snorted. "My father chilled them all. There are no clones anymore."

Just then, cheering could be heard from outside the throne room. Suddenly, the double doors were thrown open and in came a large group of laughing people, led by Glassman.

"My lord, it's a boy!" he cried, carrying the swaddled bundle into the throne room of the baron's fortress. "You have a son!"

"I have an heir!" Kinnison roared, brandishing both bandaged fists into the air. "An heir! Nobody works for the rest of the day! Wine for everybody, and it is forbidden to whip the slaves until nightfall!"

The crowd of attendees erupted into cheers, lifting high their mugs made from old 120 mm tank shells. From somewhere in the fortress a chorus began to sing, and fireworks could be heard exploding outside as could the crackle of blasters.

Reverently, a midwife placed a clean white blanket on a sturdy table, and Glassman lay the swaddled infant before the lord baron. "The ship carrying my family is long gone," he whispered. "I am yours."

"I know," Kinnison replied, leaning closer to see the child as if for the first time. The boy was large, ten, maybe twelve pounds, and had a wild stock of coal-black hair. Incredibly, he seemed to actually resemble the baron slightly. But then, it was hard to recall what the baron looked like under his layers of encrusted bandages.

"Corbet," the baron proclaimed, grinning so wide his lips bled at the corners. "His name shall be Corbet Kinnison, the twenty-seventh lord baron of the Thousand Islands!"

The room erupted in cheers once more, and now an army of slaves arrived to serve predark wine in crystal goblets. One by one, the barons lucky enough to be present for the wonderful event filed by the infant to pay their respects.

"Magnificent!" an old baron said, nodding at the tiny pink face. "A perfectly healthy norm. Congratulations."

"Thank you," Kinnison said, reaching out a hand toward the babe, then forcing himself to withdraw it. There was no way he would chance spoiling everything now by giving the little one the Red Death.

"And how is the mother?" Griffin asked, his hands tucked into the loose sleeves of his jacket.

The guards in the corners raised their blaster at the movement, and the chancellor quickly withdrew his hands and kept them in plain sight.

"Lady Susan died giving birth, noble sir," the midwife answered sadly, giving a slight curtsy. "The delivery was long and difficult."

"I see, what a tragedy," Griffin said, stroking his beard. "I will attend to her burial needs personally. Such a glorious day to be marked by tragedy."

"That is life," the old baron said.

Kinnison agreed, and carefully watched the chancellor disappear into the crowd. There was something in the way the man had spoken that greatly disturbed the baron. He debated having the man chilled on general principle. His father had always told him that only the dead couldn't hurt you.

"Looks exactly like you, my lord," a baron from the western islands said in a measured tone.

The lord baron narrowed his cold eyes and started to draw a blaster. "And what does that mean, shit-eater?" he growled in an icy voice.

The visiting baron went pale and began to sputter apologies, when a bedraggled sec man stumbled into the throne room pushing his way past the armed guards and guests.

"Who dares!" Kinnison began, then saw it was Lieutenant Brandon. The baron scowled at the man's appearance, clothes torn and bloody, his face slashed with a dozen half-healed scars, some of his black hair burned away, and an expression that announced serious trouble.

"My lord, we need to speak in private," Brandon said quickly, giving the most cursory of salutes. His hand was bandaged, and it was obvious two of his fingers had been broken.

Kinnison felt a blind rage build at the implied discourtesy, especially on such a day as this! Then he saw the grim determination in the sec chief's face and forced down his fury.

"My private chambers," he directed, and rose to his feet. "The audience is over for today. Come back tomorrow."

As the fat man waddled for the door, the slaves and bodyguards hurried to follow, but not getting close enough to chance touching their master and catching his dread sickness.

"What the fuck was that about?" a baron muttered softly.

Another sipped his wine before speaking. "Perhaps," he said in a hushed tone, "those clones that don't exist have come to call upon our lord and master."

"Wouldn't that be a shame," another added, failing to hide his smile.

"Yes, wouldn't it just be—" he paused to find the correct word "—a total disaster."

"Poor man would never be able to fight the muties and defend this island, would he?"

"That's not for me to say," the first baron replied. "At this time."

Slaves opened the door to the room before the baron, and quickly closed it behind Brandon. The brick walls were lined with longblasters, handcannons and even rapidfires. Covering an entire wall was a detailed painting of the Marshall Islands, every known landmass, island and atoll clearly in beautiful detail. Some sections of the wall map were raised higher than others, layers upon layers of corrections lifting the features until it was almost a contoured relief map.

"Well?" Kinnison demanded, the second the door closed.

"I lost the fleet," Brandon reported, taking a chair. Damn, he was tired.

"Ten ships? How is that possible?

"And Cold Harbor ville was on fire the last time I saw it," Brandon added wearily. "Probably burned to the ground by now."

"Tell me everything," Kinnison demanded, and the sec men explained in detail—the fight, the pirates, the outlanders, the mesa with the predark machinery.

"So you chilled the outlanders and smashed the device," Kinnison said. It wasn't a question.

"The machine for sure, my lord," Brandon answered truthfully. "If we don't control it, no science must be allowed in the islands."

"Correct."

"However, I didn't see the dead bodies of those outlanders. It's possible they survived the fall. I doubt it highly, but you never know."

Going behind his desk, Kinnison slumped in a massive chair built just for his bulk. "At least that machine is gone," he grunted, running his hands along the smooth polished top of the desk. "Unfortunately, we have also lost our main source of flash.''

The baron rubbed the corner of his mouth, his hand coming away stained with red. ''Were there any young girls with forked tongues involved in this?''

The lieutenant managed to keep a neutral face. How the hell did the fat bastard know about her?

''No, my lord,'' Brandon lied, ''there weren't.''

''Good,'' Kinnison said, grimacing. ''If you run across any, chill them on sight. No rape, no torture, just a round in the head. Understood?''

''Yes, my lord. It shall be done.''

''I have a son,'' Kinnison said from out of nowhere.

The comment startled Brandon, but he smiled broadly. ''My congratulations, my lord. What's his name?''

''Corbet.''

''Good name. May he rule for a hundred years!''

''Of course,'' Kinnison said, waving that away. ''With the loss of the flash, this places me in an awkward situation with the western islands. The villes are fighting each other again, and if I refuse them both black powder, I could appear weak. It is possible the fools might join forces to attack us.''

''The fact you have an heir now will slow them down some,'' Brandon replied, leaning forward in his chair.

"Not by much," Kinnison shot back, then slammed his bloody hand onto the desk. "Shitfire, I have no choice. Go the quartermaster and have him fill a hundred barrels with our best black powder, the stuff reserved for the castle defense."

"Yes, sir!"

"Then fill another hundred with charcoal dust mixed with some fireplace ashes. That should look enough like black powder to pass a brief inspection."

Brandon raised an eyebrow. "Sir? We're going to sell each ville a combination of good and bad?"

"No. We're selling the weakest villes the good powder, and that bastard O'Keefe the crap. The little villes will slaughter O'Keefe, removing a possible danger to the security of my son. Leaving only the small villes without the resources or sec men to ever challenge Maturo Island. Two problems solved, and we reap double the profit from one sale."

"It will be done," Brandon stated firmly. "I can refit my boat in a week and will personally escort the cargo to its destinations."

"I can send some other PT captain to handle that," the baron growled, glancing out the window at the bright sunny day. Lighting flashed in the clouds too far away to hear the rumble of its thunder. "Its more important to know if Cold Harbor ville is still standing. If it is gone, I'll take it over.

If it stands, then my Firebirds will level the ville, and again I take it over as abandoned.''

"And what about those outlanders?''

"I want them brought before me, dead or alive," he growled. "And I prefer alive. The dead can't be forced to talk. How did they get here from the mainland? Where did they find those rapidfire weapons? There is much I need to know.''

Brandon saluted. "I shall take care of it myself, my lord.''

"No need for that,'' Kinnison said smoothly as he drew a pistol from under the desk. "Somebody else will handle the task, not you, fool. The last time we talked, I said that failure to secure the flash meant your death. Did you doubt my word?''

"B-but my lord!'' Brandon managed to stammer, rising from his chair. "I have faithfully served you for fifteen seasons! And I brought you the news of the pirate fleet and the outlanders! Surely, that is much more important than one small mistake. I can reclaim Cold Harbor ville and bring you the bodies of the outlanders. Give me a chance! Just one chance, is all I ask!''

"No more chances,'' the baron said, and fired twice. The man toppled over clutching his belly, the bones of a shattered knee showing white through the tattered flesh of his leg. Blood pumped freely from an open artery, and Brandon did what he could to hold the flow back with his bare hands.

A heartbeat later, the door was slammed aside and sec men rushed into the room with their blasters drawn. But they paused, uncertain what to do next at the scene of their baron with a blaster and their commander lying in a pool of his own blood.

"Baron, are you okay?" a corporal asked.

"Take that prick to the playroom," Kinnison commanded, rubbing the sores on his hand. They were stinging badly from the discharge of the weapon. "And keep him alive while you peel off his skin. Let's see if it fits me better than him."

The leader of the man paled, but saluted. "At once, my lord!"

"No, please!" Brandon wailed, terror distorting his features. "Baron, don't do this!"

Kinnison made no reply, his blaster held steady on the crippled man.

As the advancing guards converged, Brandon tried to draw his blaster, and a corporal slammed the wooden stock of his longblaster into the officer's hand, shattering the bones. The weapon dropped from limp fingers, and Brandon made a mad dash for the window. But the troopers tackled him to the floor before he got ten paces, and ruthlessly beat the officer until he stopped resisting. Bloody and battered, the weeping lieutenant was hauled away, leaving a trail of blood on the freshly scrubbed floor.

As the door closed, cutting off the former sec man's anguished cries, Kinnison tucked away his blaster and reclined in the cushioned chair to debate whom he should send to find the nameless outlanders and bring them in for questioning.

Chapter Five

A week later, Ryan and the others stood on the balcony of the predark lighthouse. Their clothes were freshly washed and boots polished. Their backpacks bulged with MRE packs and their pouches were jammed with ammo. The past few days had been mostly spent sleeping, and rubbing lotion into wounds. There had been no sign of the lord baron's PT boats, and while the crabs rallied several times to try to gain entrance through the fireplace, they never made it in alive.

It was a clear, crisp day, the heat of the sun perfectly balancing the coolness of the water. A breeze carried a faint smell of living plants and flowers. Down on the beach, the crabs moved about on the shattered remains of their fallen dead, the broken shells picked clean of anything edible with ruthless efficiency. The wind moaned through the rustling weeds, and the waves gently crashed on the rocky shore. Ryan felt this had to have been what it was like before humanity was born and the world was clean and untouched. Raw. But everything changed, and humanity was now here to stay. If they could survive skydark, then nothing could get rid of Man. The world belonged to them, not the muties.

"Time," Krysty asked, hunching her shoulders. The straps of her pack would have cut into her shoulders if not for the thick bearskin coat.

"Pretty soon," Ryan announced, checking his wrist chron.

The plan was simple, as all good plans were. Create a diversion, then wade across the bay to the next island during low tide.

"Good," Mildred said, her wild hair tied back with a strip of cloth. "I hate long waits."

"That's not what you said last night," J.B. whispered out of the corner of his mouth.

Mildred hushed the man with a glance, then smiled and bumped him with her hip.

Ignoring the lovers, Ryan watched the waves on the beach, carefully noting they were cresting lower each time. Soon the tide would be going out, and that was when they would make their move.

"Now," he announced, clicking off the safety on the handle of the M-16, ready to cut loose on full-auto.

The seven chattering assault rifles sprayed a hellstorm of 5.56 mm death, and the crabs died in droves, chewed to pieces by the streams of lead. Finishing a clip, Ryan dropped it from the breech and slammed in a fresh magazine. They each had one spare, all of the live ammo they could salvage from the stacks and crates. A lot of the M-16 rounds had been bad, not corroded, but simply weak from the long decades. But J.B. had been able to cook up some guncotton and mixed it with the old cordite to get the blasters working with half charges. The rounds had just barely enough recoil to operate the feeder mechanism of the weapons, and misfires were happening constantly.

Soon they had a clear zone at the base of the tower, and J.B. rappelled down first to tether the rope and to stand guard. His M-16 sputtered flame at anything that moved, more than once chewing up weeds, but catching several blues trying to sneak closer under cover of the foliage. In a matter of minutes, the companions were on the ground, spraying lead in every direction. Crabs exploded constantly, their green blood splattering over the rocks and sand dunes.

"Shit," Jak cursed, working the bolt to free another jam. "Ammo stinks!"

"Better than throwing rocks," Dean retorted, burping the rapidfire at the thickest cluster of the muties. Seeking protection, the crabs frantically scuttled for the shoreline, and the companions concentrated their weapons in that direction to drive the muties inland and away from the water.

"I'm out," Krysty reported, dropping the rapidfire and drawing her S&W revolver.

"Same here," Doc rumbled.

''I hope this works,'' Mildred muttered, firing her rapidfire in a long burst only to have to abruptly stop. She cast away the dead blaster and pulled her ZKR in a smooth draw.

''Damn well better,'' Ryan growled. ''Light the fuse.''

Grabbing a thin string dangling among the climbing ropes, J.B. shielded the end with his body and used a butane cig lighter to start it burning. The long fuse sputtered and popped for a while, started to hiss steadily and climb toward the balcony, then out of sight.

''Thirty seconds!'' Ryan shouted, and splashed into the shoals, heading for the next island.

In ragged formation, the rest of the companions followed the man, wading into the shallow water. Walking was tricky with the outgoing tide pulling at their legs, the sand underfoot shifting as it followed the flow. They stayed to the right to avoid a deep ravine spotted days ago by Krysty while she mapped the crossing, then they jogged to the left to bypass another.

But the moment they went into the shoals, the crabs rushed for the beach. The companions started to fire their blasters, while Dean and Jak maintained cover fire with the M-16s until the clips became exhausted. The rapidfires went into the drink, and their regular blasters were hauled into view.

Suddenly, the big blue appeared and started clicking its pincers, directing the other muties. Jak fired his Magnum pistol, the blast rolling over the waves, and the slug scored a glancing blow off the shell of the huge mutie.

"Fucking windage," the teen cursed, turning to try to catch the others. They were halfway across the bay by now, and had to watch their footing to avoid another ravine full of coral.

"Any second now," Ryan warned, dropping the exhausted M-16 and pulling out the SIG-Sauer. The blaster glistened with oil, the trigger and most of the internal springs brand-new, taken from another handcannon of similar design.

"Make sure to cover your ears and keep your mouths open," Mildred warned, kneeling in the damp sand. "That way the concussion won't make you deaf."

The ground shook, and the glass Fresnel lens shattered into a million pieces as flames shot out of the lighthouse. The whole peninsula seemed to shake as the base of the tower broke apart from the titanic explosion. The structure lifted into the air on a fireball, then came crashing down, catching most of the advancing crabs under its descending tonnage of granite blocks. The muties were obliterated, the big blue screaming for only a moment before it was gone, smashed flat by the crumbling building.

Then the secondary charges went off. The concussion hit the companions, slamming them into the water as the ground under the lighthouse formed a geyser of boiling flame that licked high into the sky, the six thousand gallons of jellied diesel fuel igniting into a fireball of ungodly proportions. The chimney bricks shot into the sky, and started to fall back to earth randomly.

Soaked to the skin once more, the companions tried to dodge the falling bricks and not fall into one of the coral beds, when suddenly a group of the large blue crabs crawled menacingly into view from over the sand dune. The creatures flicked their eye stalks around the scene of destruction, stared hatefully at the two-legs, then started forward at a remarkable pace.

Ryan raised his longblaster and fired a fast four times. One stopped dead, but the others only flinched as the 7.62 mm rounds glanced off their hard shells. Fireblast! This wasn't part of the plan.

"On your ten!" the Deathlands warrior shouted, working the bolt and firing again.

The companions cut loose with their assorted collection of blasters, and two more of the giant crabs fell dead before reaching the beach. But the remaining three made it safely into the shallow waters and disappeared from sight.

Ryan fired rapidly into the water, but the rounds were visibly deflected. He would have to get a lot closer before the bullets could cause any damage. Fuck that.

"Run for it," J.B. ordered, pulling out a gren and flipping away the handle. He pulled the pin and cast the charge between them and the oncoming crabs. While the gren was still in the air, he turned and waded after the others at his best speed.

Glancing over a shoulder, Mildred saw the gren splash into the bay, closely followed by a thunderous explosion of fire, water and coral. As the noise and smoke drifted away, she saw no taint of green in the area to mark a kill.

"No blood!" Mildred warned, and fired a few rounds into the sea before turning and running for the next island with the others. Only a few more yards to go until she was safe on the beach.

The water level dropped from her waist to her knees, the rocky sea bottom changing to sand, and the physician struggled through the loose material, every step more difficult than the previous one. Several of the others had reached the shore and were watching the sea. Suddenly, J.B. gasped and fired the shotgun from the hip.

No! The woman braced herself to be torn apart by the barrage of fléchettes. There was a sharp crack to her left and something screamed loudly. She turned with her blaster in hand, and saw one of the giant blues only a yard away. It was missing a pincer, a torrent of green blood pumping from the shattered end of its limb.

Burbling and hissing, the mutie turned on her and

raised both scorpion tails high for a strike. Mildred leveled her weapon and fired once directly into its segmented mouth. The crab jerked back and trembled all over, then collapsed into the water and went still.

"Good shot," J.B. said, offering a hand and pulling her to dry land.

"Can't have an armored throat," she panted, giving a weak smile. "The .38 probably rattled around inside its thick shell, chewing up organs and doing ten times the damage of a gren."

"I'll remember that," Jak snorted, thumbing fresh rounds into his .357 Magnum pistol. These were also partial loads with only half of the usual power. The lower recoil was throwing off his aim.

The strident boom of the LeMat shook the beach as Doc triggered a round at a huge crab rushing out of the water. Five feet wide, the mutie stood over three-feet tall, its scorpion tails lashing wildly about as it headed for the companions, then moved around as if trying to dodged their bullets.

Bizarre. Sensing a trap, Ryan spun with his long-blaster spitting fire. Caught by surprise, the crab right behind him recoiled from the attack. Ryan blew off an eye stalk, then blocked a crushing blow from a pincer as large as a shovel.

J.B. stroked his shotgun's trigger, and the fléchettes removed the mutie's face. Unexpectedly blind, the creature went mad, lashing about with its good pincer and both tails in any direction. Stepping into range, Ryan aimed the Steyr and fired into its pulped mouth. The beast reared on its hind legs and stayed that way, frozen in death.

Caught alone, the remaining crab started for the safety of the ocean and was easily chilled by the combined firepower of the companions' blasters.

"Anybody hurt?" Ryan demanded, shaking his blaster to get rid of the excess water. Droplets flew from the weapon as he jacked the slide to keep the breech clean. Good thing it had been freshly oiled.

"No blood showing," Mildred announced in relief.

"Good," he said. "Let's get moving. We've got six more of these to cross before reaching the main island."

IT WAS LATE in the afternoon by the time the companions reached their goal, the big island with the ville. By now the tide was coming in again, and forced them away during the last crossing. The group was barely able to wade to shore before missing the island entirely and getting swept out to sea.

On the secluded beach, the companions poured salt water from their boots and pulled on dry clothes from their backpacks. There were no footprints on the beach nor any other sign of the place being inhabited, but then, they were a good distance from the ville.

Leaving the beach, Ryan led the group into the jungle and headed westward. It was cool in the lush greenery, but the heavy tangle of vines made for slow travel. Monkeys scampered in the treetops, screaming at the presence of the humans, which sent off the flocks of birds, and soon the jungle was filled with the cacophony of animal screams. Hacking through a cluster of vines with his panga, Ryan fought the urge to chill the noisy bastards. So much for sneaking in close on the quiet. Anybody not deaf knew that strangers were nearby.

"Should we hit the beach?" Dean asked. "Easier walking."

Jak answered, "They know coming. But not which way."

"Gotcha."

Tall palm trees laden with green coconuts festooned the sky, and the lower trees were heavy with breadfruit. No starvation here. The greenery stopped abruptly and Ryan found himself standing on the edge of a twenty-foot drop. At the bottom was a flat plain that stretched into the distance only to rise into jungle again after fifty or so yards. A thin creek flowed down the middle, some small birds drinking from the stream. Just around the bend on the other side, they could see the top of the wall around the ville. J.B. unfolded his telescope and gave it a once-over. Odd, no sign of guards.

"Riverbed," Jak identified.

Doc beamed a smile, flashing his perfect teeth. "Ah, a most excellent location for a ville. The sea for fish, and the river brings freshwater to your door."

"Dumb," the teen corrected. "Coldhearts attack, only escape has no cover. Easy chilling."

"Dark night," J.B. muttered. "From the lighthouse, I thought the wall had iron plate bolted to the outside, but that's wrong. It's made of cargo containers stacked on top each other."

Pushing some leaves aside, Ryan took a look through the scope. Damn, the man was right. A wall of cargo containers. The Deathlands warrior had encountered them before in the ruins of dockyards, just never this many of them all at once. There had to be a hundred of them in the wall.

The containers were always exactly the same, ten feet high, twenty feet wide, thirty feet long. According to Mildred, folks would pack them with whatever, and then load the containers on ships. That kept things fast and easy, with no juggling around in the hold of the vessel to try to fit one more item. Modular—that was the word she used. Like bullets in a blaster.

"Damn good wall," Krysty said, passing the longeyes to somebody else. "Just stack two of the containers on top of each other and repeat. Could fill them with sand if you wanted, and no pirate cannon ever made would breach that wall."

"You wouldn't have to fill them," Mildred said slowly, "if they were already packed. These boxes are air- and watertight. Sometimes they were welded shut if the cargo was valuable. If they haven't been opened, the wealth of the old world is sitting right there, ready to be found."

"Could be filled with anything," J.B. said, compacting the longeyes and tucking the device away in his pack. He glanced at the others. "Wonder if the local baron knows this?"

"Let's find out," Ryan said, and started forward along the edge of the riverbank.

Reaching the beach once more, they headed for the ville, walking in the open with hands on their blasters, but no weapons drawn. They didn't want to appear hostile and start a fight, or walk naked into a slaver camp. If possible, they would trade the two M-16 rapidfires they had with them for that purpose, or the secret of the cargo containers, for a ship, and leave without incident. Spilled blood would only make cutting a deal with the sec men that much tougher.

As Ryan rounded the bend and the ville came full into view, the first thing he noticed was the ruined dockyard. The smashed hulls of burned ships and rowboats lined the crude wooden docks, tiny birds pecking at the bodies sprawled everywhere. Not a soul could be seen moving about in the dock, or on the top of the wall. No guards were in sight, and no alarm bells rang at the approach of outlanders.

"I don't like this," Mildred said, drawing her piece and thumbing back the hammer. A wave crashed on the rock formations along the beach, spraying the woman with salt water, and she moved away from the shore.

"This could be Spider Island all over again," Krysty said, her hair flaring outward.

Jacking the slide on his semiautomatic pistol, Dean concentrated on the ocean. No ships of any kind were in sight at the moment. But that didn't mean a pirate ship, or one of those damn steam-powered PT boats wouldn't appear at any moment with blasters blazing.

There was a gap in the steel box wall surrounding the ville, a section where only one of the shipping containers sat on the ground instead of two. Sand-bags lined the top of the container, the cloth sacks bristling with deadly pungi sticks made from sharp-ened bamboo. A formidable barrier to cross.

"There's the gate," Ryan said, sliding the Steyr off his shoulder. "Let's see if there's anybody in-side. I'm on point. J.B. cover the rear. Five-yard spread."

"Got you covered," J.B. said, working the bolt on the Uzi machine pistol.

Spreading out so as to not offer a group target to any snipers, the companions slowly walked toward the gate, the sand crunching under their new boots. In the jungle, monkeys ran amuck in the treetops screeching at the top of their lungs.

"Something has them spooked," Krysty observed.

"Cannon fire?" Dean asked.

She shook her head. "Something a lot worse than pirates."

The boy didn't reply, but loosened the bowie knife in the sheath at the small of his back.

As Ryan got closer, he saw the gate box was shoved back a few feet, leaving a gap in the defenses. Raising a hand to call for a halt, he jerked his head in both directions and the companions split apart, half going to either side of the opening. Then Ryan charged forward and threw his back to the steel box, blaster at the ready. After a few moments, he eased to the corner of the container, then proceeded down the dark ten-foot passageway between the gate and the wall. His nerves were taut. This was the perfect spot for an ambush. Nearing the end of gate, he listened closely and heard birds, lots of them. Not good. Wriggling closer, the man chanced a quick peek inside.

"Fireblast," he snapped, easing his stance and lowering the blaster. "Mildred, check this out."

Quickly, the puzzled physician came down the pass and stopped dead in her tracks. A hundred different types of birds covered the ground, steadily pecking at something lying on the ground. Aiming at the scavengers, Mildred fired a shot and the creatures took flight, their beating wings sounding as loud as thunder until they were gone into the blue shy.

"Yeah, just what I thought," Ryan said. Decomposing corpses lay everywhere in the ville, sprawled on the ground, some halfway through windows as if trying to escape, while others were locked together with knives drawn. The dead were dressed in rags, many wearing loose garments made of woven grass. All of them were barefoot. The ripe smell of rotting flesh was thick in the air.

"Plague," Doc said, a quaver of fear in his voice. "We should not go any closer."

"What? Oh, horseshit," Mildred countered, and kicked over a desiccated corpse lying sprawled in the sand. The birds and insects had done a good job of stripping away the flesh on most of the dead, but this one was fresh, no more than a day or two old. Rigor had come and gone. There was very little meat on the dead man, which told her a lot.

"See? There are no pustules or skin eruptions," Mildred said, drawing a knife to slit open the men's chest. Some insects scampered from his lungs, carrying away tiny morsels of food.

She pointed with the blade. "Hmm, yes, look at the kidney, and the belly. This man died of *Vibrio cholerae*…he died of cholera, I mean. Not the bubonic plague.''

''What is?'' Jak asked, holding a handkerchief in front of his face. ''Like brain rot or bloodfire?''

''An enterotoxin. It comes from bad water,'' Mildred said, cleaning her blade on the rags of the corpse, then stabbing it into the ground before playing the flame of her lighter along the steel. Alcohol would have been better, but she had none. This would have to do for sterilization. ''I'd bet live rounds we'll find their latrine right next to the drinking well. Damn fools did it to themselves.''

''Masks,'' Ryan commanded in a no-nonsense voice, pulling a handkerchief out of his pocket. All of the companions tied some sort of cloth across their faces to cover nose and mouth.

''Not necessary,'' Mildred said. ''It's spread by oral consumption, not breathing.''

''Can we stay?'' Ryan asked bluntly. In battle, or cutting a deal with a baron, he knew what to do. But sickness like this was more Mildred's speciality, and only a triple stupe would make a guess when he had an expert standing three feet away.

''Keep the handkerchiefs over your faces,'' she directed. ''Don't touch anything with your bare hands, and for God's sake don't eat or drink anything unless it's in a sealed can. We'll be okay.''

''Must have hit like lightning,'' Krysty muttered,

looking away from tiny corpses, still clutched in their mother's arms.

"Goddamn it!" Mildred raged, clenching her fists. "I could have saved this whole ville with a pocketful of rehydration salt and some tetracycline. Or even old furazolidone!"

Jak stared at the physician, wondering if she was making up those words.

"Got any of the chems?" Krysty asked bluntly. "Do they exist anymore, even in the redoubts?" The physician sometimes got this way over her inability to cure diseases that were such simple matters in her day, and now were the unstoppable plagues of the reality that was Deathlands.

"Can't even remember what penicillin tastes like anymore," Mildred admitted gloomily. Her med kit hung heavy at her side. She had the skill to cure the people, but not the tools. Sometimes the physician got so frustrated she thought she'd go as mad as Doc.

Going to the other side of the gate, J.B. found that a bulldozer was attached with lots of heavy chains to pull the gate open, its shovel flat against the container to keep it closed again. It was one hell of an impressive gate. Going to the driver's seat, the Armorer found a corpse sprawled in the chair, skinny arms still on the controls.

"Aced trying to get out," J.B. said, climbing into the dozer and checking the gauges.

"Nuke batteries have plenty of power," he reported, thumping a control board. Rust fell from under the dashboard like dried blood. "But it's out of fuel."

"Let it stay there," Ryan decided. He had no intention of wasting any of their precious fuel on operating the big wag. They would need every drop for the gateway to get them out of here. He only hoped it was still intact. People often destroyed predark technology simply out of fear. If that had happened to the gateway, well, he had another plan to get them out of the Cific, but it was a hell of a lot more risky than using the gateway.

"Wonder how they moved the boxes," Doc rumbled, leaning on his stick, hands clasped on the silver lion's-head handle.

"No biggie," Dean said, pointing. "See? They're empty."

Ryan looked closer and noted that all of the containers had holes cut in the side to serve as doorways and windows. But there was no glass, and the doors were only hanging sheets of canvas.

"They lived inside the wall," Ryan said, rubbing his chin. "Smart. Anybody tried to get in, and you'd hear them on the metal roof."

"Must have been a bitch cutting the doors," J.B. stated, tilting back his hat. "Those aren't plas-ex holes. Mebbe they used chisels and hacksaws."

"Take weeks," Jak said grimly. "Months."

"Mebbe the locals needed the steel boxes to keep out something no sandbag-and-wood barricade could," Krysty said, her hair stirring to unfelt breezes. The sense of death in the ville was strong, but somewhere life was stirring weakly. It was like a tickle with a feather, almost too soft to feel. Then as quickly as it came, the sensation was gone.

"Triple red," Ryan whispered softly. The hairs rising on the back of his neck, he raised the Steyr and scanned the area quickly.

"So you felt it, too?" Krysty said, clicking back the hammer on her S&W .38 revolver.

"We're being watched," Mildred agreed. "Don't know from where." The hundred holes in the encircling wall each seemed to stare blankly at the companions below. But from one of those dark holes, living eyes watched their every move.

"Could be the birds. Got to clear this place out," J.B. said. Sliding the shotgun off his shoulder, he jacked the action and fired a 12-gauge round into the birds. The flock erupted in bloody feathers, the rest lifted into the air, only to settle down again and begin to feed once more.

Doc tried this time, the LeMat roaring louder than a cannon. Some birds rose into the sky, but most roosted on the top of the wall, settling in to simply wait until it was safe to return.

"Never leave," Jak stated, leaning forward slightly so that his white hair cascaded down to

cover his face. "Too much food, not enough us."
The position was a combat stance, something he did
unconsciously to hide his eyes and thus mask what
direction he would attack.

"When the belly speaks," Mildred growled, "the
ears become deaf."

"Indeed, madam." Doc arched an eyebrow.
"Buddha?"

"Who else?"

Looking over the aced ville, Ryan scowled
deeply. This was no place to make camp. The smell
of the dead was attracting swarms of dragonflies,
which had discovered the companions as a new
source of nourishment. J.B. hauled a Molotov cock-
tail from his munitions bag, and the group passed
around the bottle of fuel, rubbing small amounts on
their exposed skin. The flies departed immediately,
but they knew the bugs would return once the gas
vapors had dissipated.

"Okay, we do a fast recce," Ryan stated, hoisting
his longblaster. "In pairs only. Stay alert, watch for
traps. Check for any boats, or even canoes we might
use. Krysty, with me. J.B. stay with Mildred. Dean
with Jak. Doc, you're the anchor."

"Once more, I am Balador at the gate, my dear
Ryan," the old man said, thrusting his stick into the
ground and drawing the monstrous LeMat. "None
shall pass without a greeting from my trusty Mjol-
nir!"

"Crazy old coot," Mildred grumbled. "Everybody in your time period talk like that?"

Doc smiled. "Only the educated, madam."

As the others spread out to follow the wall, Krysty and Ryan cut directly through the middle of the settlement. The corpses carpeted the ground, and more than once they were forced to tread on the dead to keep going straight.

In the center of the ville, they found a huge cooking pit, now converted into a pyre. Bodies and cords of wood were mixed together, waiting for a lit match. The stench was unimaginable.

"Gaia! They tossed the poor bastards in, dead or alive," Krysty said.

The man merely grunted in reply. He'd seen folks do a lot worse than that to stay alive. Ryan was no stranger to the savagery of man.

"Let's try over there," he said, indicating a box with iron bars over the windows. It was the only such cargo container with anything added to the Spartan exterior.

"Must be the baron's home," she guessed.

"Makes sense," he agreed.

But as they started to leave, a whispery voice spoke from out of nowhere. "H-help…me…"

The man and woman swung about in a crouch, their blasters sweeping the nearby corpses for any hostile signs. But nothing was stirring, except the

swarms of fat flies feeding on the festering dead.
Then the voice came again.

"Ryan..." the voice called from the depths of the
reeking pit. "For God's sake, Ryan. It's...me...."

Chapter Six

With white-knuckled hands, Henry Glassman grimly held on to the control board of the pitching PT boat. The spray whipped back his hair and stung his eyes as it came howling over the cracked windshield of the open cabin at the front of the craft. Its speed was phenomenal, and the huge steam engine aft of the vessel thumped louder than a cannon. The crew said that was normal, and he wondered if it was true.

Glassman still couldn't believe this PT boat and its sec men were his to command. The healer had played for as much time as possible with Kinnison, praying his family would escape the clutches of the lord baron. But Kinnison had outmaneuvered him once more, and with his family under guard back on Maturo Island, Glassman had no choice but to do the baron's dirty work yet again.

He had no idea why he was chosen for this task. The healer knew next to nothing about the sea, and even less about the steam-powered boats called peteys by the sec men who rode them, and PT boats by everybody else. Rebuilt from the wreckage of some predark navy, the craft moved faster than arrows and carried enough weaponry and blasters to level a small ville. No pirate ship would dare to approach one of the deadly boats, even the huge four-masted windjammers that carried dozens of black powder cannons.

The sec men who served as crew on the vessels were fiercely proud of their status, and wore facial tattoos to show their rank and boat. Once you were made crew, you were crew for life. And the sailors feared nothing but the wrath of their master and the deepers, the terrible muties that lived in the cold depths of the limitless ocean and rose only after the worst storms to devour anything they could find. The sea muties were the main reason nobody tried to sail out of the archipelago and reach the mainland anymore. As soon as any vessel sailed past the last island of the Cific chain, the currents forced it back, and then the deepers attacked, dragging the vessels down whole into the sea. Volcanoes, hurricanes, pirates, slavers and Kinnison, this hellish prison was the extent of their world, as sure as if there were solid granite walls sealing the people inside.

Dripping with spray, Glassman ran a finger around the stiff collar of his new uniform, trying to get more comfortable. As befitting his rank of captain, Glassman wore loose gray clothing, and woven sandals that were easy to kick off if a man went overboard. Heavy boots could drag a sailor into the cold embrace of Davey faster than a knife to the neck. Around his waist was a wide leather belt with a flintlock sitting in a holster smack in the middle of his stomach, and a machete slung just below his armpit. The rest of the crew was dressed the same, except for the pilot, Sergeant Campbell. He alone carried a predark revolver. It was blatantly obvious he was the jailer assigned to watch over the healer, and to assure his obedience.

"How far to the next island?" Glassman shouted over the crash of the waves and the roar of the steam engine.

The man at the wheel started to reply when the aft engine cut loose with a long, loud blast of its steam whistle to equalize pressure. Some of the old-sters said that back in the predark days, there was something called a relief switch that could keep a boiler from exploding from too much pressure. But that tech was lost, and the whistle was sounded reg-ularly to keep the machine functioning.

"About fifty miles," Campbell replied. "Say, an-other hour, sir."

"Thank you, Sergeant," Glassman replied, sud-denly reaching out to grab hold of the dashboard as the boat lurched. Alongside the pilot was an empty chair, bolted to the deck and his to use whenever he wished. But it seemed using it was something only a landlubber would do and would greatly decrease his authority over the crew. Swallowing hard, the man fought the roiling sensation in his gut and tried to rock to the motion of the vessel as it skimmed rapidly over the choppy waters. He had to be the baron's sec man in every possible way if his wife and children were to stay this side of the soil.

So far, the crew of PT 312 had visited a dozen islands, leaving messages with the local barons about the reward for the capture of the outlander Ryan and his crew of murdering coldhearts. A dozen out of a thousand. This journey to all of the major islands was going to take weeks, if not months to complete. Some of the larger islands like Namorik and Alinglapala supported numerous villes. Most were on the beach, and each of the barons agreed to send runners to the inland villes with the news. On the crescent-moon-shaped Oma atoll, Glassman had found two villes on opposite points of the landmass at war with each other. The healer had his crew use the big .50-caliber machine gun to chill a score of people fighting on the beach. The combat paused, and he relayed the message to the barons and departed, leaving them to their battle. Lord Baron Kinnison didn't give a spent brass if the villes fought with each other, or much of anything else—as long as they obeyed.

Unfortunately, the last baron visited had slyly suggested cleaning up some slaves and pretending they were the strangers to turn them in for the reward. Glassman agreed to the plan, sailed away from the docks and had the crew blow the entire ville apart with a barrage of Firebirds from the main missile pod. Dozens, maybe hundreds were aced on his command. The healer felt the deaths inside his guts like hot stones. But there had been no choice. It was either chill strangers or be dragged back to the dungeon of the baron to watch his family skinned alive.

"Captain!" a sec man called out from the port cannon. "The waves are cresting white!"

"Is that important?" Glassman responded.

The sailor stole a glance at the others on the deck of PT 312 before answering. "Ah, yes, sir," he replied, trying to mask a surly smile. "Means a storm is coming! Maybe we should find a cove to anchor in, just in case."

A storm? Glassman glanced at the sky. The heavy clouds rumbled with sheet lightning as always. He recalled less than a week of clear blue in his whole life. Some of the oldsters said the clear days were coming less often, as if the atmosphere was becoming more polluted with toxic chems and rads. But that was impossible. Sheer nonsense.

"What's your opinion, Sarge?" Glassman asked the pilot.

Campbell looked out of the corner of his eyes. "I know of a small atoll only a few miles to the norwest, Cap'n," the pilot replied, trimming their speed. "Good harbor, no villes, though."

Which meant no more blood to be spilled, for a while at least.

"Take us there," Glassman ordered. "Best speed." Then releasing the stanchion, he climbed into the empty chair. Ah, better. He was tired of standing, and if he was supposed to be the goddamn captain then he could do whatever he wanted. Including sitting down.

"Aye, sir," Campbell replied, then leaned sideways to shout down a bamboo tube sticking out of the deck. "Engine room! Skipper wants all she's got! We're racing a storm!"

"Aye, aye, sir!" a muffled voice replied, and the speed of the boat increased noticeably.

The healer looked hard at the sergeant. That was the first time he had been called the skipper of the vessel. Briefly, he wondered if by taking the chair he had just passed some sort of test.

"Okay, swabs, batten down the hatches!" a bosun called out from amidships, his wet shirt clinging to his muscular chest. "Or do ya wanna swim home!"

Glassman watched as the crew hustled into action, lashing down loose items of equipment, tightening ropes and covering the machine guns and torpedoes with old plastic sheeting that was heavily patched.

Just then, the speeding craft gently rose and fell as something colossal disturbed the water directly under the petey and continued onward, heading directly for the brewing storm on the horizon. The pilot went pale, the crew whispered curses and

Glassman felt clammy, his heart pounding in his chest. They had just sailed past death itself, a sea mutie.

With an effort of will, the captain put the event out of his mind and concentrated on the work at hand. There was nothing to be afraid of; death was just part of life in the Cific. And often a welcome release.

PAUSING, Krysty pointed with the barrel of her weapon. Only a few yards away, the form of a woman was sprawled on the filthy soil. Feebly, she raised a hand, struggling to accomplish the action as if her limb weighed a million pounds.

"Here…" the ghostly voice whispered once more. "R-Ryan."

It was a woman, dressed in rags, her body covered with dark discolored bruises. Her arms were skeleton thin, her cheeks sunken and sallow. On her arm was the brand of a slave.

"Who the hell are you?" Ryan asked, scowling, his blaster pointing directly at her heart.

"I w-was on…" she gasped, "S-Spider Island."

Ryan's scowl deepened, but he moved aside the blaster. There was no way a local slave could know that. Quickly, he dragged the dead man off her legs as Krysty knelt on the ground and opened her canteen to trickle some of the tepid water into the woman's mouth. She drank it greedily and sighed in relief.

"Been so long…" she croaked, then broke into a ragged cough. "You're really here. Not another dream…"

"We're real," Krysty said softly, trying to brush aside the tangles of hair covering the woman's face. But the hair was stuck to her skin in spots from the dried residue of sickness.

"You were on the *Constellation*, right?" Krysty asked, drawing a blade. Cutting a relatively clean shirt off a dead man, she splashed some more water from her canteen onto the rag and mopped the woman's face clean. The smell from the dead around them was terrible. Most were lying in dried pools of their own vomit and feces.

Blinking to focus her eyes, the woman nodded. "I was…one of the slaves who refused to join the crew."

When her face was clear of filth, Krysty could see the woman was actually a girl about Dean's age. Once she might have been pretty, but the enduring scars of privation had shrunk her features into a gnarled visage. She looked a hundred seasons old, Gaia help her. Food and rest might make her strong again, but nothing would remove these scars of hunger.

"Part of the crew, eh?" Ryan demanded, glancing around them. There was no other movement in sight, nor anybody else who looked familiar. But then, the corpses were all so thin and emaciated, the Trader himself could be ten feet away and Ryan would never know it.

"What was wrong? Didn't like the deal I offered, eh?" Ryan said smoothly, studying her reaction.

Licking cracked lips, the girl frowned. "Wasn't you. Old man, silver hair…"

Good enough. Kneeling in the muck, Ryan slid his powerful arms under her frail body and lifted the girl. She weighed next to nothing. His ammo pouch felt heavier.

"What are you doing?" she demanded, her eyes unnaturally large in her sunken face.

"Taking you with us," he said. "Gave you my word back on that island, and it's still good."

"Thank you…"

"Shut up," Ryan said with surprising gentleness. "Go to sleep."

"Ann," she croaked, closing her eyes. "My name is Ann."

"Go to sleep, Ann," he repeated. "You're safe now. My word."

"Safe," she said, the word becoming a whimper, and a tear rolled down her cheek. Then she touched his face with a trembling hand. "I know where it is, the machine you want."

Startled, Ryan stared at the women hard and started to speak, but she went limp, fallen unconscious. The strain of talking had to have been too much for her in that weakened condition.

Inhaling deeply, Ryan sharply whistled three long times. Three short whistles replied, and soon the rest of the companions came running up, weapons out, looking for trouble.

"By the Three Kennedys, what a stench in this area," Doc rumbled, holding his embroidered swallow-eyed handkerchief to his nose. Not even the pig pit of his slave days smelled as bad as this ville. Never before had he prayed for acid rain before, but it was just what this hellhole needed to wash it clean.

"Good Lord, is she alive?" Mildred asked, and went straight to the girl in Ryan's arms. She felt for a pulse in the wrist, then tried again on the neck.

"Aced?" Jak asked, looking over her shoulder.

"Alive," the physician stated. "But just barely. Let's get her out of here."

"Located the baron's box at the other end of the ville," J.B. said, wrinkling his nose. "Or mebbe it'd be better if we got her out of here, get some fresh air."

"We can make camp outside the wall," Dean suggested. "Digging a fire pit is easy in sand."

"Too cold on the beach with the wind," Mildred said. "Warmth is the important thing right now."

"This way," J.B. said, starting across the compound.

"Hate to leave the gate unguarded," Doc rumbled, glancing that way. "Visigoths and rapscallions abound in these islands."

"You mean coldhearts?" Dean asked.

Doc smiled. "Indeed, my young friend. That is exactly what I mean. Men with cold hearts."

"Leave it," Ryan said, shaking his head to dispel the returning clouds of flies. "There's nothing here anybody would want."

"'Cept us," Jak stated.

After J.B. passed around some more fuel, the flies departed again. Crossing the open center of the ville, the companions found the baron's box at the opposite end of the ville away from the gate. Iron bars covered the windows, and a crude wooden door leaned against the open doorway. Bamboo racks of crude spears stood in place, ready to repel invaders. A rusty bed frame stood upright in the ground, a damaged fishing net spread over it for repairs. Only a few yards away was a brick well, standing right next to a bamboo hut that clearly was a public latrine.

"Idiots," Mildred muttered under her breath.

Watching the empty windows lining the two layers of steel boxes, Krysty felt her hair fan outward when a cough sounded from somewhere, echoes disguising the distance and direction.

"More folks dying," Ryan said, scanning his

good eye over the curved wall of identical containers.

"Poor bastards," Doc said, but he kept a hand resting on the grip of the LeMat in its holster.

Going to a window, Jak waited for J.B. to cover the door with his Uzi, then he tossed a stone into the box. It hit something wooden, then rattled around on the metal floor. After waiting a moment, the teenager chanced a look inside.

"Clear," he reported.

Doc and Dean pulled the heavy door aside, and Ryan walked into the box, careful not to hit Ann's head on the badly cut doorway. Inside, there were tables made from wooden spools for holding coils of cables, and chairs of bamboo tied together with vines. Most of the knots were already frayed and unraveling. A ratty bed with rags sticking out of the mattress stood in a corner, and there was a stone fireplace with stacks of seasoned wood. Inside was an empty aluminum pot sitting on a triangle of bricks. One of the tables was stacked with pieces of blasters, flintlocks and predark revolvers, mixed together. Lying in alabaster clamshells was a collection of tools—worn hammers, blunt chisels, twisted screwdrivers and the like. Everything was smeared with fatty grease to keep away rust, and bunches of dried herbs hung from the metal wall to keep flies off the protective lard.

There was no sign of the baron, or any sec men.

"Set her here," Mildred directed, going to the only bed.

Ryan placed the girl on the dirty mattress and looked around for a blanket of some kind to cover her. Nothing was in sight. Without comment, Doc slid off his frock coat and placed it over the still girl.

"Would have thought steel boxes would make for a good home," J.B. said, pushing back his hat. "Obviously not." There was no second floor, or another door to use for escape. Probably too tough to cut the plate steel.

Dean took a seat on one of the tables, the old wood creaking under his weight. "Think that dozer moved the boxes to make the wall?" he asked.

"No, they used slaves," his father replied bluntly, lifting a set of shackles from the tool bench. "I'll bet there's a lot of flesh and blood crushed between these layers of steel."

"Get a fire going," Mildred ordered, pulling a chair close to the bed. "We need more heat in here, and make some bouillon. No coffee or tea. She needs salt."

Jak went to the fireplace and got busy. Doc dropped his backpack and began to rummage around for MRE packs.

"Can you save her?" Ryan asked, leaning against the wall. "She knows something about the gateway."

Mildred shrugged. In a proper hospital with a full medical staff, there would be no problem. Ann was warm, and cleaner. She had received clean water, and broth was coming. Antibiotics was what she needed now. Spreading the canvas flap of her med kit, Mildred took out a plastic sandwich box, popped the top and removed a plastic film canister, the kind photographers kept undeveloped rolls of film in. Burping the top, Mildred opened the canister and removed a folded foil board. Military antibiotics, the good stuff. She hadn't seen better in years. However, even under ideal conditions the medicine would stay potent for ten years. Mildred could only hope there was a little life left after a full century.

Using a thumb, she pressed five of the tablets out of their bubbles and tucked the rest away. Knowing the stuff would taste as bitter as hell, Mildred crushed the tablets and mixed them with a full pack of sugar from a MRE pack. Adding some water, she swirled the mixture around and poured it down the throat of her patient. Ann murmured in response and made a face.

"Sour," Ann said, smacking her lips.

"Okay, what happened on Spider Island?" Ryan asked, kneeling so they were face to face.

"Lieutenant Brandon had his sec men raid our ville," Ann whispered, new strength in her voice. "He was looking for you." She broke into a ragged cough.

Ryan frowned. Fireblast! He hadn't considered that possibility. After blowing the bridge, the sec men did a recce on both islands and tortured the escaped slaves for any info they had on the companions. The women knew nothing, but that wouldn't have stopped Brandon.

"Brandon. This was a big man, dark hair, lots of scars," Ryan asked.

She nodded. "Th-that's him. W-wanted you bad."

"We aced a lot of his troops," Ryan explained briefly.

Ann almost smiled. "Good."

The water in the pot was boiling now, and Jak added a couple of envelopes of brown powder. Soon the tantalizing aroma of beef soup filled the cramped quarters. A cup was brought over, and Mildred spoon-fed the girl tiny sips. The broth seemed to bring her back to life, and soon she was gulping down the brew.

"Not too much," Mildred warned, taking away the cup. "Your stomach isn't used to anything yet. Give it a while."

Ann nodded obediently, but constantly gazed at the tin cup with open avarice.

"How did you get away from Brandon?" Krysty asked.

Feebly, the girl showed her scarred wrists. "Bit through my ropes, jumped into the ocean and swam away. They fired a few shots, but I kept swimming. Anything was better than being tortured by them. Half the other girls were already aced. Some ocean current caught me, and I was dragged here.''

''Just like it did us,'' Dean commented.

A great rustling noise sounded from outside the box, and J.B. went to the window for a look. All of the birds were taking wing, swarming into the sky and flying away. Bad.

''Be right back,'' he said, and slipped out the doorway.

Doc and Jak placed the wooden board back over the entrance, and Ryan gestured for the girl to continue.

''The ville was mostly dead when I washed ashore. Bodies everywhere. I tried to help and got...taken by some of the men. Thought it would cure them.'' Ann shifted the frock coat to hide the bruises on her thighs. ''Then I got sick, too, and they tossed me in the hole.''

''Bastards,'' Mildred growled. ''Hope they died hard.''

''What about the machine they found,'' Ryan said, returning to the original topic. ''Did they take it with them?''

''He, Brandon, suspected you wanted it for something,'' Ann replied slowly, as if afraid to speak. ''So he had the sec men smash it to pieces.''

"Fuck!" Ryan cursed, rocking back on his heels. The gateway was destroyed.

"We're trapped," Krysty said in a hollow voice.

"No, we're not," Ryan said, worrying a fist into the palm of his other hand. "Remember that map in the lighthouse."

"Those weird symbols?" Mildred scoffed. "Could mean anything."

"Mebbe so. But it's our best chance for leaving," Ryan shot back. "Our destination may have changed, but the plan is the same. We find a ville, buy a ride on a ship and leave. Only now we're going to Forbidden Island."

"Well, our rad counters will help us avoid the blast craters there," Doc mused aloud, pursing his lips. "But we shall need to locate another ville. There are no vessels for hire here."

"Not even a canoe," Dean said in a serious tone.

"I know where there is a ship," Ann said, levering herself upward on an elbow. "And I'll show you, but only if you take me with you. Please…"

J.B. appeared at the doorway. "Company coming," he reported. "Lots of them."

"Brandon?"

"Don't think so."

"Triple red," the Deathlands warrior barked, sliding the Steyr off his shoulder and working the bolt.

Going to the window, Ryan watched as whistling objects arced over the wall to land among the dead and bounce along the ground, spewing forth thick streams of black fumes. A bird caught in the gas gave no reaction and continued feasting. Not poison gas, then, which was good. Spreading across the compound, thick tendrils of dark smoke crept along the ground, hiding the dead. Then dim figures on horseback appeared in the smoke, stopping occasionally to stab at the corpses with long spears. Testing to see if any were still alive. Had to be slavers come for fresh muscle.

"Dig in here?" Dean asked, jacking the slide on his Browning semiautomatic pistol.

"Fish in a barrel," his father answered curtly. "We'll have to snipe these bastards to pieces. Dean, stay with Mildred and the girl. Everybody else, spread out. Now move!"

Going to the bed, Jak gestured and a knife was in his hand. Kneeling, he pressed it into the palm of the girl. "Any probs, whisper about blasters," he said fast. "They lean close to hear, stab in throat."

She silently thanked him with her eyes, and Jak moved off at a run.

Dashing outside, the companions separated into the thickening smoke, not daring to fire their blasters yet and draw unwanted attention to the baron's home. As soon as the companions were gone, Mildred and Dean manhandled the door into position and dropped down the wooden arms on each side. The slats held the door in place, but Mildred highly doubted its ability to withstand any kind of an attack.

"Best we got," Mildred said, wiping her hands.

"Watch the windows," Dean replied grimly.

Hoofbeats pounded in the smoky compound. So they had horses. Good. Keeping his back toward the wall, Ryan drew the SIG-Sauer and waited until a dimly seen figure came closer. He fired, there was a muffled cry and the rider tumbled to the ground. Small as the sound of the silenced pistol had been, it drew a barrage of return fire, tongues of flame stabbing into the smoke from a dozen flintlocks, the telltale thud-clack sounding before the powder ignited. Lead balls slammed into the steel wall around him, one plowing into the dirt between his boots. Diving out of the line of fire, Ryan rolled to get some distance. Rising, he fired again, another rider dropped and again the flintlocks delivered a brutal retaliation.

Dark swirling clouds filled the ville, the galloping of horse hooves thudding onto the soil forming a low rumble like an approaching storm. It was difficult to know which direction the riders were coming from, but Ryan realized the smoke worked both ways. The companions couldn't see the invaders very well, and the coldhearts would have no idea how many defenders there were. Might be able to use that in their favor.

Somewhere close by, a revolver snapped off

rounds, followed by the thundering roar of the LeMat. Flintlocks responded, accompanied by several thrown spears. Then Jak's Magnum pistol boomed, and a horse screamed in pain. More flintlocks spoke, lead balls ricocheting off the wall and rebounding back into the compound. Ryan felt the hot passage of a near miss and started zigzagging across the ground.

Leaping over a corpse, he stopped just in time before tumbling into the firepit full of decomposing bodies. A sputtering smoke bomb lay on top of a dead man, charring the flesh and clothes. Odd place for it to land. Damn thing should have rolled right off. On impulse, Ryan kicked the charge into the firepit. Almost instantly, a spear jabbed from the billowing clouds and he fired from the hip, the cough of the SIG-Sauer heralding the wet smack of lead hitting flesh. The figure staggered and dropped its weapon to grab an arm, but the coldheart didn't cry out in pain. Swiftly, he retreated into the smoke and disappeared. But now Ryan knew why they were so hard to spot. The enemy was wrapped in gray cloth the same color as the smoke. Camou clothing. Clever.

From the distance came the stutter of a rapidfire, the fiery flower of the discharges brightening the clouds in a brief strobe effect. J.B. was in action. But the sound stopped almost as quickly as it had started, and Ryan feared the worst.

Moving sideways, the man headed in that direction and after only a few yards discovered that the body of the man he had aced was gone. The coldhearts took their dead? Suddenly, Ryan wasn't sure they were facing just slavers anymore, but something infinitely worse.

More gunfire and flintlocks spoke as the one-eyed man reached into a pocket and pulled out a rebuilt gren from the lighthouse. Ryan couldn't use the explosive in the smoky field; that would be a sure way to chill his own people. But he could toss it into the firepit. That would contain the deadly shrapnel and hopefully the noise of the detonation would rattle the unseen enemy. Slim chance, but worth a try. This whole fight could turn against them with lightning speed.

Something long went by the man, as silent as a dream, but he saw what it was and drew the panga with his free hand. Then another lasso snaked out of the clouds and Ryan caught it on the blade, slicing the loop apart, and firing back along the rope. A man cried out and the rope went slack.

As if in response, Krysty's voice cried out, her blaster blazing steadily. More voices were raised, the smoke and steel walls distorting their origins. A riderless horse galloped past Ryan, almost knocking him down. The LeMat discharged five, six, seven times in a row, the last answered by an anguished scream. Slapping in a fresh clip, Ryan grunted in approval.

Suddenly, he heard the sound of splintering wood, followed by the sound of two blasters firing together. Then it abruptly stopped. Pocketing the gren, Ryan headed for the baron's home. As he went past the well, a spear stabbed out of the swirling fumes, the shaft coming so close it passed through his black hair, ripping some out by the roots. Ignoring the minor pain, Ryan spun and fired from the hip. There was the meaty thump of a slug hitting flesh, but again no cry of pain. The invaders seemed to make noise only when they died; wounds meant nothing to them.

Huffing horses were running everywhere in the compound, the bones of the dead audibly cracking under their hooves. A flintlock discharged, a revolver answered, and then there was silence. No sound or movement for several minutes.

Barely breathing, Ryan stood stock-still, straining to hear anything. But the eerie quiet continued. Even the scavenger birds were gone, and the complete lack of noise seemed thicker than the roiling clouds of gray smoke.

Chapter Seven

Chaos and pain filled J.B.'s world as he sluggishly came awake.

He was tied wrist to ankle, bouncing on something hard that kept slamming into his stomach, knocking the breath out of his lungs, and he was facedown with the ground moving past his face at great speed. Dark night! He was tied over the back of a galloping horse. A big one, white with black stripes on its rump.

There were a lot of horses, fifteen, maybe twenty, and he caught jumping glimpses of the riders. Gray camou! So that's how they did it. Clever bastards. The group was racing along the dried riverbed, the hard-packed earth cracked in a mosaic pattern. The stink of sour horse sweat and badly cured leather nearly made him vomit, but he fought it. With his mouth gagged, he could easily drown if his stomach rebelled. Out of the hundreds of ways to die, that was suddenly the worst he could think of.

Struggling against his bonds, he tried to see the rider on his horse, but there was a bundle in the way. In horror he realized it was three of the gray men roped together and stacked across the back of the beast. J.B. was near the rump, which explained the severe jostling. They took their dead? Oh, no.

Then a familiar sight swung into view, bouncing off the chest of the huge animal. His munitions bag was hanging from the bone pommel of the saddle, the wire stock of the Uzi sticking out the top flap. Now he had a goal. J.B. tightened his stomach muscles to handle the pounding, and worked out a couple of plans in his mind. He knew that time was against him; moments, not minutes counted here. Two plans came to mind, each seeming more dangerous than the other as he mentally reviewed them. But the man couldn't think of a third, so he had to use one of these.

Decision made, J.B. pulled on his bonds as hard as he could, the ropes tightening painfully on his wrists and ankles, but that gave him some slack. Bracing himself, the Armorer dived forward to slide around the beast and was suddenly looking at its stomach. The hind legs started banging into his side like sledgehammers, and the ground slammed into his back so hard he feared bones would break. Breathing was impossible in this position, and J.B. fought to suck in enough air through his nostrils to stay alive. His arms felt as if they were coming out their sockets, and he squinted as hard as possible to keep his glasses from flying off.

Dark night, this was the worst idea he had ever come up with, but it was too late now to stop. They'd chill him, or blind him once they discovered he was trying to escape. This was his only chance.

Swinging back and forth to the rhythm of the hind legs, J.B. got the timing down and jabbed out with his elbow to stab the horse directly in the testes. The stallion screamed and kicked backward. Caught by surprise, the rider tumbled over the animal and hit the ground hard, rolling wildly with his arms and legs failing like a broken puppet.

Guttural laughter sounded from the riders of other horses, and the mount he was on abruptly slowed to a canter, the beast turned to snap at the man dangling under its vulnerable stomach, bringing the munitions bag close enough for J.B. to snatch the wire stock and haul the Uzi free. Timing pencils and coils of fuse came with the blaster and tumbled away, but the Armorer paid them no attention.

Several horses came to a stop, and men began to dismount when a woman screamed, and the startled riders turned their attention to her for a moment.

But that split second was all that J.B. needed. Flipping the weapon over, he worked the bolt with his jaw and clumsily placed the barrel of the blaster to the knotted ropes and fired a short burst. The horse bucked wildly at the blaster fire from underneath, making him drop the weapon, but the rope was torn to pieces and he fell to the ground.

Heavy hooves stomped all around J.B., sinking inches into the soil, and he frantically rolled clear. Then he threw himself back under the beast to reclaim his blaster. Angry voices sounded from the advancing gray men, and several drew big flintlock pistols. Another uncoiled a lasso from his belt.

"Fuck you!" J.B. shouted through his mouthful of rag and started firing on full-auto, spraying the coldhearts with half a clip, turning quickly in a full circle. Those closest to him fell over riddled with copper-jacketed lead. Startled by the noise, the horses bucked, and the riders cried out, clutching the reins with both hands, unable to attack for the moment. Then the Uzi jammed, and J.B. feverishly worked the bolt to clear the malfunctioning cartridge. Not now.

Horses circled him, kicking up clouds of dust. A blaster fired in a thunderous boom, the black powder blowing an acrid cloud of smoke over the area, and his fedora was yanked off his head by the near miss. Shitfire, too close! Cold adrenaline filled his body and, slamming his fist onto the breech, J.B. got the round loose and started to fire 9 mm rounds at the masked riders. He jerked the barrel of the Uzi away from a horse with a woman bound across its back exactly as he had been. Then he recognized, the ragged clothing. It was Ann!

Just then a lasso snaked out of nowhere to land around the man's shoulders. As J.B. jerked away, the rope drew tight and he was yanked off his feet, but he kept hold of the Uzi. This was how the bastards got him in the ville. It wasn't going to work twice.

Another landed on his boots, and he managed to slip out of the closing loop. Running toward the rider holding the rope loosened the lasso, and J.B. shrugged his way out. A third flew toward him, and the Armorer blew it out of the air with a hip shot. Going to single rounds, he fired again and again, constantly moving to avoid any more of the those freakishly accurate lassos.

A riderless horse slammed into his side, knocking J.B. to the ground. Hooves pounded everywhere, one coming so close it grazed his cheek. Hugging the Uzi, he rolled away to avoid the smashing hooves. He fired twice more and the blaster clicked empty.

Throwing the weapon at a gray man, J.B. took off at a run, pelting down the riverbed with all of his strength. The banks were too high to climb easily. He had to find another section where he could get into the jungle. The horses and lassos would be useless there. He'd have a fighting chance to live.

Flintlocks fired from behind, and the ground puffed as the miniballs plowed into the hard soil. That only spurred him on to greater speed. Then he heard galloping hooves, and he knew they were after him again. No way could he outrun a horse, even with the load of dead bodies each was carrying.

Turning in midstep, J.B. dashed for the nearest embankment and started to scramble up the side of the riverbed. The soil broke loose under his hands, and he kept sliding back down. But he was still making headway. Less than a yard to go, then he slid back two feet. Throwing himself for the edge so tantalizingly close, J.B. grabbed hold of the grassy top when a flurry of blasterfire rang out, and he braced for the arrival of the hot pain.

Then the blasters roared again, and he realized those weren't flintlocks shooting. Glancing over a shoulder, J.B. saw the rest of the companions charging up the riverbed in the old bulldozer, Ryan in the shovel and steadily triggering the Steyr. Another gray rider fell, and the last one turned to flee when Doc unleashed the LeMat. The handcannon boomed like doomsday in the confines of the riverbed, and the rider flew out of the saddle to land on the ground in a crumpled heap with most of his skull blown away.

"Get those horses!" J.B. shouted, then released his grip and slid down the embankment on the seat of his pants.

As Ryan turned off the dozer, several of the companions started to walk toward the horses, talking softly and making clucking noises with their tongues. The beasts were skittish, but obviously well-trained as they didn't bolt. Soon the five horses were gathered by the reins and brought back to the dozer.

"Whoa, there. Easy does it," Krysty said in a soothing voice, tethering the reins to one of the hydraulic lifters of the dozer. The animals sniffed curiously at the huge machine, but didn't shy away. Then she noticed the heavy scarring on their flanks, not from spurs, but whips. The horses had been beaten into submission like any human slave, the will to rebel crushed completely. They wouldn't have dared to run away. Fear ruled their hearts.

"We're going to need those animals to get Ann," J.B. said, limping over to the dozer. His clothes were torn and bloody in spots, his hands turning purple from the tight ropes cutting off the circulation.

"We know," Jak said, producing a blade. Carefully, he cut away the remnants of rope from the man's wrists.

"Thanks," J.B. said, rubbing his sore wrists. There were chafe marks on top of his old scars. It wasn't the first time he'd been bound by rope.

"They came in through the windows. Almost got me and Mildred, too," Dean stated. "I think they knew it was the baron's home."

"Want a drink?" Krysty offered.

"Dark night, yes!"

The canteen was passed over and the Armorer drank greedily, the excess running down his cheeks. Then he poured some into his palms and washed the dirt off his face.

"Better," he said, returning the canteen. Then he hawked and spit, and bloody saliva hit the ground. Damn, busted a tooth. "Got my hat?"

"In the dozer. What happened?" Mildred asked, checking his face and ribs. There didn't seem to be any serious damage, just a lot of fresh bruises forming. The wiry little man was as tough as old boot leather.

Briefly, J.B. explained while reclaiming his dropped blaster. The Uzi was dusty and dirty, but undamaged. Ryan passed over a box of 9 mm rounds, and the man reloaded the 30-round clip. All of the Armorer's spare clips and ammo were now with the gray men. Plus his munitions bag.

A few yards away, Doc went to one of the corpses and pulled off a gray mask. The face underneath seemed perfectly normal, no obvious mutations or differences. How odd. One at a time, he went through their clothing and found several flintlocks, plus several pounds of black powder and lead shot. He filled his ammo pouch and left the rest. As far as the old man was concerned, the abundance of black powder for his Civil War blaster was the only good thing about these wretched islands.

"Five horses, seven people," Ryan said, checking the cinches on the saddles. "Going to be slow traveling. But we've got no choice. Ann helped me escape. We have to at least try to get her free."

"Agreed."

Stroking the neck of a horse, Krysty looked up the riverbed. "They'll know we're coming."

"But not when," Ryan said. "We'll use that."

"We had best tend our mounts before departing," Doc rumbled in his deep voice. "They have been used most strenuously for quite a while."

While Dean climbed the bank and got some green grass for the animals, the companions let the horses drink from cupped hands, but not too much. They didn't want to slow them down. When the grass arrived, the poor things ate as if ravenous. Afterward, Mildred went to the clear stream, intending to refill the canteens, but upon testing the water she found it was heavily polluted. Totally undrinkable.

"You okay to ride?" Krysty asked in concern. "Took quite a beating."

J.B. slapped the clip into the rapidfire and worked the bolt, chambering a round. "Try and stop me."

"The dozer works," Dean offered, "and we

have juice. Found a cache in one of the cargo containers.''

"Too slow, and they'd hear us coming for miles," Ryan stated. "Besides, we used most of the juice getting here. Had it in high gear all the way. Damn near blew the engine.''

"Correction," Mildred replied, looking at the growing puddle of fluids on the ground. "We did blow the engine. Looks like a cracked block.''

"Aced," Jak agreed.

"Then we ride," Ryan said, stepping into the stirrup of a big stallion and hoisting himself into the saddle. The animal was larger than a normal horse, like those back at Front Royal. Its rib cage was noticeably wider, its legs longer. It probably could run forever without getting tired. With practiced hands, he patted its muscular neck and scratched behind the ears. The horse snuffled with pleasure in response. Even as a kid, Ryan had always liked horses, and any animal worth its brass responded to kindness better than the whip. The gray men were triple stupe.

"Just like the Carolinas," Dean said, climbing into the saddle behind Jak.

"Wish we had the Leviathan," Mildred said, as J.B. offered her a hand, and she awkwardly climbed onto the beast right behind him.

"When find, what do with girl?" Jak asked, adjusting the reins. He was pleasantly surprised to find the horse was bridle wise and well tempered. "Could make litter and drag behind."

"Ann will ride on her own horse," Ryan said, gently kicking his heels into the stallion's flank. "There'll be plenty of extra mounts by then."

The companions started off in single file, staying very close to the left bank to hide their approach from any scouts in the northern trees. The majority of the island stretched to the north, so that would be the logical place for the gray men to go. The plan made sense, but it was only a guess. They could have a ship moored in the southern harbor.

Keeping the animals at a leisurely trot, the companions watched the embankments for any sign that the riders had climbed out of the natural passageway. The miles passed and the sides slowly lowered in height until only a few feet tall, easy passage for the long-legged horses.

"Over there," Doc whispered, gesturing with his stick at the embankment. Dark earth showed where the ground had been churned from the passage of hooves.

Shaking the reins, Jak rode over to that section and studied the pattern of the scuff marks in the dirt.

"Bullshit," he announced. "Fake trail."

Walking his mount to the other side of the riverbed, he slid off and looked over the ground. Not a mark showed in the soil, and not a leaf was out of place in the grass.

"This way," Jak stated without hesitation. Drawing his blaster, the teen stepped out of the riverbed and started through the field of green grass.

Dean took the reins and led the way, the rest of the companions following close behind. Nobody questioned the Cajun. Jak was the best tracker among them.

Ryan moved to the left, the Steyr resting across the saddle, and J.B. took the right side, the Uzi tight in his fist. Both men scrutinized the trees ahead of them, while Doc and Mildred kept a watch behind.

The field stretched for more than a mile, trees growing in scattered stands, which grew closer and closer together until the companions were proceeding through a lush grove. The trees gave off the rich aroma of eucalyptus, and Mildred pulled off several handfuls to stuff into her med kit.

Several times, Jak altered course for no discernible reason, and the others followed, even though there was no indication of anything having passed that way.

"Damn, they're good," Krysty said softly, in annoyance.

"We're better," Ryan answered, tracking a motion in the trees. Then a monkey with four arms scampered out of the greenery, pursued by a gang of norm chimps, who snarled and slavered in blind fury, the bull males culling the troop of a mutie.

The sky was darkening when they arrived at a large vista of black stone. The irregular plan of congealed lava extended for hundreds of yards. Jak didn't even pause as he changed direction and headed for a low rise, a momentary swell in the lava flow that had become trapped forever in time. Cresting the rise, he easily walked down a gentle slope into a deep ravine. At the bottom was a predark road, the pavement stained and cracked, weeds growing tall through every crevice.

Even in the early-evening light, Ryan could see that several of the stalks were bending back into shape from something recent pushing them aside.

"Here less than an hour ago," he said softly.

Jak nodded his agreement.

The ancient road meandered through the dense weeds as if based upon the path of a snake. The cracks became wider and more pronounced until the slabs of pavement were islands in the soggy earth. Soon they were riding through a marsh, the muddy water almost a foot deep. Clumps of decaying trees dotted the surface, and occasionally the bloated body of a drowned animal floated by.

"Watch for pools of still water," Ryan warned, slowing his horse. "Could be a sinkhole. Break a leg stepping into one of those."

"Or quicksand," Dean added, frowning.

Following the wash of the stagnant water, the companions walked their mounts through the sodden landscape until the mud turned to grass, and they were back on dry ground again. Another forest of tropical trees grew to the east, stretching to the mountains, tall peaks of brown stone that reached for the clouds. To the west and north was the start of the jungle, the array of bushes, bamboo and vines seeming impassable without machinery.

"Gate," Jak said, pointing.

Moving incredibly fast, Ryan fired the SIG-Sauer twice, the silenced weapon coughing gently. There was a stirring in the bushes, and two men dressed in mottled green dropped their flintlock longblasters and fell to the ground, both of them bleeding from the throat.

Spreading out, the companions did a quick recce of the area and found no more hidden guards. Dismounting, they checked the fallen guards and found one of them still breathing, the blood bubbling from the ghastly wound in his neck. Ryan cut the man's throat with a smooth stroke of the panga, the blade curving along the neck as if designed specifically for that function.

On closer inspection, the wall of bamboo was false, the tubular plants resting on some old splintery wood with a central pivot buried in the soil. Ryan pushed on one side, and the other swung outward. Ryan took the point and went inside first. To the left was a corral of horses, to the right a bubbling spring of naturally carbonated water. He whistled like a mountain lark, and the others came through the gate, weapons in hand.

Tethering their mounts on the outside of the corral in case they needed to leave quickly, they fell into line, Ryan on point, Doc in the middle, J.B. at the rear. A wide path led through the bamboo groove, and Ryan found two more hidden guards. The first was a massive hound. It wasted its only chance to give a warning by growling at the companions. Ryan aced the dog nice and quiet, the SIG-Sauer delivering a 9 mm round directly into its left eye. The other guard was a man who burst from cover to throw a spear. Ryan dodged the spear, but his slug only grazed the man's neck, a geyser of blood spurting from the nicked artery. Grabbing the wound, the man opened his mouth to scream and a knife slammed into his temple. With a sigh, the guard collapsed to the ground and died. Jak reclaimed his blade and wiped it clean on the corpse's shirt.

There was a clearing in the bamboo forest, and the land started to slope toward an imposing barrier of pungi sticks and thorny vines. A click sounded from the companions, and Ryan and J.B. quickly looked at the rad counters on their lapels. The background count had increased, but not significantly.

"They live in a rad pit," Ryan muttered in disgust.

An inclined earthen ramp offered direct access through the pungi sticks and into the pit. Sounds could be heard coming from below now, laughter, a steady thumping, the murmur of voices. As quietly as possible, the companions crept along the outer perimeter of the hole until locating a vantage point in a pool of shadows cast by the setting sun.

Distant thunder rumbled, warning of an approaching storm as J.B. swept the ville below with his longeyes. About a dozen huts stood at the bottom of the blast crater, simple arrangements of tanned skin over a hinged skeleton of aged wood, similar to the yurts of the Mongol hordes. There were several work areas with oldsters busy making things with their bare hands. An old man sat on a rock carving a comb from bone, and a young woman with full breasts was using a scrap piece of rock to scrape a stretched piece of hide as a preparation for curing.

A stream trickled out of the bamboo forest, going down the sloped side of the crater and through the pungi-stick wall and forming a pool at one end of the ville. In the center was a banked pile of glowing red coals ready to cook dinner. About forty people, adults and children, were walking about in loincloths and crude sandals. Here in the safety of their home, the gray men had removed their camou.

They were covered with tattoos, but appeared to be norms.

Near the center of the ville was a pit in the ground covered with a lid of stout logs and guarded by several of the women, each armed with a long spear. As the companions watched, an arm clawed through the wooden grating and the women stabbed it back down into the pit, the tips of their spears becoming dabbed with crimson in the process.

The lid was removed and the gray men jabbed at the trapped people until one was forced to exit the prison. Instantly, he was swarmed upon and ropes tied to his arms and legs. With five or six tattooed people on each rope, the chosen prisoner was hauled to a tree and held there helpless while old women jabbed out his eyes with sharp sticks, and then cut the tendons in his legs. Even if set free, the man would never walk again.

Now his clothes were cut away with great care not to damage the skin. Naked, he was bound tight and the ropes looped over a tree branch, then he was hauled off his feet to dangle upside down. Next, a barrel was shoved underneath. Doc and Jak muttered curses. Born and raised on farms, they knew what was coming next.

Without a qualm, the prisoner's throat was slit and his blood flowed into the barrel. When the corpse was completely drained, the stomach was slit apart and the intestines slithered free to be saved in a woven basket. Evidently, all body parts were consumed.

The sun was nearing the horizon, and the rad pit was illuminated by the banked coals, giving the ville a reddish tone like a nightmare, but it was all terribly real.

Now the head was sawed off and given to an old man who peeled off the scalp as an aid to plucking out the hairs, probably to make ropes. Another old-ster broke off the jaw and removed the teeth, for saws and arrowheads. Meanwhile, young woman neatly removed the skin from the corpse, and the raw carcass had a wooden pole shoved down the neck stump until it exited the anus. The limply dan-gling arms and legs were cut away and put into a tent filled with smoke, curing the meat to make it last.

Sprinkled with herbs, the skinless torso was placed on a spit above the coals, and old women started turning the food slowly, chatting among themselves as dinner began to cook. Sticks with rags tied to the ends caught the melting fat and were used to baste the meat in its own juices. Soon the smell reached the companions, and they fought the urge to retch.

"Cannies," Doc muttered, looking away. He had encountered man-eaters before, but this methodical processing of the aced man was demonic. It de-meaned humans to no more than cattle.

"Any sign of Ann?" Ryan asked, squinting into the crimson pit.

"Not yet," J.B. answered, moving the brass scope around the camp. "Got a live round says she's in that hole, though."

"Need diversion," Jak stated forcibly. "Stampede horses, set fire bamboo?"

"We could use several diversions, my friend," Doc stated. "There are a lot more cannies than there are us."

Ryan rubbed his jaw. If they knew which tent contained the stores of black powder for the blasters, they could toss in some firebombs and rock the whole ville. The stampede wasn't a bad idea, except that the horses were as passive as an old eunuch. And most of their explosives were in the lost munitions bag. This was going to require some thought.

"Whatever we're going to do had better be soon," Krysty warned, pointing below. "They're getting the tree ready for another prisoner."

Unslinging his longblaster, Ryan handed it to Mildred, along with most of his spare ammo mags. Then he pulled out the panga and started drawing in the dirt.

"Okay," he said, "here's the plan."

Chapter Eight

Searching around, Krysty found a flat rock and slid it carefully to the very edge of the crater, then wiggled it snugly into the dirt to make sure it wouldn't move. Setting the Steyr SSG-70 on the rock, the woman placed a handkerchief on the ground nearby and laid out a neat row of the extra mags for the longblaster. Taking a look through the scope, she could see the cannies in wire-sharp detail, and practiced moving the crosshairs from one to another. Very soon now.

TAKING POSITION inside a clump of young bamboo, Mildred used a knife to gently saw through some of the jointed tubes until she had a good view of the secret ville below. Taking a tiny piece of a bandage from her med kit, the physician rubbed it in the dirt until it was no longer white, but a dull brown. Tying it to the end of a bamboo stick, Mildred eased it into the open where a breeze stirred the strip of cloth. Thrusting the other end of the stick into the ground, the physician watched the fluttering rag and tried to gauge the wind shear. She had never attempted this great a distance with her ZKR target pistol, not even back when she went for the gold medal in the Olympics. But lives were riding on her accuracy today, not just a medal.

If they wanted to live the night, there was blood to be spilled. Somehow, the physician didn't think the Olympic committee would have approved.

FORCING HIS WAY into the stands of tough bamboo, Dean got his blaster ready for a fight. If the advance party was found, Krysty and Mildred would give them cover to reach the top, then he was to give everybody cover to reach the horses. Then they would cover his own escape. It was a good plan, but something deep inside the boy, honed from surviving a hundred fights, warned that this wasn't how it was going to happen this night.

CIRCLING THE RIM of the crater, Ryan crawled on his belly until he was at the top of the ramp going down into the ville. Staying low, he continued onward until reaching the flow of carbonated water from the spring. Easing gently into the water, the man felt his clothes soak through in an instant, and a chill swept over his body. Damn stuff was cold. Sliding along the muddy creek, Ryan paused every couple of feet to listen for any reactions to his presence, then moved on.

Getting through the wall of pungi sticks was a

lot easier than he had thought. The flowing water had undercut many of the sticks, making them very loose. Very gently, Ryan pulled them out of the sucking mud, placed them aside and moved forward a little. A cannie guard would have to be watching very carefully to detect his passage.

Past the defensive wall, the creek ended a few feet off the ground above a stagnant pool thick with green scum. Sliding into the filthy water, Ryan crouched low so that only his face was in the air. The banks were lined with reeds and cattail punks, fat and brown, waving gently in the breeze. Murmurs of conversation could be heard from the campsite, the thud of a heavy cleaver, a whimper of pain, low laughter.

Peering through the weeds, he saw the cannies haul somebody from the pit, but the shadows hid the face. Then the men began to laugh and run their hands over the struggling captive, and Ryan knew it was a woman. Whether it was Ann or not, he still couldn't tell. He'd have to find out before they could start shooting.

A disturbance in the water made Ryan turn with a knife in hand. But it was just the others arriving in his wake. As silent as ghosts, Jak, J.B. and Doc eased through the muck. Each man carried his blaster just above the water level, then Doc gave a gasp as he sank out of sight, sending out ripples and waves that shook the reeds. The scholar was completely submerged, except for the hand holding his blaster aloft, a scant inch above the surface of the pond. A moment later, he emerged from the reeking pond, snorting green water from his nose and mouth, and wiping his face clean as best he could with a dripping hand.

"Okay?" Ryan asked, raising the SIG-Sauer higher to protect it from the waves.

"My weapon is still dry," Doc whispered, spitting the filth from his mouth.

If there had been time, Ryan would have made some catapults from the more sturdy stands of bamboo and propelled flaming arrows to set the whole ville on fire. But he had to settle for something more wasteful. Each of the M-16 rifles they were saving for trade had three full clips of ammo. Ryan took one clip from each to throw into the campfire. When the ball ammo cooked off, that would give them the edge needed to get Ann. Unfortunately, the ammo clips didn't skim well, and the companions would have to be close to get them into the fire. Very close.

Doc also had the military blasters with him, wrapped in several layers of plastic to keep them dry. That was their key out of the crater in case everything went to hell. Hopefully, they wouldn't have to be used. Ryan would prefer to buy the use of a ship, rather than just steal one.

Just then a fat woman in mismatched clothing

waddled to the pond and threw in a bucket of was-
tewater. Ryan tracked her approached and departure with the bulbous end of the SIG-Sauer, two
pounds of pressure on the six-pound trigger. A
breath on his part and the big cannie would be
blown away. Squatting, she lifted her skirts and
sent a yellow stream into the scum. The men
flinched, realizing that this was the latrine for the
ville. No wonder it was so far away from the rest
of the camp. By sheer effort of will, they didn't
move or speak. When finally finished, the woman
stood, smoothed out her patched skirt and waddled
away.

As the obese woman went around a tent and
ducked out of sight, she started to scream in an
unknown language. Across the ville, the cannies
dropped whatever they were doing and dived for
weapons, coming up with spears, knives and more
than a few flintlock handcannons.

Moving through the reeds, Ryan fired a fast three
times directly into the animal-skin tent, and the fat
cannie stumbled into view, blood covering her
back. Wailing in agony, she fell to the ground, trying to staunch the loss of blood with her pudgy
fingers. There was no hope of success.

Stepping onto dry land, J.B. burped the Uzi at
the nearest group of armed cannies, sending them
to hell, but he refrained from spraying the entire
ville. The unknown female, possibly Ann, was

somewhere loose among the deviant flesh-eaters, and he could easily ace her going for the big chill. He had to do this the hard way.

A beautiful woman carrying a spear charged at the companions, then jumped forward, throwing away her weapon. She hit the ground hard just as the boom of the Steyr rolled down from above. A sharp crack followed, and a man loading a flintlock spun like a top, a hole in his face where a nose used to exist. Krysty and Mildred were on the job.

Darting from the reeds to behind a stack of firewood, Ryan chose his targets and aced everybody who wasn't screaming in panic. The more disorganized the bastards were, the better. Just then a pounding hail of miniballs hit the cord of wood, slamming it apart and almost trapping Ryan under the falling logs. A roll of thunder shattered the night as Doc triggered the LeMat, the deafening report illuminating the battle scene in brutal clarity, and three cannies flipped sideways.

Small children were running everywhere, and a pregnant cannie shuffled for safety behind a tree. Ryan's blaster tracked their movements, but he didn't pull the trigger. They were no danger. No sense wasting ammo.

Withering cross fire filled the air, chips of bark flying off the trees, and the cooking torso jerking in a ghastly pantomime of trying to escape from the spit. Just then, a woman dressed in dirty rags staggered from behind the killing tree and headed for the inclined ramp out of the crater. Ryan bolted across the open ground to catch her in his arms. Blood was pumping freely from a terrible wound on her chest; most of one breast had been torn away by a miniball. She tried to fight off Ryan as he carried her into the weeds. A chest wound. No way could he get a tourniquet around that, and he had nothing to use as a pressure bandage.

"Sorry," he said, dropping a clip and reloading to fire into the thinning mob of cannies.

Clutching a ruined hand, one man just stood there, howling at the stars until Ryan shot him again and the noise ceased.

Several men dressed in gray charged from a tent into view, large clay pots with dangling fuses in their hands. J.B. swung the Uzi in their direction. No way he was going to let them do that smoke trick again. The Uzi spoke, and the gray men fell, the smoke bombs rolling away. Then there came a fast series of sharp bangs from above and each one burst apart, totally destroyed. J.B. nodded at the unseen women and moved on, firing single rounds to conserve ammo.

Dropping his spent brass, Jak reloaded and sent three booming messengers toward two cannies trying to sneak behind Doc. Both men fell as if hit with sledgehammers, the hollowpoint rounds tearing holes in their bellies the size of a fist. As the flintlocks hit the soil, the blasters discharged, sending the .75 miniball rounds randomly into the ville.

A gang of old women carrying axes came after them now, and J.B. used the rest of the clip to blow them away. The survivors ran for the ramp to reach the safety of the bamboo forest. But as they reached the top, Krysty and Mildred mowed them down in ruthless efficiency.

A spear sailed by overhead, forcing Ryan to duck. Then a trembling hand touched him, and Ryan briefly glanced at the dying woman. Her mouth filled with blood, she burbled something impossible to hear and went still. Then Doc fired again, and in the flash Ryan got a good look at her face. She was beautiful and badly scarred, but this woman was much too old, an adult, deeply tanned with pirate-style earrings.

"She's still in the pit!" Ryan shouted through cupped hands.

That was all the others needed. J.B. stood and cut loose with the Uzi, mowing down the cannies with a deadly storm of the copper-jacketed 9 mm rounds. Darting out of the shadows, Jak flipped both of the 30-round mags into the campfire and dived for cover. In less than a heartbeat, the ammo started cooking off, the irregular series of detonations throwing hot coals and deformed lead everywhere. Clay pots shattered, a man fell, clutching his ankle, two more fell over lifeless, a tent hit with coals burst into flames and another cannie insanely rushed the campfire and struck at the exploding magazines with a war club. That close, he caught all of the next rounds and was torn apart. The corpse fell forward into the campfire, and the reek of burning hair soon mingled with the wretched aroma of roasting human flesh from the torso on the spit.

In raw terror, the last few cannie warriors broke ranks and dashed for a tent set off by itself in the ville. Going inside, a grisly cannie came back out with a flintlock rifle and a pouch of ammo. Jak shifted his position to get closer. That longblaster was trouble. As the warrior started to load the weapon, Jak aimed carefully and shot him with the Magnum pistol. His face gone, the hideous corpse fell backward into the tent, and the other men started firing their weapons from within the flimsy structure.

Whistling sharply, Ryan gestured at the tent, and J.B. rolled their only gren through the opening. The companions took cover and the whole crater shook with the strident blast, a roiling fireball spreading out to engulf a dozen other tents. In moments, the whole ville was in flames.

Suddenly, a young boy charged out of a burning hut, brandishing a bone dagger. Most of his body was covered with burn marks, the skin cracked and covered with large blisters. Shouting more in pain than anger, the child charged straight at Ryan and he aced the boy with one careful shot to the heart. Death was instantaneous.

When the campfire stopped spitting lead, Ryan headed for the holding pit to check on the prisoners. But as he passed the smoking ruins of the exploded tent, Ryan saw no bodies strewed around in the wreckage. Only a neat square hole in the ground, a sturdy bamboo ladder going down into the darkness. Ryan set his mouth in a thin line. Tricked again!

Whistling sharply, he signaled the others over and they cautiously gathered around the hole. Doc dropped down a torch, and a group of cannies standing at the bottom of the ladder started firing flintlocks in reply. Moving out of the way, Ryan fired blindly over the edge until the others stopped.

"Son of a bitch, this is just the top!" J.B. raged, shouldering the exhausted Uzi. "The rest of the ville is underground!"

"Seal it," Jak said, passing over the munitions bag. "Found this in other tent." The bag was splashed with fresh blood, none of it from the Cajun.

Making the catch with one hand, J.B. dug into his bag and pulled out a block of C-4 salvaged from the lighthouse. Actually, it was the C-4 taken from forty grens whose firing mechanisms had been rusted useless. He removed the small pats of plas and molded them into a block. Safe inside the airtight gren, the high-explosive plastique was as good as ever.

"Half block," Ryan said, estimating the size of the tunnel. He wanted it sealed tight, with no chance of their digging their way out again.

"Hell with that," J.B. retorted, the raw marks of his wrists aching as he stabbed a timing pencil into the full block. Snapping off the length of the pencil at thirty seconds, he tossed the whole primed charge down the hole.

Wasting no time, the companions raced away from the area and were almost to the filthy pool when there was a tremendous detonation and the entire valley shook. The torso fell off the spit, large sections of the pungi-stick wall collapsed and the horses in the corral screamed in fear.

Checking the results, the men saw the ground had fallen into a deep depression about twenty feet wide and just as deep. There was no way the cannies were going to dig their way out of that avalanche, if anybody survived the blast.

"Let's find Ann," Ryan said, heading across the ville.

Going over to the holding pen, Ryan passed a moaning cannie twitching on the ground, a piece of tent stake protruding through his side. Holstering his piece, the Deathlands warrior drew his panga and silenced the noise with one quick stroke.

Reaching the pen, Ryan called out for the woman, but there was no reply. He tried again, but still nothing. Fireblast, she might have been knocked unconscious. Taking a torch from a bucket of tree resin, Jak lit it with his butane lighter and looked inside. The crackling torchlight brightly illuminated the small cramped hole. There was nobody in sight, and an open door led deeper underground. Soft light came through the opening from somewhere on the other side.

"They took them with them," Ryan growled, drawing his blaster. "Stand back."

Firing the SIG-Sauer twice, he blew off the lock and, kicking aside the wooden grating, Ryan jumped into the damp pit. He landed in a crouch and stayed that way, waiting for his eye to become adjusted to the darkness. Without warning, a screaming cannie rushed in through the doorway, brandishing a wooden club studded with human teeth. Ryan shot him in the belly, and the man doubled over, dropping the club and howling with pain, clutching his middle with both arms. Kicking the club out of reach, Ryan saved ammo and used the panga once more.

There was a shadow cast from overhead and Doc landed in the prison cell, an M-16 cradled in his arms. "Prudence dictates decorum," the scholar said, working the bolt on the rapidfire.

"Sweep it," Ryan ordered, jerking a thumb at the door.

Doc stuck the fluted barrel of the M-16 out of the doorway and fired a burst in both directions. Screams announced hits, and the two men charged out of the cell, blasters firing. Already wounded, the cannies waiting in ambush were aced in seconds, their flintlocks remaining unfired. Stooping, Ryan picked up two of the weapons and fired one, then screamed as if in pain and fired the other.

"That'll make them think we're wounded," he said, casting the spent blasters away. "They'll get brave, easier to chill."

"Exemplary, my dear Mr. Cawdor," Doc rumbled, tucking one of the ammo pouches from the dead into a pocket of his frock coat.

With catlike speed, Jak appeared from the cell with the second M-16. J.B. was right behind, the Uzi sweeping for targets. A spare ammo clip from the recovered munitions bag was tucked into his belt for fast access.

"What this?" Jak demanded, squinting in the dim light.

"Some sort of underground lair," Doc said. "Highly appropriate for eaters of the dead. Almost ironic."

The corridor walls were stacked rows of bamboo tucked into place behind thick wooden beams that supported a jigsaw of wooden pieces: roofing shingles, tabletops, decorative louvered doors, plywood, ship planks, anything that would serve as roofing. Every few yards, there was a niche in the wall with a clay bowl full of some greasy substance, a burning piece of cloth serving as a crude wick. The passageway extended to the left for only a short distance before ending at a mound of fresh-turned earth—the cave-in from the C-4 blast. The right ended at a sharp left turn. There was no noise or voices discernible, only the slow echoing drip of water striking stone from somewhere distant.

"Smells odd," Jak stated, crinkling his nose.

"They're burning human fat in the lamps," Ryan said grimly.

"Devs."

"Agreed."

"Well, leaving won't be a problem," Ryan stated, looking over the collapsed tunnel. "We can climb the cave-in and reach the ground easy."

"Indeed. As long as the folks on the other side don't dig their way out," Doc reminded him curtly. "Perhaps I should stay as rear guard, to prevent such an occurrence."

"Good idea," Ryan said. "Anybody with us when we came back, and I'll use code."

Hesitating for a moment, Doc offered the man the M-16, but he pushed it back. "You may need it," Ryan said, glancing at the ton of collapsed soil.

The scholar nodded. "Understood."

"Hey, what that?" Jak asked, retrieving a small piece of dirty cloth from the floor. It wasn't a wick for one of the candle bowls, or a used snot rag. On a hunch, he held it to the clothing of the dead men and it was completely different.

"This Ann?" the teenager asked, showing it to the others.

Ryan took the rag and looked it over closely. "Same color," he said thoughtfully. "And it has been ripped loose, not cut. Mebbe she's laying a trail for us to follow."

"Or a trap for us to walk blindly into," J.B. stated, straightening his glasses.

"Come on," Ryan said, advancing, "Let's find her and get out of here."

He took the point and crouched to sneak a peek around the corner of the tunnel. There was a long passageway beyond that stretched for yards before ending at another intersection. Rising, he led the way down the corridor, pausing at a dark section of earth that rose ever so slightly above the rest of the floor. Ryan scuffed his combat boot on the ground and detected a subtle movement under the newly turned soil. He fired twice into the ground. There was a muffled cry and blood began to ooze from the earth.

"Triple stupe," he stated coldly. "Old trick. Trader taught it to us over beers at Charlie's bar."

"Called it a Hanoi Handjob," J.B. added.

''No shit?'' Jak asked nervously, brushing back his snowy hair. The cannies buried a man to wait like a land mine for one of them to step on, and then he'd attack. It was brilliant. The teenager now scrutinized the dirt floor and the jigsaw-puzzle ceiling much more closely for any additional living traps.

Reaching the intersection, the companions found the tunnel went in both directions for a good distance, the walls lined with doors. Most were unlocked and led to sleeping quarters for families, empty now. A few were locked, and contained clothing from the prisoners, one room packed to the ceiling with assorted boots. But no weapons.

Every corridor ended in another intersection, each branching out into more corridors and side passages. Closed doors lined the bamboo walls, and they had to check each one before risking to leave it behind them. It was slow going, and they worried about the cannies preparing another trap. The gray men were smart and ruthless, a dangerous combination.

''Place is a bastard maze,'' Ryan growled, using a pencil stub to draw a map of the tunnel on a piece of the lighthouse journal. He had kept the page because it showed the strange symbol from the gateway. He had hoped to ask some of the locals to see if they knew what it was. Now he simply needed it as paper. No way he was going to let them get lost down here for the cannies to trap and slowly starve them into submission. He'd rather take a round than go into a stew pot.

Another bit of rag led them to the left of an intersection. This corridor was dark, all of the wall lamps extinguished. Ryan nudged J.B. and motioned behind them. The Armorer nodded and passed the warning onto Jak. He silently agreed, then started down the darkened corridor as if unaware they were walking directly into a trap.

Almost at once, there came the slamming of a door, followed by the barks and howls of dogs. In unison, the three men turned and opened fire at the floor, the fusillade of rounds tearing the hounds to pieces, blowing away ears, legs and eyes. Only a large bitch managed to reach the men, bleeding but still alive. J.B. kicked its head into the wall, Jak used the butt of the M-16 to smash its jaw and Ryan buried a blade into its spine. Still snarling, the beast dropped and lay there heaving for breath, crippled but not dead.

"Couple more of those and we would have been on the last train west," Ryan stated, reloading the SIG-Sauer.

"Tough like hellhound," Jak said, checking the clip on the rapidfire.

"What's that?" J.B. asked.

"Big mutie in bayou. Tough kill."

J.B. pulled the clip and checked inside. "Ten

left,'' he announced, slamming it back into the breech.

"Out," Jak said, dropping the rapidfire to draw his .357 Magnum pistol.

"See big black dog, shoot in eyes," he said cryptically, cocking the hammer with a callused thumb. "Just eyes. Not stop firing till say."

Using their butane lighters, they lit the lamps along the corridor but stopped when they found a piece of rag caught between a door and the jamb. J.B. checked for boobies, while Ryan and Jak stood guard. When satisfied it was safe, J.B. picked the old lock and got out of the way. Then Ryan kicked the door open without entering. Taking a lamp from the wall, he thrust it into the darkness. Dirty human faces stared back. People were sitting on the floor, and one of them stood to walk toward the light, a hand covering her face.

"You okay?" Ryan asked, looking her over for injuries that might slow her. The longer they stayed down here, the more time the cannies had to regroup. Time wasn't on their side.

"Ryan? You came!" Ann cried, then threw herself at the man, weeping uncontrollably.

Holding her by the shoulders, Ryan pushed the woman away and slapped her hard across the face. She recoiled in shock.

"Stay focused if you want to live," Ryan

snapped. ''We're up to our ass in dreck and low on ammo. Where's the ship?''

Ann blinked in confusion. ''What?''

He squeezed her arm. Pain always made a person more aware. ''Said you know where a ship was to be found. Tell me and we all leave together.''

''There is—'' Ann hiccuped with nerves and tried again ''—there's a ville, on the far side of the island, past the Black Mountains. It's a port. Lots of ships dock there.''

''You know the way,'' Ryan said. It wasn't a question.

''Yes! Of course, I do. Used to live before—''

''I know the way,'' someone said, hobbling to the doorway. He was a big man, gaunt from hunger, but his former strength was clearly visible in his sheer size. Black hair and almond skin, he was dressed in bloody and torn clothes of very good cloth. A wide leather belt around his waist proclaimed the man a sailor.

''Ann said you would come after her,'' he added. ''Guess she was right.''

''Here for her. Not you,'' Ryan said bluntly, and jerked a thumb. ''Leave if you want. But don't follow us. Get in the way and you're zero days.''

''I know the way through their pungi-stick wall,'' the man said, reaching out with his hand.

''The creek. Found it already.''

The man lowered his gaze to the 9 mm pistol in

Ryan's grip. "Then again, mebbe you don't need us," he said in awe. "Does that thing actually work?"

"It's how we got here," J.B. stated, lifting the Uzi for the prisoners to see. The men gasped at the sight, and backed away deeper into their cell.

"Stop talking. We have to leave!" Ann urged, impatiently moving from foot to foot. The motion made her dress sway and exposed a lot of skin. There had been little of the dress remaining before she started ripping off pieces. "They can come back any tic. Hundreds of them!"

"Who the hell are you?" Ryan demanded, ignoring the interruption. Every minute wasted was ammo against them. But with more men they had a better chance of reaching the surface alive—if he could trust the prisoners not to throw the companions to the cannies to slow down pursuit. Better to travel alone than with enemies.

"I'm Cal Mitchum, sec man for Baron Thayer of Ratak ville. That's the ville she was talking about on the far side of the island. There's more, but they're rad-pit dreck holes, without a single working blaster or a tin pot to piss in. But you want a ship, you got it. Just take us with you."

"Big words. You got the powder to deliver that lead?" Ryan asked. The SIG-Sauer was still in his hand, the barrel pointing steadily at the stranger.

The others in the room stared longingly at the

open doorway, but the dead black eye of Ryan's blaster kept them at bay.

"Fucking right I do! I'll get you a ship if I've got to steal one," Mitchum stated forcibly.

He was too confident, too sure of himself, Ryan decided and took a chance. "Major, behind you!" he shouted, and pointed the blaster away from the sec man.

Mitchum spun, hands reaching for a blaster not there. Then he turned, his face a controlled mask of rage.

"Tricky bastard. Okay, I'm Colonel Mitchum," he stated through grit teeth. "Sec chief for Ratak ville."

"Ryan," the Deathlands warrior said, "J.B. and Jak."

"The rest of the prisoners are my troops. Can't leave them behind."

"Can and will," Ryan stated firmly. "Unless I decide they're useful."

"Need them to get me," Mitchum shot back.

A noise echoed down the corridor, and Jak moved out of sight.

"They're coming back!" Ann whispered. "We must leave now!"

"Do we have a deal?" the sec man insisted, sweat on his brow.

Ryan knew he was negotiating for the lives of

his troops. That said a lot about the man. ''Deal,'' Ryan said.

Relief easing his countenance, Mitchum exhaled. He extended his hand, and the men shook.

''Everybody start walking,'' Ryan ordered. ''We have horses at the surface. Lag behind and we leave you, deal or not.''

. The companions herded the freed prisoners along the corridor, carefully retracing their steps. Ryan was very glad he had made a map. The scraps of cloth had been moved to new locations and they would have been seriously lost following those.

Rounding a corner, Ryan and Jak opened fire as a gang of teenagers burst out of a room, their arms full of flintlocks. The teens cried out as the SIG-Sauer and Colt Python took their lives, displaying their sharply filed teeth. Bleeding badly, a girl tried to bring a weapon to bear, but J.B. emptied the Uzi into her, driving the body backward under the brutal assault of the copper-jacketed rounds.

Stepping over the twitching bodies, Ryan checked the room they had come from and saw it was an armory. Big wooden barrels of black powder filled the room, wall racks held dozens of flintlock rifles and a barrel was jammed full of Navy cutlasses. The cannies had to have eaten a lot of pirates. Good for them. Ryan smiled as he noticed a couple of Firebirds on display, the lacquered tubes resting on wooden pegs jutting from the wall for fast access. He debated taking one, but the risk of their being booby-trapped was far too great. It's what he would have done, and he always had to consider what the enemy could do, not what they might. However, the flintlocks should be safe.

"Everybody grab a blaster and ammo," Ryan said, taking a pistol and tucking it into his belt. There was a post covered with short pegs, plump ammo pouches hanging conveniently near the door. Whoever the cannie quartermaster was, he knew his stuff.

"Flintlocks?" Jak said, arching an eyebrow.

"Take spares for Doc, and the others also," he added.

"Camou. Gotcha," J.B. said, his face brightening in understanding, and he shoved several handcannons into his munitions bag. Next he added a coiled length of dried grass as a fuse. Then he spied the S&W M-4000 shotgun on a table. Reclaiming his alley-sweeper, J.B. checked the weapon to make sure it was okay, then draped it over a shoulder. Back in business.

The sec men eagerly armed themselves, passing over a few of the flintlocks to take others. Mitchum tested the black powder by licking some from a palm, and nodded in approval. Trained hands loaded their weapons in amazing speed, and the group exited the armory with longblasters in their hands, and two handcannons tucked into every belt.

J.B. was the last to leave the room, and he spent a few moments breaking the lock on the door. Then he jammed a copper knife blade into the jamb and snapped off the handle.

"Wouldn't open that easily," he smirked, tossing the handle away.

"How long?" Ryan asked.

"Roughly minutes. It's not my fuse, so I can't know for sure. Might be eight, could be twelve."

"Fair enough. Everybody, double time!" Ryan shouted, and took off at a run.

The group hustled through the zigzagging corridors, encountering no resistance until reaching the last intersection. Two cannies were dragging away the pile of dead dogs on a bamboo litter. The men dropped the animals and hastily ran away at the sight of the heavily armed party. Ruthlessly, the prisoners gunned down the cannies from behind, and spit on the corpses as they hurried by.

Reaching the collapsed section of the warren, Ryan paused at the right turn and signaled it was all-clear to Doc.

"Lady Ann, we meet once more." The scholar smiled, then looked over the sec men. They were as rough and tumble a group as he had ever seen. "Your entourage, I assume?"

"Six minutes and counting," J.B. said brusquely, patting his munitions bag.

Doc said nothing, but his eyes went wide, and

he started up the mound of loose dirt. Reaching the surface, Doc unlimbered the M-16 and stood guard while the others clambered out of the blast crater. Exiting the tunnel, the group quickly got away from the depression in the ground as the rim was soft and crumbled easily under their boots and bare feet.

"This way!" Mitchum cried, waving a blaster and heading for the water pool.

"Forget it! Follow me," Ryan countered, and started up the inclined ramp at a full sprint.

In ragged formation, the group charged past the pungi-stick wall, and braked to a halt upon reaching level ground. Masked by moon shadows, Krysty and Mildred were waiting there with blasters drawn. Dean was nowhere in sight.

"Hello, Adam," Mildred said, her blaster out, but not quite pointing in the direction of the sec men.

"Hey, Claire," Ryan responded, and the women relaxed.

Mitchum arched an eyebrow at the exchange and said nothing. But it was patently obvious they were exchanging some kind of a code. Who exactly were these outlanders?

"Nice to see you again, lover," Krysty said, resting the barrel of the Steyr on a shapely shoulder.

Ryan pulled her close for a hard kiss and took the longblaster. "Move fast. We lit their armory."

"Dean, get the horses!" Mildred shouted.

Instantly, the boy bolted from the stand of bamboo and dashed into the darkness of the night.

"Horses? Scorch me, we might live to see daylight yet!" a sec man said, grinning widely.

J.B. tossed Mildred the scattergun. She caught the blaster and pumped the action to chamber a round. Watching the exchange, Colonel Mitchum was impressed that a lowly woman knew anything about blasters.

Just then there was a loud bang and a sec man fell to the ground, a jagged hole in his chest. In unison, the companions turned and fired down into the ville. A group of cannies armed with longblasters took cover in the smoking rubble, and started to reload.

Leading the way, Ryan sprinted along the path through the bamboo forest and found Dean slashing the ropes tethering the horses. Most of the animals were bareback but there was no time to find and cinch on saddles. Clumsily, the people climbed onto the placid animals and rode out the swinging gate. Once outside, they kicked the beasts hard and started to gallop away from the hidden ville at top speed.

The companions and the sec men had just cleared the patch of dry land and were splashing through the beginnings of the swamp when a flash of light lit up the sky. As wind buffeted man and horse, they watched as a column of fire and smoke formed a classic mushroom shape that reached for the stars.

"Mother of God," Mildred said, watching the mushroom cloud expand over the shaking bamboo. "How much powder did you use?"

"Everything they had," J.B. replied curtly.

Just then the ground tremors arrived, and the horses reared on their hind legs, screaming in terror. The riders fought to control their mounts.

"Watch for debris!" Ryan warned, even as the first of the wreckage started to plummet from the sky.

Charred heads splashed into the soggy landscape, along with bent blasters and unrecognizable things blackened by smoke and fire. Racing into the trees, the group waited until the grisly rain finally ceased. A reddish light swelled to fill the world, and they could see the bamboo forest was on fire, the flames illuminating the surrounding countryside for miles.

"Which direction to the ville?" Ryan asked, settling the Steyr into a more comfortable position across his back. He was dirty and tired, but they couldn't make camp until far away from here. A few of the cannies might have survived and could come after them in a nightcreep. Best to get some distance for safety.

Gazing at the stars overhead, Ann turned in the saddle and pointed. "That way. North."

"No, we should go east from here," Colonel Mitchum corrected her. "Then north after passing the rad zones."

Reining in his horse to keep it steady, Ryan studied the two people, debating their answers.

"How far?" he asked suddenly.

"A week on foot," the girl answered after a hesitation.

"Day or so, on horseback," Mitchum added. "Easy traveling, flat land, lots of freshwater."

Moaning across the land, a warm wind blew over the group, rustling the leaves on the trees and carrying the smell of fiery death.

"East it is," Ryan said, not believing a word said by either of them. Personally, he much preferred fighting cannies. At least you could see them coming.

Chapter Nine

The bedroom was lit only by candles, the flickering light playing across the waiting people. Dried flower petals mixed into the wax gave off a sweet perfume. The only door was shut tight and locked with a heavy wooden bar, and a cheery blaze burned in the predark fireplace, giving off soothing waves of warmth. The window shutters were closed, and the silence was broken only by the soft crackle of the burning logs in the fireplace.

Standing on a small rug in the middle of the room, a slim woman with long blond hair slowly unbuttoned her shirt and let it slide off her body. The cloth fluttered to the floor, and she ran delicate hands across her taut stomach, then upward to cup her heavy breasts. The pink nipples hardened immediately, and the tip of her tongue played along her sensuous lips. Tugging on her waistband, she released her skirt to join the shirt on the floor. She was shaved clean, ready for this special evening, and small tattoos adorned her pale skin, which only made her appear even more naked, if that were possible. A finger was missing from her left hand, and

the brand of a slave was burned into the satiny skin
of her shoulder.

"You, too," the giant man on the bed said, taking another sip from his 40 mm brass goblet of
wine.

The other woman removed her top and held it
out at arm's length for a moment before letting it
fall. Her breasts were small but firm, the oversize
nipples already protruding. She laughed, the sound
as gentle as the rain, and ran her long hands down
her waist to push off her cotton pants. She stepped
out of the pile of clothing, and kept her legs spread
wide, then ran her fingers across her taut stomach
and down to the juncture of her thighs. Her skin
was as dark as coffee, her raven hair set in bouncy
coils that dangled loosely and partially hid her features. There was an acid scar on her neck from
when she had been caught out in the rain as a child.
Her nails were long and sharply pointed. The brand
of a slave marked her bare shoulder.

"Come close," the huge sec man ordered, slurping his wine. He shifted position on the bed and let
his robe fall open, showing that he was fully ready
for the women. His body was colossal, and more
heavily muscled than a field slave's. White dots
marred his thickly hairy chest, showing where he
had been shot many times. A thin scar ran across
his forearm where he had blocked a knife thrust,
and a small gold ring glistened from his right ear,

disguising the fact the lobe was gone, bitten off in a bar fight.

"Do me," the giant demanded, placing aside the artillery shell of red wine. "Do me now."

The women joined him on the bed. Going to either side, the gaudy sluts pressed breasts onto his face and both wrapped their hands around his throbbing cock. Almost suffocating from the delicious softness, he ran rough hands over their bodies as he sucked on one nipple, then bit another.

The blonde lifted a leg onto the mattress and guided his hand to her moist softness. His stubby fingers played with the delicate folds as the brunette wrapped her strong fingers around his shaft and started to stroke the sec man, but he pushed her off. Not yet, too soon. He wanted this to last the whole scorching night.

"You," he panted, grabbing the blonde by the shoulder hauling her to the floor.

Obediently, the woman took him fully into her mouth and began to use her talented tongue. He groaned in lust as she rotated her head around his throbbing shaft, playfully using her teeth at just the right spot.

"Nuke me," he hoarsely whispered. "Again. Do that again!"

"No, that's quite enough," a new voice said calmly.

The giant snapped his head around and tried to

focus on the figure standing in one corner of the room. A thousand questions filled his mind, but his hand instinctively darted for the blaster in the gun belt hanging from the nearby bedpost, only to find the weapon gone. Frantically, the sec man tried to extract himself from the ministrations of the two naked sluts, so pleasurable before, now a deadly trap. But the women hung on tighter, digging in their nails to hold him in place.

As he struggled to get loose, the stranger walked into the firelight, raised an ax and brought it down with unbridled fury. The blade passed through the arm the sec man raised to protect himself. The pain rooted him to the spot, and as he tried to scream, the women pulled long thin needles from within their hair and stabbed upward through his jaw, pinning his mouth shut.

Unstoppable, the ax fell again, opening his chest, and the women hastily backed away as his beating organs slithered out of the red body cavity.

The giant fell backward, reeling from the loss of blood, and the ax descended once more, permanently ending the matter.

As the stranger yanked the ax free from the dead man's head, he saw the exposed heart suddenly beat a brief flurry, and then go still. Nukeshit, the huge man had been hell to chill. Perhaps the hired coldhearts hadn't been lax in their failed attempts to ace the battle-scarred goliath. Pity he couldn't be bought. He would have made a wonderful body-guard.

"Good work, my pets," Chancellor Griffin said, wiping the crimson blade on the sheets. Blood was still flowing from the warm corpse, and he had trouble locating a dry patch to clean his weapon. As he shifted a blanket, the gun belt became visible tucked far underneath the bed. Completely out of reach.

The two slaves bowed to their master, then raised smiling faces, plush lips smeared with blood.

"You're filthy. Get washed and visit the next man on the list," the chancellor commanded. "And be quick, there is much to do tonight."

Gathering their clothes, the women hurried off, exiting through the same hidden doorway their master had entered.

Removing a bit of skull from his weapon, Griffin tested the nicked edge of the blade and decided it was still in good enough shape for one more kill. After that, silence wouldn't be necessary, and he could move openly.

Lifting the brass cup, he drank the wine in a victory toast. Everything was going precisely on schedule. Nothing could stop him now. Not even the mighty Lord Bastard himself.

ARMED GUARDS walking in front and behind, Kinnison walked down the main corridor of the mansion, waving and smiling at the cheering people lining the way. He had a son, an heir to carry on his reign! Triple-damn fools had better cheer, or he'd rip the bones from their flesh.

The pain in his limbs was especially bad today, but the baron forced a smile and continued along with the procession. Slaves threw rose petals in the air, an old man blew a tune on a harmonica and the sec men stayed very close to the chained midwife carrying the newborn baron.

But Kinnison was annoyed his preparations for the parade had failed so miserably. Every step was agony even though he was wearing fresh bandages boiled in clean water, had smeared ointment on every open sore, and even took an extra dose of jolt to ward off the pain from his disease. The baron knew the drug was rotting his mind even as the disease did his flesh, but he had no choice. Twelve more winters and he could die. Not until then would the boy be big enough to rule the islands, and their hundred villes. That was the age he was when he pushed his own father off a balcony to seize the Iron Throne.

His grandfather had once told him how the secret of black powder was found in an old book. Just a book, sitting forgotten on a shelf for decades. Amazing. Unfortunately, it wasn't the strange silvery stuff in predark military blasters. Nobody had ever been able to duplicate that smokeless brew.

But the grainy black powder did operate muzzle-loading blasters, and if ground very fine it would work in rapidfires, at least for a while. They always jammed.

Only his family knew the formula for the precious black powder, and protected that prize by having a hundred different chems delivered to the mills when he needed only three. In recent years, Kinnison thought he would be the last of the noble line, taking the knowledge to his grave. But now he had a son to carry on the reign. In some indescribable way, that made him feel immortal.

Oddly, while black powder was the source of his island's wealth, the Firebirds were its strength, the power that made his words into law. The sleek missiles obeyed his commands as if alive, and would never swerve from a target once it was in view.

More than a dozen times since skydark, other barons, coldhearts, pirates and muties had attempted to seize control of Maturo Island. But the Firebirds always slaughtered the invaders, and nobody had tried open rebellion for quite a while. However, the local barons were constantly testing him by sending old fish and sick slaves as their tribute. Sometimes even beer they watered down with piss. Each "mistake" was savagely answered by a barrage of Firebirds, and there would be no more trouble for years. That was, until some fool decided to try again. The dockyard dogs of his island feasted richly on the entrails of those who dared to challenge his power.

Approaching the throne room, trumpeters blared a herald for the arrival of the baron and his son, which naturally made the infant start to wail in fear. Seriously annoyed, Baron Kinnison glared at the men, and they quickly retreated down a side passage. Fused-brain idiots.

"My lord, a moment!" a sec man called from the attending crowd.

Turning in the doorway, Kinnison stared at the disturbance. It was a corporal from the coast watch. Evander something, good man, had chilled a guard with his bare hands for sleeping on a watch.

"What?" the baron demanded.

"My lord, pirate ships have been spotted on the horizon," he reported. "And the quartermaster is unhappy with the number of Firebirds we have ready. I understand this is an important moment, the coronation of your first son—congratulations, my lord—but the safety of the ville may be in danger. Would it be completely out of the question to—?"

"You talk too much," Kinnison snapped, and turned to the midwife.

"Take my son to his room. Double the guards and stay there until called. Understood?"

"Yes, my lord," she said, bowing her head. "I shall guard the boy with my life."

"You better," the baron growled, touching the blaster at his side. The woman paled and raced away with a full squad of sec men in her wake.

Anxiously, the crowd waited to be told what was happening.

"Evander, with me, the rest of you stay here," the baron commanded, and started along a corridor at his fastest pace.

Murmuring among themselves, the attendees did as ordered, nobody wanting to be the first to leave and risk the wrath of their brutal lord and master.

The sec men easily matched the speed of the ill man, and spread out in a standard defensive arc as he reached a massive door set in the stone block wall. It was a new section of the mansion, formed of solid granite blocks taken from the ruins of a lighthouse at the far end of the island.

Kinnison unlocked the door and opened it a crack to reach through and fumble with something on the inside. When the booby trap was deactivated, the baron swung the door wide and marched straight inside. The room was narrow and dimly lit by a single oil lantern hanging from the ceiling, the wick barely glowing red it was turned down so low. At the back was a honeycomb of bamboo tubes, every one filled with a Firebird, and both of the walls were lined with shelves filled with small bowls. Something in the bowls splashed about at his approach, and tiny tentacles writhed in the air as if waving in greeting.

Suddenly, Evander entered the room with a torch, the crackling light filling the tiny room with brilliant illumination. The things in the bowls began to shriek and wildly thrash their tentacles in blind panic.

"Out!" Kinnison yelled, and shoved the man into the corridor.

Evander stumbled from the room and dropped the torch. It rolled away, leaving a trail of burning pitch on the cold stone.

Leaving the room, Kinnison ever so gently closed the door, then turned on the sec man. "Idiot!" the baron shouted, backhanding the officer to the floor.

"I just wanted to see..." Evander began hesitantly. Suddenly, he felt the cold gaze of the other sec men directed toward him.

"The pilots are terrified of fire!" Kinnison raged. "You've weakened the defensives of the entire island! If the pirates attack now, we may lose because of this. It will be days, even weeks before the pilots calm down!"

Kinnison found he had trouble speaking, his mind was a hurricane of dark thoughts. To lose everything because of one small mistake. There was no torture awful enough to serve as punishment for this crime. Wait. Yes, there was.

"Guards, seize the traitor," Kinnison commanded. "But no blasters! I want him alive when we feed him to the pilots."

Evander went pale and backed away, clawing for his blaster. But the other sec men pounced on the former guard, easily disarmed him, then bound his hands behind his back.

"Mercy, my lord," Evander stammered, tears running down his bruised face. "Castrate me, burn me at the stake. But not this! Anything but this, please!"

Kinnison said nothing as he watched the weeping prisoner dragged away, then sighed and sagged against the stone wall. He was feeling weaker every day, and the drugs were helping less and less. Death would be a sweet release. But this unexpected excitement of pirates and Evander had drained him completely. He felt sick to his stomach, and itchy.

"Here, my lord," a sergeant said, offering a gourd. It sloshed from the slight motion.

"And what is this?" Kinnison demanded suspiciously, not accepting the container.

"Chancellor Griffin commanded us to start carrying some of your medicine with us while on duty," the guard explained smoothly. "There is no reason our baron should ever be in pain."

Kinnison looked at the gourd as if it were a fanged insect. "Thank you, Sergeant," he spoke in an even tone. "Take that to the launch pods on the roof. I'll be there shortly to direct the attack."

"But..." The sec man stopped and saluted. "As you command, my lord."

As the guards marched away, Kinnison decided that Griffin had to go to Davey. This was the most clumsy attempt on his life ever, and if the chancellor was this poor at his job, then of what possible use could he be to the ville? None. Simply more jetsam for the sea.

Flanked by the remaining sec men, Kinnison rushed along the corridor as quickly as he could, and forced himself up a flight of stairs to reach his private level. The guards at the iron gate saluted as he went through. Going directly to his bedroom, Kinnison used two keys to unlock the steel door. The guards stayed in the hallway as he went inside and threw the heavy bolts. Then he paused to catch his breath. His temples were throbbing like a ship's cannons, his bandages felt tight, breathing was difficult and his skin felt prickly as if he were standing near a roaring fire. That sec man had been right; he needed more jolt immediately. But he wasn't accepting any as a gift. How stupid did Griffin think he was? Something was happening, and the baron began to strongly doubt there were any pirates in the waters around his island. The real danger was under his own roof.

Rushing to a hidden compartment in the headboard of his bed, Kinnison slid back a grooved wooden panel that perfectly matched the rest of the intricately carved mahogany. Quickly, he extracted a jar full of white powder and shook some into his trembling palm. There was spring water in a crystal pitcher on the table, and red wine in sealed bottles filling a shelf near the rack of longblasters, but those were much too distant. Lapping the drug from his hand, he stayed kneeling on the quilt until the tremors passed. Feeling better by the second, he drained the pitcher of water and sat down in relief.

Kinnison first knew something was terribly wrong when a fuzzy warmth spread outward from his enormous belly, stealing the strength from his limbs. He tried to rise and found it impossible. What was happening? Had he finally crossed the line and was dying of an overdose? The baron had to concentrate to breathe. His fingers twitched for the bell rope to summon his healer, but the effort was too great. He felt woozy and confused, and trying for the rope was too great an effort.

The door swung open, and in walked Griffin with a huge revolver in his grip. Kinnison recognized it instantly; it was a gift to Samson, one of his personal guards, for saving the baron from a nightcreep attack. But the sec man was fanatically loyal to Kinnison and would never give up the weapon. Unless he was chilled.

"Yes, he's gone," Griffin said with a grin, cocking back the hammer. "And the ones I didn't ace personally, my gaudy sluts did. Every man and woman who supported you is dead. The palace is mine."

A great well of fury boiled inside Kinnison, but he could do nothing. The chancellor seemed to be at the far end of a long white tunnel. The baron mouthed the word *traitor,* but nothing came out.

"Oh, I'm much more than that, you fat bag of pus." The man chuckled and went to the door to slide back the heavy bolts.

As the door swung open, in came a dozen young sec men, their faces grim, hands full of rope.

"Hi, tubby," Evander said, grinning. "Was I a convincing enough fool to bring on one of your fucking attacks?"

"I am baron," Kinnison managed to whisper hoarsely. "This is my ville!"

"Was," Griffin corrected with a grim smile. "Report, Colonel, how goes the revolt?"

"The mansion and armory are under our control. A few of his guards escaped into the jungle, but we released the Hunters to bring them down, so they're meat in the ground. The gates of the ville are closed, the petey boats have only our men on board, and we have control of the Firebirds on the roof. The slaves tried to escape in the chaos, as you said they would. We shot some, and the rest went back to work. There is some fighting at the docks, but nothing we can't handle. All is secure.''

It was so easily said. Maturo Island had fallen. Kinnison couldn't believe he heard the words. Nightmare. This was another wild hallucination brought on by the jolt, nothing more. His ville was fine, everything was fine.

''Excellent work, Colonel,'' Griffin said.

''Thank you, my lord.''

There it was. Chancellor no more.

''You and you,'' Baron Griffin said, gesturing. ''Bind that sack of shit with rope. Don't worry about cutting off his circulation. It isn't important.''

Pulling on canvas gloves to protect them from his sickness, the sec men bound Kinnison tightly. He wanted to fight back, to reach the machine pistol hidden in the bed, but his strength was gone. He felt like a fish on the beach, fighting to move, trying to breathe.

''How…?'' Kinnison said, then broke into a cough, bloody flecks staining the floor. The sec men moved farther away. Dragging in a lungful of air, he tried again. ''What…did you…give me?''

''Exactly what you came here for, fat boy,'' Baron Griffin said with a sneer. ''The jar was full of jolt. Not your painkillers and flash, with a trace of the drug. But pure quill jolt. Enough to stun a whale. I guessed it should be enough to dull your quivering bulk. Your own healer told me of the secret stash. I knew if a sec man offered you some openly, your natural paranoia would make you rush here for some clean drugs. You fell right into my hands.''

"And if you died," a corporal said, "who'd give a fuck?''

The others agreed, some laughing, others staring with open hatred. Kinnison gave no reply, the growing buzz in his ears drowning out the world. He began to surrender to the warmth and closed his eyes. Then pain took the baron as his head snapped to the side, and he realized somebody was slapping him awake.

"Don't you die on me," Griffin snarled, backhanding his prisoner again. "I haven't begun to take my revenge yet. Colonel, send some of your men to cast that new brat of his into the sea with a stone tied around its neck."

"Yes, my lord.'' The man grinned and exited the room.

"No!" Kinnison screamed, and in a rush of strength stood and charged for the usurper. Two sec man grabbed his bandaged arms, and he shook them off, the urge to kill driving him onward like a Firebird in flight. But Griffin merely laughed as the sec men wrestled him to the wall, pinned helpless under their combined weight.

"Not even a good try," Griffin said haughtily.

"You'll never keep the throne," Kinnison growled, feeling the rush of strength ebbing away like the tide. "You can't control the Firebirds!"

Leaning past the guards, Griffin whispered something into his ear and Kinnison went pale.

"Did you really think I never followed you?" Griffin asked, delighted at the expression on the man's face. "Or listened at a keyhole? The rockets will obey my commands. I am in absolute control."

"There's still Lieutenant Brandon, sir," a burly sec man reminded. "He's got a dozen peteys, could be trouble. The ass is actually loyal to this blubbering thing."

Griffin waved that aside. "Brandon is dead. That healer, Glassman, is in charge of those boats, spreading the word about the outlanders. If Captain Glassman tries anything, we nail his family to the front wall until he surrenders. Then we blow him out of the water with my Firebirds."

Kinnison narrowed his piggy eyes and said nothing. For once he was thankful for the bandages that masked his features.

"What about the outlanders?" a sergeant asked. "I heard they took Cold Harbor ville in less than a day."

"Send the word, chill them on sight."

"Yes, my lord."

Exhaling loudly through his nose, a guard moved his head away from the huge prisoner. "Shitfire, this diseased pus bag stinks something awful!'' he stated.

The other guards muttered in agreement. They had never been this close to the former baron before, and were beginning to understand why dogs wouldn't go near him, and his bed partners got drunk before and after sex. He reeked worse than a dead seal on a hot beach.

Baron Griffin sniffed the air and made a face. "Nuke me, he is pungent. Well, he'll smell a lot worse when I'm done with him. Sergeant, have your men haul his wretched ass to the dungeon. I have something very special planned for our former lord and master.''

"Yes, sir!''

Dragging Kinnison into motion, the sec men kicked and shoved the fat man along the stony corridors of the mansion and down into the cellar. When Kinnison heard the telltale booming of the heavy door closing, he knew that there was every possibility that he would never leave the dungeon alive. A flare of pride overlook him, and he found the notion intolerable that the hideous tortures he did so often to others would now be done to him. Kinnison decided to try for a clean death. When the guards cut off the rope to shackle him to the wall, he'd grab a blaster and start shooting. They would be forced to chill him then, and he would be spared the humiliation of being taken apart under the sharp knives and red-hot tongs of his enemies.

But the sec men seemed to have expected that move on his part, because they shackled him first, and then cut away the ropes. Dangling helpless from the iron cuffs attached to the ceiling, Kinnison stood before the jeering men utterly helpless. They could do as they pleased with him now, and there was no way he could stop them. He was already dead. If he had a single minute alone, he might have a fleeting chance of escape, but that would never happen. Griffin was proving himself worthy to be a baron in every way.

"Let's carve him up a little first," a guard said, poking at the man with the tip of his knife. "Mebbe set him on fire first."

"Cut off his fingers, feed them to the dogs!" another shouted.

"Don't be ridiculous," Griffin said, testing the anchor bolt that held the chains. It was good and solid. "His heir is dead, his reign is over. Let him live out the rest of his miserable life down here in the cold and wet. The sickness will eat him alive, and without his drugs or shine, it'll be a much more painful death than anything we could do to him."

Dribbling blood and pus from tied hands, Kinnison heaved for breath and remained quiet.

That wasn't the reaction he wanted, so Baron Griffin took a bottle from a nearby table, grabbed

Kinnison by the chin and forced him to look upward.

"Live forever," he whispered, and pulled the
cork with his teeth to pour the contents over the
man, front and back.

Kinnison had only a moment to wonder what
was happening before he smelled the strong aroma
of alcohol. He watched in horror as the clear liquid
seeped through his bandages and reached the open
sores covering his skin. The screams exploded from
him as searing pain burned into his flesh, his anguished cries almost drowning out the laughter of
his captors. The agony seemed to last for years as
he was doused with more shine, and then again,
until he was finally swallowed whole by sweet
blackness.

KINNISON AWAKENED with a scream, and it took a
moment for him to realize he was alone in the cell.
Then he shuddered in memory of what they had
done. He ached from the beatings, and every sore
felt brand-new, as tender as a bullet wound. Plus
his clothes were filthy. The blood and pus had
soaked through the bandages and stained his shirt
and pants. His sandals were gone, his bare feet resting on the cold stone floor, and his left arm was
broken, the job expertly done. There were no splin-
ters of bone through the skin to cause major blood
loss and a fast death. He could feel the splintered

ends grinding against each other, but after a decade of pain, it was only a minor annoyance.

The cell was as he remembered, small and damp. There was only ambient light in the cell, a soft glow seeping around the door from the torches in the corridor outside. The wall shelf had been emptied of any tools. There were no sounds, but the scurrying of rats in the dank straw piled near the waste bucket.

Patiently, the man forced himself to wait, making sure he was truly alone. Griffin had made a terrible mistake letting him live. Soon he would answer for his crimes against the state. And for the death of his son.

Suddenly, Kinnison not could wait another second, and he clumsily swung the broken arm to his mouth and started tugging at the shirtsleeve with his teeth. The fine cloth ripped easily, and he started on the stained bandages. Steeling his stomach to the task, the man started chewing off the filthy strips. The smell of his diseased flesh turned his stomach, but he continued until inadvertently swallowing some saliva. The taste convulsed his entire body, and he violently retched.

Gasping for breath, he heard the rats arrive as if they knew what the sound was. They gathered around the sour puddle, and he crushed one underfoot, then kicked it into the corner. The rest converged on their wounded member and started to feast. Dripping sweat, Kinnison redoubled his efforts to get the putrid strips of cloth off his arm. They would be even more hungry when finished and would immediately turn on him. Now it was a race.

Ignoring the pain and taste, he ripped at the bandages madly until the last layer peeled away making the sores bleed anew. But there it was, a small iron key taped just below the break. Breathing through his nose, he lipped the item out of the slimy sore, and quickly jerked his head to the right, grabbed the key from his mouth and retched again, until his body was racked with dry heaves. The rats didn't seem to notice or care.

Commanding himself, Kinnison twisted about and brought his hands close, awkwardly inserting the key into the lock of the manacles and turning it ever so gently. As the catch released, his arm dropped free and he bit back a scream, trembling with the effort. As the circulation was restored, the pain subsided, and he forced the shaking limb to reach up and unlock his right wrist. The click was like music, and he quickly caught the broken arm so it wouldn't drop again. Very gently, he tucked the aching arm into his shirt, then rigged a crude sling with his own bandages. It was uncomfortable, but more important, he was free, although locked in a rat-infested cell deep underground, surrounded by traitors.

Trembling with weakness and covered in filth, Kinnison grimaced in triumph as he climbed onto the pile of straw and fumbled with the ceiling. Even in bright lantern light it appeared to be solid stone. Finally, his fingertips found the pattern of a Firebird carved into a stone, and he started to pound with his right fist. After a few minutes, the stone came loose and he reached into the hole to start removing handfuls of items: a zip-top plastic bag full of fresh white bandages, plastic film canisters of his drugs, clean clothing, candles, a tinderbox, a gourd of wine, glass jars of food and clean water. Then came the weapons: a slim dagger and a pre-dark revolver in oiled cloth, with a full box of live rounds. His emergency supplies in case of a rebellion. This hadn't been done with every cell in the dungeon. That would have been too dangerous. Only this special one had been kept empty of prisoners, even when he had five or six packed into the others.

Now taking his time, Lord Baron Kinnison lit the candle, the light making the rats flee back into the walls. Stripping naked, the fat man washed the filth from his body and plotted revenge as he wrapped his sores and began to dress. By the time he was rigging a new sling for the broken arm, Kinnison already had a plan to bring down Griffin and the rest of the cowardly traitors who had planned this Judas strike.

"Live forever," Kinnison throated through his gritted teeth, tightening the sling. "No, I won't, but I'll live longer than you bastards. Oh, yes, I will."

Chapter Ten

As the train of horses plodded along the mountain-
ous trail, Ryan fought off a shiver, his coat offering
little protection against the strong winds.

There had been enough horses for everybody,
more in fact, but only saddles for about half and
no supplies. Most of the freed sec man were in thin
clothing. As the group climbed into the hills and
the temperature quickly dropped, Krysty had gotten
the horse blankets from under the saddles, and cut
holes in the centers to make crude ponchos for the
cold men. It helped, but not much. The horses were
unhappy, but they didn't have a vote in the matter.

Good thing the companions were wearing jackets, although only Krysty was actually warm in her
bearskin coat. And those fingerless gloves J.B.
wore were a godsend. Ryan's own coat was too thin
to be much protection against the bitter winds of
the higher peaks, but it was a hell of a lot better
than those ponchos. Mildred had loaned Ann some
of her spare clothing, but the thin girl still looked
pale and weak. Ryan wasn't sure she could last

much longer without a hot meal. The cholera had taken a lot out of her.

And everybody was hungry. The cannies hadn't fed their prisoners since they had planned on eating them, and while the companions had lots of MRE food packs, they hesitated to display the predark wealth of the foil envelopes. Ryan had convinced Mitchum that the companions found their rapidfires and revolvers in the cannie armory. The lie was accepted at face value, but if they started showing MRE packs, flashlights, rad counters and such, the only possible conclusion would be that they were outlanders, and strangers got aced in these islands by order of the lord baron.

With a week's worth of food in their backpacks, the companions rode along with Mitchum and his troops, stomachs growling, and watching the landscape for anything they could shoot for dinner, then breakfast and now lunch. Thankfully, there was lots of grass for the horses to munch on the lower hills, and plenty of snow for water. Filling a canteen only gave a few cupfuls after it melted from body heat. But it tasted pure and clean.

"Ville much farther?" Jak asked, his teeth chattering. The albino teenager had one hand stuffed into a pocket, the other holding the reins. And he switched them often. He couldn't understand how it could be so damn cold in the tropics. But then, he'd seen a swamp turn into a desert in under a year in the Deathlands. Bastard weather was screwy across the globe.

"Mebbe by tomorrow morning we'll see Ratak ville," Colonel Mitchum said, tightening the belt strapped around his poncho. The wind kicked up tiny blizzards of snow and constantly dusted them with flakes. The officer filled his mind with memories of warm days on the beach, and savored what little heat came from the animal he rode.

"Ah! This reminds me of those carefree days in Moscow," Doc said, his frock coat buttoned to the collar. "We were with a colonel then, too. Nasty fellow at first, but he turned out a decent enough chap."

"Moscow? Where's that?" a sec man asked, hunched under his dirty blanket. His breath fogged in the air, often hiding his unshaved face.

"It's an island to the south of here," Mildred lied, remembering only at the last second that the farther south you traveled in this hemisphere the colder it got. Almost said it backward. "Little place, lots of wolves."

"Folks nice?"

"Baron was tough, but excellent shine."

"Good enough." Ann tried to laugh, but the sound died away in the cold breeze moaning around the craggy peaks and bare outcroppings.

"What the hell," Dean muttered, slowing his mount and staring off to the side. There was a tiny cloud that appeared, and disappeared, near one of the snowbanks. Breathing out of the side of his mouth to see better, the boy suddenly realized the odd cloud was exactly like breath foggy from the cold. He drew his Browning semiautomatic pistol, and jacked the slide. Could be another buried cold-heart like back in the cannie camp. Should he warn the others quietly or attack?

The decision was taken away when the snow-bank charged at the group with only the soft crunching of the new-fallen snow under its soft paws.

"Mutie!" Dean cried and fired, both rounds missing. Hot pipe, that sucker was fast.

The rest of the mixed group spun as the snow-bank leaped on Ann, the blow shoving her off her horse. The girl hit the ground, rolling with the thing, blood spurting from deep gashes in her chest. Instantly, everybody had their blasters out, but withheld firing. The girl and mutie were so entangled it would be impossible to shoot one without hitting the other.

"Shoot it!" Ann screamed, beating at the snowy white creature with both fists. Her blanket was ripped, taking most of her clothing with it, and she pulled the big flintlock from her belt and fired, the boom echoing along the crags sounding like a hundred blasters. The discharge cloud masked the two until the wind pushed it away. Shapeless white covered her neck for a moment, then went away and blood fountained into the air from severed arteries as her throat was neatly removed. She gurgled horribly, her hands at the ragged flesh of her neck, then the snow mutie moved to her belly and once more hot blood spewed.

"Ann's dead, chill the fucker!" Ryan ordered leveling the Steyr and firing. The round missed striking the dying girl and only startled the creature.

As the companions fired a barrage of lead, the creature turned toward them and Ryan could only see a vague outline of a bestial face under the blood; the rest was only shapeless white. Good enough.

Working the bolt, he aimed between the eyes and pulled the trigger. The mutie flipped over sideways and hit the snow, green blood pumping onto the ground like a chem spill. Framed by its own blood, the thing was now an easy target. Mildred used the shotgun, tearing the carcass apart with a full charge of fléchettes. Dean got it in the face again, while Jak, Doc and Krysty aimed for the chest. Facing the opposite direction, J.B. was sweeping the wintery landscape with the Uzi for any more of the strange creatures.

Dismounting, Mitchum and Ryan slowly approached the mutie with drawn blasters, the others holding back, controlling the scared horses and reloading their assorted weapons. The strained breathing of the creature could clearly be heard, but even at ten feet away it was difficult to focus clearly on the thing. It was a blob of fuzzy white floating in green—that was all. Jacking in a fresh round, Ryan fired the longblaster at point-blank range. The creature bucked from the impact and went still. The puffing of its breath disappearing for good.

"It's aced," Mitchum reported, holstering his piece.

"Something local?" Ryan asked, looking over the thing.

The officer frowned. "Never saw or heard anything like it before. Must be a newbie."

"A new mutant," Ryan translated.

"Yeah, sure, get them all the time from the north."

The direction of the Bikini Atoll where the American government tested all those nukes in the past. Made sense.

Sliding off her mount, Mildred passed the reins to J.B. and hurried over. The physician burned with curiosity to see the mutation closer. Moving past the men, she stepped into the blood and crouched near the body, running her hands over the cold corpse. It couldn't have lost body heat that fast. It had to be cold-blooded, like a lizard. But then, how could it move so fast?

The body was huge and draped with gossamer-fine fur as pale as the snow. It was broad daylight, but the sun didn't reflect off the hair filaments. The nose, even the eyes, were as pale as ice, and the entire body was draped with a fringe of the translucent fur, including the face.

"Some sort of cat, like a cougar," Mildred said, lifting a paw for study. The claws were six inches long, as sharp as knives and a smooth dull white where they weren't coated with blood. She opened its mouth and noted that even its gums and tongue were white, only some plaque on the lower teeth adding the smallest tinge of yellow. It was the most amazing natural camouflage she had ever seen. Made stick-bugs and chameleons pale in comparison. No way this was a result of natural selection; it was much too perfect. *Designed* was the word that came to mind.

"Bitch to see," a sec man stated, squinting at the mutie. "There be snow falling, it could have easily chilled the whole group."

"I saw its breath, but wasn't sure until it moved," Dean said, his expression of a mixture of serious and embarrassed. "Then it was too late."

"Not your fault," Ryan said, resting the stock of the Steyr on a hip.

"Strangest mutie I have ever seen," Mitchum said, hitching his blanket closed more against the wind. "Only hope it's traveling alone."

Jak slid off his horse and walked closer to it. "Want see paws," he said. "Case find tracks elsewhere."

"Good idea," Mildred said, and pressed a paw into the snow. Together, they scrutinized the pattern closely, logging the details of the pattern into memory.

"How odd. It's sort of like that symbol for Forbidden Island," Mildred whispered softly.

"Yeah," the teenager agreed. "Not like."

Walking her mount to the dead girl, Krysty bowed her head in prayer for a minute, then said, "We should bury Ann. But without shovels, I don't see how."

"Leave her for the birds," Ryan stated, glancing at the sky. Condors were already circling the area. Blasterfire always meant food for the scavengers. Also gave away their position. The one-eyed man didn't like that, but there was nothing he could do about birds. What could not be changed, had to be endured, as Doc liked to say.

But more important, with Ann on the last train west, it meant the companions now depended on the goodwill of Mitchum and his sec men. And Ryan didn't like that one bit. Ann owed them her life; these folks only owed them their freedom. It wasn't the same thing.

"This is bullshit," a sec man grumbled, rubbing his blaster as if it were a source of warmth. The air fogged before the man, his visible breath mixing with the exhalations of the horse. "Colonel, how do we know these folks ain't tricking us somehow. Get the ville gates open and in pour the cannies!"

"Shut up, trooper," Mitchum snapped, glaring at the shivering man. "These are the folks who hauled us out of the stew pot. I'll trust them with my life."

Ryan said nothing, hoping it was true.

"Yeah?" the sec man said rudely, then pointed. "Including the freak?"

Jak looked up from studying the mutie, his snowy hair billowing in the cold wind, his red eyes and ruddy cheeks the only touches of faint color in his pale face.

"Got prob?" the teenager asked, in a dangerous tone of voice.

"Bet your ass I do! You look like the thing!" the sec men raved on. "Sir, mebbe he worships it or something."

"A mutie? What a load of spent brass," Mitchum shot back. "Listen up, feeb. They saved us from the cannies to feed to the mountain cats?"

"I say we should ace the freak to make sure!" the sec man shouted, grabbing the flintlock at his side to brandish the weapon in the air. "Who's with me?"

Nobody said a word, the only movement the windblown snow and the horses shifting their legs to stay warm. The companions exchanged glances and judiciously walked their horses out of the line of fire. They could smell death coming.

"You can see he's a stinking mutie!" the sec man shouted in argument. "By the baron's law, we're supposed to ace any human muties!"

Feeling her red hair flare angrily at the pronouncement, Krysty kept her features neutral, but filed that information away.

"Shut mouth," Jak said, opening his jacket to expose the Colt Python holstered at his side. "Or go steel."

"Think I can't take you, freak?" the trooper said, sneering, the flintlock already in his hand.

Reaching behind his back, Jak pulled his jacket out of the way. "Any time, stupe," he said softly, flexing his blaster hand.

"You in on this?" Mitchum asked, flicking a look at Ryan.

He shook his head. "Between them."

"Agreed," the colonel said. "Anybody helps this asshole gets on the wrong side of me. Natch?"

The rest of the troopers nodded in agreement and moved away from the lone gunman. Suddenly realizing he was without backup, the sec man dropped the blaster to his side, then whipped out a second pistol from inside the blanket, the hammer already cocked and ready to fire.

As the weapon swung toward Jak, the teenager

drew his own piece and jerked his wrist the second it cleared the holster to shoot from the hip. The booming Magnum round hit the sec man square in the face, eyes and teeth blowing into the wind as the primed flintlock discharged, the miniball buzzing past Jak so close he felt the passage of its wind on his cheek.

The sec man toppled from the saddle to hit the ground in a crumpled ball. Red blood puddled around the corpse, wisps of steam rising off the warm pool of life fluid.

"Nuke me." Mitchum exhaled a held breath, creating a small fog. "Never seen speed like that. You're good, boy, damn good."

Jak shrugged in response, then slid his Colt Python back into its holster and zipped his jacket over the blaster to help keep it warm. There was nothing special about chilling a stupe. World was full of them, always making noise and getting in the way. They were just a minor annoyance, like skeeters or flies.

"Sir, I could use his boots," another sec man said eagerly. Then others called out for his blasters and poncho.

"Ain't mine to give," Mitchum said, tilting his head toward the albino teenager. "Talk to the owner."

"Help self. Not want any," Jak said, climbing back on his horse.

The troopers grinned in delight and proceeded to strip the faceless corpse. Ryan was pleased. Letting them have his stuff was another point in favor of the companions. Besides, it was painfully obvious that nobody had liked the dead man very much, or seemed to mourn his passing.

"It has occurred to me," Doc said in his deep voice, "that such a creation as this should naturally be antithetic to heat. If we traveled with some torches, the flames should hold off any more of its kind."

"Most animals hate fire," Dean agreed.

"Except stickies," J.B. added, leaning forward. "But it's a damn good idea. I still got some juice left."

"What'll we burn?" Mitchum asked, hugging his blanket tighter. There was nothing in sight but a few bare trees, icy rocks and snow in every direction.

Crunching through the ankle-deep snow, Ryan went to Ann and started cutting away her clothing. Dean rode off to get some branches from a tree with Krysty and Jak on his flanks for protection. Until they had the torches, nobody was going anywhere alone.

Unexpectedly, there was a sharp crack and a riderless horse dropped lifeless to the frozen earth.

"Dinner is served," Mildred announced, holstering her smoking ZKR and drawing a sharp knife.

WITH RAW HORSE filling their bellies, the mood of
the group improved noticeably and tempers cooled.
Riding through the day and into night, the travelers
kept the torches burning with strips of diesel-
soaked clothing and took turns sleeping in the saddles. Along the way, the nervous sec men fired a
dozen times into the snow, chilling a couple of rab-
bits and wounding something that bled green, but
it ran off so fast nobody was able to get a second
shot. Might have been a snow cat, or it might not.
It was impossible to say.

By dawn, the group was past the frost line and
descending into the warmth once more. As the sun
crested the horizon, the torches were tossed away
and everybody relaxed. Now that they were past
the snow, the snow cats wouldn't dare to attack.
Here in the green grass and trees, their weird color
would only make them incredibly visible. Easy targets for anybody.

"Better." Jak sighed and unzipped his jacket.

"This is my fav time of day," Mitchum said,
smiling, luxuriating in the golden dawn. "It's what
Ratak means in some old speak, sunrise."

"Any more meat?" Dean asked, riding over to
Krysty.

"Sure," she answered, passing over a strip. The
dead animal had been skinned, and its hide made
into a sack stuffed with snow and the best cuts of
meat. Now that they were warming up, the snow

wouldn't last long, but with any luck it was only a few hours to the ville.

"You know, I once read that the ancient Mongols used to place raw meat under the saddles first thing in the morning, and when they stopped at night would eat the meat cooked by the heat of their horses."

"That's just an old wive's tale," Mildred retorted. "The Mongols put raw steaks on their horses to help heal saddle sores. Nothing more."

"Work?" Jak asked, stroking the neck of his mount. The horse whinnied in response and bent closer to the teenager's touch.

"Works fine, or so I've been told," Mildred replied.

"Raw meat as a bandage," Colonel Mitchum muttered. "Pretty smart. Must remember that."

Reaching level ground, the group found grass for their horses and let them eat their fill, before kicking their mounts into an easy gallop. The riders had no wish to tire the beasts after the long walk over the mountain.

The sun rose toward its azimuth as the miles flew by without incident. Birds exploded from the trees as they rode by, and monkeys of various sizes chattered furiously at the invasion of their territory and threw handfuls of fresh feces at the riders to seriously discourage them from returning. A near hit made a sec man fire his flintlock, and the chimps disappeared into the thick canopy of flowers of vines, screaming and chattering in fear.

"There!" a corporal called out, gesturing ahead of the group. "Tide bridge, sir! We're nearly home."

Brushing the hair out of his eye, Ryan could see they were approaching another shallow bay like the one on Crab Island. But here rocks had been piled in the water until forming a wide bridge over the ocean. Old rusty pipes stuck out of the rocks below the surface to allow the tide to flow freely.

"Will that support a horse and rider?" J.B. asked in concern. The bridge had no mortar or concrete. It was just a pile of rocks, nothing more.

"Always has before," Mitchum said, guiding his mount down the bank and onto the rocks. They moved at every step, but the sec men rode their animals along the crude construct with no real difficulties, so the companions soon followed. There was no sign of crabs anywhere.

Reaching the far side, Ryan noticed a wide area where there was no grass, and in the center was a deep hole. Checking his rad counter, he saw no dangerous readings, and there wasn't any glassy slag at the bottom from a tac nuke.

"See that? Our fathers killed a tin can there," a sergeant said with pride, slowing so the others could take a look. "Fifty sec men died, but they aced the mofu."

"Tin can," Krysty repeated. "Some sort of machine?"

"They say it was a crazy thing," Mitchum answered grimly. "Didn't resemble a wag, or a boat. It was built like a cartridge, round and flat on the bottom. Had rotating red eyes and floated off the ground like a soap bubble, but it was made of steel. They say miniballs only dented it at close range."

The companions knew the description well. It was a sec hunter droid, and it had to have already been damaged for a bunch of sec men with blasters to bring it down. Ryan had one chase him and J.B. for miles a while back, and it had been a triple bitch to stop. Damn near aced both men.

"I assume it detonated once damaged sufficiently," Doc inquired politely. This was clearly a site of great importance to the local sec force, and it was only wise to pay it proper respect. In his own time period, Doc would expect no less of a visitor from another country upon viewing Gettysburg or Bunker Hill.

"Detonated?" the sergeant snorted a laugh. "Naw, that's what everybody thinks, but it's the other way 'round."

"Our fathers dug a hole, filled it with kegs of black powder and lured the tin can there, then lit the fuse," Mitchum said, his vision unfocused as he imagined the past event. "The blast blew it to dreck."

"The shrapnel aced most of the sec men," Mitchum said. "Lost my father and two uncles in that fight. But they saved the ville."

"Good men," Ryan said.

"Damn straight they were."

Riding onward, they found a path leading through the jungle, the dirt road speckled with a layer of loose gravel pounded into the soil under countless hooves. Protection against erosion from the rain.

"Bad storms here?" Jak asked.

Mitchum snorted in reply. "Like nothing you've ever seen," he stated bitterly.

The roadway was fairly level, although filled with potholes, and in a short while, they exited the jungle and rode onto a grassy plain with countless tree stumps dotting the land. A lot of the stumps were deeply charred. Krysty knew that was how you removed a stump, burn it deep and the roots died, then after a year it could be easily chopped from the ground. Lacking machines and explosives, there was no other way to do the job.

A ville rose in the distance, its wall made of tree trunks notched and laid on top one another in layers to form a zigzag pattern for maximum strength. Bits of broken glass and shards of clam shells jutted from every crack, making climbing the wall a risky proposition. Thorny vines were draped over the top in the manner of barbed wire, and armed sec men walked the parapets with muzzle-loading flintlock rifles in their arms.

The front gate was very small, only slightly larger than a regular door, just barely big enough to walk a horse through. Riding into the ville would have been out of the question. There was no way coldhearts or pirates could force enough troops through the door to forcibly hold the passage open. A handful of sec men could defend the door with nothing more than axes. With blasters it would be a slaughter.

"Impressive," Krysty said.

"Best ville in the Thousand Islands," Mitchum boasted.

Looking around, J.B. noticed a break in the trees to the far right, indicating another road. "That lead to the docks?"

"Where we keep the ships," the colonel corrected. "Wouldn't call them docks, exactly."

Ryan reined in his horse. "Before we go any farther, you and I need to talk."

"Yeah? What about?" Mitchum asked suspiciously, a hand moving dangerously near his blaster.

"Our deal. A ship for your freedom."

"I'll pay your price," the officer said. "Don't worry about that. Just one of these flintlocks will buy you a rowboat large enough for everything but the horses."

"And you can keep the horses once we're gone. All we want is a boat."

"Fair enough, but you better hide those fancy blasters. I know you got them from the cannies, but if Thayer spots those, he'll take them away. Road tax, defense budget, whatever he feels like calling it this month."

"He can try," Dean said stoically.

"Won't just try, lad. Baron Thayer would get them any way necessary," Mitchum stated. "That's a fact. And we'll help him do it, too. We owe you big, but the baron has our oath."

Yeah, Ryan thought as much. But they had walked this razor's edge before and survived. Briefly, he considered having J.B. stay outside and keep watch, but decided it would be wiser to keep everybody together. Otherwise, they might have come back for the Armorer through an army of sec men. Besides, they had a few special items that Mitchum knew nothing about in case of trouble.

"Hide the weapons," Ryan commanded.

Reluctantly, the companions removed their gun belts and holsters, hiding the blasters and ammo inside their bedrolls and backpacks. Flintlocks were tucked into their belts now, ammo bags of black powder and lead shot slung across shoulders to distribute the weight.

Shaking the reins, Ryan made a clucking sound with his tongue and started the horse at a canter through the field heading toward Ratak ville. Mitchum galloped to catch up and stayed alongside, while the rest of the group followed close behind.

Chapter Eleven

As the companions and the sec men rode toward the jungle ville, Mitchum started to wave at the guards on the wall.

"Gotta show we're friendly," he said, "or we don't even get close. Standing orders are to shoot on sight."

"Shoot who?" Mildred asked, rocking to the movement of her mount.

"Everybody," the colonel answered. Then he pointed at a sec man on the wall, who was sitting with his legs dangling over the top and sipping from a gourd. "Pierce! Put down that shine!"

The startled sec man dropped the gourd and quickly stood, wiping his mouth on a sleeve. Squinting down at the riders, he broke into a smile. "Fuck a mutie, it's the colonel. Hey, Sarge! Colonel Mitchum's back!"

"I saw him five minutes ago," the sergeant stated calmly.

Raising a hand, Mitchum brought the riders to a halt a short distance from the front door.

"Open the gate, Sergeant Whyte."

"Sure thing, sir!" the man said, lowering his blaster to point at them. "Be glad to, just as soon as your new friends back away."

"Better do as he asks," Mitchum told the others. "And don't draw a blaster or he'll shoot without warning."

"Tight security," Ryan said, noting the placement of the guards. "Must have a lot of enemies."

"Not anymore."

Shaking the reins, the companions walked their mounts away from the sec men and watched the group enter the ville through the door. It closed behind them. But after a few moments, the door swung open again, and Mitchum waved them inside.

Ryan took the lead, and single file the companions guided their mounts through the narrow doorway. Doc was the last, and as it thudded closed the sound reminded him of a coffin lid slamming shut. An unnerving comparison.

After the gate closed, armed sec men struggled to slide a wooden beam as thick as a horse across the portal.

Mitchum and his troopers had stopped in the middle of a street and slid off their mounts to look around the ville and clap each other on the back. It was obvious they were glad to be back home.

Sidling closer to the sec men, Ryan studied the place. Logs with steps cut into them served as a

ladder to reach the walkway set along the inside of
the wall. Boxes and barrels placed at regular inter-
vals probably held ammo, arrows and such for the
sec men to use in case of attack. That was smart.
Ryan had seen many a ville fall because the baron
kept every round of ammo in his home, and didn't
arm his guards fast enough to stop an attack.

The streets were dirt with gravel walked into the
ground as protection from the rain. The ramshackle
buildings were mostly trailer homes, with a few log
cabins and one big structure made of brick and
stone. The baron's home, obviously. A well stood
in the middle of a stone plaza, a bamboo-and-thatch
roof standing guard over the precious clean water.
A door stood wide on a blacksmith shop, tan men
pounding iron on an anvil made of stone, and a
thick waxy smell came from a tiny van whose chassis was sunk into the ground, smoke rising from a
vent in the roof and rows of candles hanging from
a clothesline to cool and harden in the sea breeze.
And looming darkly over the ville was a row of
gallows, the light-color palm-tree wood stained
with blood.

From somewhere there came the steady crack of
a whip, followed by an anguished cry. The noise
continued, with the cries becoming weaker.

Straggling in, a crowd of people was forming in
the street to greet Mitchum and his troops. The locals were dressed in the usual assortment of home-

made hides and bits of predark junk. Many wore sandals cut from tires, and there were lots of vests and skirts made from shag carpeting. An old man was smoking a wooden pipe, and a young girl was suckling a newborn in her arms.

Suddenly, the crowd parted for a big man in shiny boots and tight denim pants worn light blue at the knees. The big man was shirtless, revealing his hairy chest and massive muscles with long arms that nearly reached his knees. Mildred thought he looked like an ape, the man was so simian in nature. As the only person carrying a blaster, he had to be the baron. The weapon was a .22 revolver, small cartridges filling half the loops lining his rainbow-colored belt. Some sort of lizard skin, the physician assumed.

Covertly, J.B. and Ryan exchanged looks. If that was what the baron carried, then the man would happily chill them to get his hands on the .357 Colt Magnum or the Uzi machine pistol.

As the ape man came closer, Mitchum and his troops quickly stood in a rough line.

"Sir!" they chorused and snapped salutes.

He tried not to show it, but Ryan was impressed. He hadn't seen disciplined troops since the Shiloh slave camp of that crazy whitecoat.

"At ease, you bastards," the baron grunted in greeting, returning the gesture. "Mitchum, glad as hell to see you and the troops alive. After a week I figured you were aced.''

The colonel frowned. ''Damn near, my lord, but we're still sucking air thanks to these folks,'' Mitchum said, looking at the companions.

''That so,'' Baron Thayer said, glancing at them for only a second. ''So what happened, pirates attack?''

''It was those cannies that been hunting us since last winter,'' Mitchum explained. ''Aced half my squad, and was working their way through the rest when Ryan and his people busted in and blew the place apart.''

''What do you mean?'' the baron asked, confused.

''They set fire to the armory, Baron,'' the colonel said. ''You should have seen it!''

''Those cannies won't ever be bothering us again,'' a private added.

''That true?'' Thayer demanded, scowling in disbelief.

''Close enough,'' Ryan said, sliding out of the saddle to talk with the man on an even keel. The Trader always said that talking face-to-face put a man more at ease, and they needed the baron's goodwill to acquire that boat.

Rubbing his chin, Thayer studied the companions closely, a thumb in his pocket, resting his hand inches from the little blaster. ''I'm Harlan Thayer,'' he said at last, "the baron of Ratak ville. Who the hell are you folks?"

"Just some explorers," Ryan said, crossing his arms, so that his own hands hung near the loaded flintlocks tucked into his Army belt. "A forest fire burned down our ville of Moscow, and we set out to find a better place."

"Lord Baron Kinnison doesn't like wanderers," Thayer growled. "Says they're often spies working for pirates."

The statement sounded like a trap of some kind, so Ryan took the offensive. "Don't give a hot shit what the Lord Bastard likes," he stated firmly. "And if somebody stuffed a Firebird up his ass, I'd gladly light the fuse."

The crowd froze in terror, but the sec man laughed and Thayer shifted his frown into a momentary grin. "Well, you got balls, One-eye, that's for sure. Everybody hates the fat rotbag, but few dare to say it aloud. What are your names?"

Introductions were made all around.

"Mighty good horse," Thayer said, going to a mare and stroking its neck. The animal stayed in place and shuffled its hooves in pleasure under the petting. "What'll you take for them?"

"The ones ridden by Mitchum and his men are yours," Ryan said. "As are the blasters they carry. They bought them with blood."

Thayer continued to stroke the beast, but seemed

confused that the offer of payment had been declined, the animals and weapons turned into a gift. If he didn't know better, the baron would have sworn the stranger was trying to buy his goodwill.

"Sell you these others," Krysty countered, draping the reins over the pommel of her saddle. "Food and good beds for a week."

Amused, Thayer looked over the red-haired beauty. He had thought she was only Ryan's bed warmer, but now he saw she carried a blaster. Odd folks these outlanders. A memory tickled the back of his brain, something about strangers with fancy blasters. But these folks had only flintlocks, so it couldn't have been about them.

"Keep the horses. I'm offering food and good beds for a month," Baron Thayer stated loudly. "That's what I pay as reward to anybody who aces a hundred cannies and saves my men from the pot. Food and beds, or three full pounds of black powder. Your choice."

The old man dropped his pipe, and the crowd gasped at the incredible offer, unable to believe what they were hearing.

"Take the food and beds," Ryan said, easing his stance and offering a hand.

"Agreed, Blackie," the baron replied.

They shook on the deal, and Thayer added, "Mitchum, take these folks to the Grotto and tell Sal they're my guests. And after they're fed, bring them to the palace for drinks. Got some coconut wine that'll melt a cannonball, and I'd like a talk with folks who have seen other islands.''

"Yes, Baron," Colonel Mitchum answered, snapping a salute.

"Just a second there, dead man," a gruff voice said from the crowd, and the people parted to admit a burly officer.

"Colliers," Mitchum growled, drawing his blaster. The rest of the sec men did the same, and the cocking of hammers sounded like tree branches snapping in the sudden quiet.

"You were gone for a week! Now I'm the sec chief in this ville!" Colliers stated, stabbing his chest with a thumb. "Ain't just going to roll over like a gaudy slut and give it back to a feeb who let cannies catch him!"

"A fight to the death," Mitchum said, his weapon neither moving nor wavering. "Not first blood, but a chilling. No quarter, no rules."

"Fine by me," Colliers snarled, and pulled a blade with lightning speed.

"No rules at all?" Mitchum insisted.

"Agreed!" Colliers spit, starting for the man.

Calmly, Mitchum fired the flintlock in his hand, the .75 miniball punching a round hole in the other man's face and blowing out the back of his head, spraying bones, brains and blood over the crowd.

Most of the people broke ranks and ran; only a few stayed to watch more.

"Only a triple stupe would agree to no rules," Mitchum said, holstering the smoking weapon, "when you got a loaded blaster pointed at your guts."

"Wondered how you two would settle this," Baron Thayer said, waving away the cloud of gun smoke. "Was going to make it a formal match, in the pit with no weapons but bare hands. Don't have to do that now."

"No, sir," Mitchum stated. "Private, drag the body to the cliff and toss him into the sea. But keep the boots and that blade. We'll give those to the sec man we take on to fill his place."

"I'll do it," a teenager said, stepping forward. "Want to be a sec man. Chill me some pirates."

Baron Thayer arched an eyebrow, but Mitchum looked the boy over closely. He was barefoot and dressed in a piece of canvas, crudely stitched into shapeless clothing. His face was gaunt, but the teen stood a good head above the rest of the crowd, and his hands were gnarled weapons of grisly scars. Good food would fill in as solid muscle, and the ville would have a useful chilling machine in their fighting ranks.

"Name?" he snapped.

"Samms, Virgil Samms, sir. I live down by the docks, in the dolphin cove with the—"

"Shut up! Never waste an officer's time with horseshit, boy. Now help dispose of the body, and remember," the colonel added sternly, "Brad Colliers was a stupe, but also a sec man. He gets full honors and prayers before going to Davey. You'll taste the lash if I hear about you missing a single word. Get me?"

"Aye, aye, sir," Virgil said and saluted.

"Sailors say that dreck, not sec men," the sergeant said, smacking the boy in the back of the head. "Now salute your baron, and get to work!"

The fledgling sec man shakily gave Thayer a salute and held it until the baron returned the gesture. Then a couple of the sec men joined the boy and helped drag the dead man away, leaving a gory trail in the dusty ground.

"Waste of a fisherman," the baron said, tucking thumbs into his belt.

Pulling out a pouch, Mitchum reloaded his blaster. "Just green, that's all, my lord. Started off that dumb myself."

"Your call," the baron said. "First time he fucks up bad, you get the lash for him." The baron gave Ryan and his crew a long look as if somehow they were involved in the fight, then turned his back and started to walk up the street toward his palace.

"Sharp move," J.B. said.

Mitchum closed the pouch by pulling on the drawstring with his teeth, then tucked blaster and ammo away. "Not really. Colliers always had a tough time controlling his temper. That made him a bad commander. Bastard had to die for the sake of the ville."

Ryan filed that information away. There was a lot more to Mitchum than was readily apparent.

"But now that he's gone, I'm in charge again." The colonel grinned as he freed the reins of his mount and passed them to a private. "Put her in the stable and have them give her a good rub-down."

"Yes, sir," the sec man said, and started off with the animal in tow. It followed placidly, waiting to be beaten or fed, whatever was the choice of its new masters.

Then Mitchum slapped Ryan on the shoulder. "Come on, let's get chow. Don't know about you folks, but I'm starving."

"Could do with a bite," Ryan admitted. Taking his own horse by the reins, he began leading it down the street of the ocean ville.

"Hot food sounds good," Dean said, rubbing his stomach.

Then Mitchum bumped shoulders with Ryan. "Also got a gaudy house," he added.

"Brought his own," Krysty said, a touch of ice in her voice.

The officer broke into a grin. "No offense meant."

"None taken," she replied. "This time."

Walking their horses down the street, the companions found that between the trailers were tiny plots of farmland, set out in neat squares, edged with brick and covered with oily canvas supported by rusty poles.

"Protection from acid rain," Mildred said, excited. Before they sailed away, she had to find out what the locals used to coat the canvas. That was info she could trade to villes across the Deathlands and help save a lot of lives.

The public latrine was far from the wells, and noisy chickens were in a bamboo coop behind a woven wicker fence. Big dogs were on rope leashes before a lot of the trailers, and there were no slaves in sight. No decomposing bodies hung from torture poles, or any of the things they normally found in a ville.

"Nice place," Doc said, resting his ebony stick on a shoulder.

The sword cane was too long to hide easily in their bedrolls. Besides, there was no reason anybody would think it wasn't just a support for the old man.

"Best in the world," Mitchum stated proudly.

Since the colonel had never seen Front Royal in Virginia, Ryan held his peace and let the man enjoy the fantasy.

Leaning out of a second-story window, a beautiful girl allowed her robe to gap open in front and expose a lot of cleavage. Several men passing by on the street took notice, but there was no reaction from the strangers walking with their horses. Still they were new, and that was nice. The gaudy slut smiled at the prospect of meeting outlanders, and for a moment the twin tips of her forked tongue darted into view. She could almost taste them already.

Then the boy in the group glanced her way and gasped. She smiled gently, letting her robe part to expose her perfect breasts. A knock on the bedroom door made her turn away, and in walked a grisly sec men and an old skinny woman.

"There you go, Lieutenant," the madam of the gaudy house announced. "You pay for the best, you get the best."

"Fantastic," he exhaled in admiration.

The slut by the window had the figure of a nubile young girl barely in her teens, but when she turned there was the face of an adult. Long black hair reached to her knees, and her shape was something out of a predark girlie mag.

He'd been saving a long time for this. She cost a lot, and only the baron had her on a regular basis. But now that the sec man saw her, he knew she was worth it for looks alone. And if the tales were true about two tongues, one in her mouth and the other elsewhere, this was going to be one hell of a ride. Sure, she was a mutie, but he wasn't here to breed with the slut. Just bed her.

Impatiently, he slapped the pouch of black powder into the old woman's hand. "I'll take her for the whole day," the lieutenant said.

"Oh, that'll cost more than this," she said quickly. The madam could hear the sound of raw lust in a man's voice. He'd pay all he possessed to have the girl just once.

The lieutenant turned on the madam and drew his blaster. "Going back on our deal?" he growled.

The madam shrugged in response and walked from the room. She had tried; that was enough.

"Come here, girl," he said loudly, but there was already a loss in his words. He could borrow, but never possess.

"Lucinda," she lisped, knowing the human name emphasized her forked tongue.

The man repeated her name in a whisper.

Chuckling to herself, she padded across the room, dropping the robe to expose her flawless body. Her breasts swayed at each step, and she mentally commanded her aureoles to tighten. The sec man began to rip off his clothes, buttons scattering across the bare wood floor.

As their eyes met, his expression softened from lust to love, and she decided to pleasure the fool all the way, in every way, then more, and make him her absolute slave. Already her brethren had taken over a ville to the south. Now she would start the process again here. One day all of the villes would be owned by the Sisters, and the humans who created the skyfire would be no more. Purged from the New Earth.

It was only a matter of time.

ON THE STREET, Krysty shivered and glanced around quickly.

"Something wrong?" Ryan asked, a hand snaking inside his coat to touch the grip of the SIG-Sauer.

The woman didn't reply, but hugged herself tight and kept walking. There had just been the oddest sensation, almost as if the companions had walked past a deadly predator and it let them go only because there was bigger prey to feed upon. Unseen danger lurked in the ville, and Krysty would warn the others to stay alert.

A group of men was in the street rolling dice made from carved bone, knives and animal pelts passed back and forth as bets were won or lost.

"Move," Ryan growled.

"Fuck off," a man said, glancing up from the game. Then he saw the amount of weapons on display and tried to grin, but failed miserably.

"My friend said move," Mitchum added in a dangerous tone.

Scrambling to their feet, the gamblers left their dice and pelts to race away, never once looking back. Continuing onward, the companions walked their horses over the spot, crushing the skins and dice to bits under the pounding horse hooves.

"Sailors," Mitchum said in explanation. "Useless bastards."

"Local ship?" Ryan asked as casually as he could.

"Naw, I know those men. They're off a trader from the Rougelap Islands."

"That's north of here, right?" J.B. asked. "Near Forbidden Island."

"Pretty close, yeah," Mitchum said, then grimaced. "Wherever you're going with your own boat, be sure to stay away from that hellzone. Bitch of a place. The currents can tear the hull off a ship, and on shore, there's nothing but rad pits and muties."

Ryan and the others said nothing, not even daring to exchange glances. But now they had a goal. Why row through the shark-infested waters when they could buy a ride? Finally, some good luck was coming their way.

Turning a corner, the companions dropped off their horses at a stable and walked over to the inn. A big sign hanging out front was decorated with the single word Grotto and a hand-painted picture of a fork for those who couldn't read. The front door led to a foyer with another door and a metal turnstile. Inside, the pink walls were heavily decorated with faded pictures and torn posters of nude women. A row of small booths along the back wall was full of wire racks holding garish paperback books whose outlandish covers left nothing to the sexual imagination.

"It's a converted porn bookstore," Mildred said in disgust. No wonder the inn was so popular with the sec men.

"What that?" Jak asked, studying a poster. Nice.

The physician scratched her head before answering. "Sort of a gaudy house," she said slowly. "For folks who didn't actually want to have sex."

Jak stared at the woman as if she were insane, and Mildred shrugged. She couldn't think of another way to explain the establishments.

Vacant redwood picnic tables filled the room, and the only customers were a couple of sailors eating a roast of some kind at the far end of the room. As the companions took the largest table, Mitchum went into the kitchen to talk with the cook, and then departed to handle some official duties. But he swore to come back around dusk to take them to the baron for drinks.

Easing straps off shoulders, the group removed their backpacks and eagerly settled down to wait for the food. The cold horse meat had fueled their bodies, but tasted like red clay. There were no utensils of any kind in view, so each dug out a wooden spoon from their clothing, being very careful not to reveal any of the military hardware hidden under their clothes.

Ryan placed his two muzzle-loaders blatantly on the table, with both hammers cocked to forestall any trouble from the locals. The sailors at the far table noticed the weapons, and immediately stopped talking to concentrate on their own meal.

A few minutes later, the kitchen door swung open and out came two girls carrying an enormous iron pot. The servers dripped sweat as they hauled the cauldron of soup to the table, while an old man with no teeth placed cracked bowls before each person. The bowls were clean, but had seen hard use. Mildred recognized it as a nearly unbreakable brand, which was guaranteed to last a lifetime. She had to admit, for once, Madison Avenue hadn't lied about the durability of a product.

Careful as if they were delivering liquid nitro, the girls ladled the hot soup into each bowl, filling them to capacity. Not a drop fell as the plastic ladle conveyed the steaming brew. As they hauled their cauldron back to the steamy kitchen, the old man returned with small loaves of bread. They were all of a different shape, but a smooth even brown and smelled wonderful.

Jak snatched one from the platter and took a bite.

"Made breadfruit," he announced, chewing steadily. "Good."

"At least they didn't serve us fish heads," J.B. said, stirring the contents of his bowl.

"No, sir, please sir!" the oldster gasped, backing away in fear. "No sweepings for nobles! Is good stew! Please, don't beat me, sir!"

"The stew is fine," Ryan said, unmoved by the display of fear. He had seen similar faces all his life. In most villes the people were little more than slaves, tortured and chilled at the whim of the sec men who ruled. Apparently, the same was true here; the strong ruled the weak. At least until the weak got blasters, then everything went to hell.

"Could we have some water, please?" Krysty asked politely.

Bobbing his head nonstop, the man hurried away. "Yes, sir! At once, sir. Without delay, sir!"

"Sweepings," Dean said thoughtfully. "Must use the stuff that falls on the floor to make soup."

"Probably what's left over in other folks' bowls, too," J.B. agreed.

"Horrid," Doc muttered.

From somewhere outside the sound of a whip was audible again, but this time the cries were female.

"Seen dogs treated better than these people," Krysty said softly, tasting the stew. It was very good, hot and thick, full of fish meat, crab, mussels, some odd veggies, with floating bits of herbs for flavor.

The girls returned with coconut shells cut in two, the bottoms flattened to make crude mugs. The other put a bamboo bucket full of water amid the dinner, and Mildred slipped some bread into the girl's pocket. The child glanced once sideways, but made no other indication that she knew what had happened.

"Baron idiot," Jak said, dipping a loaf into the soup and tearing off a chunk. "No food, folks can't work."

"They'll turn on him," Krysty agreed, "and I hope they win."

"When we sail away," Dean said softly, "mebbe we could leave these flintlocks behind."

Slurping clean a spoon, J.B. nodded agreement. "Won't need them once we're at sea. Might even make some friends in case we come back this way."

"An exemplary idea." Doc smiled. "The enemy of my enemy, and all that."

"Freeze, outlanders!" a voice cried out from the doorway.

The companions looked up to see three sec men enter the room, blasters in their hands. Two of the men were dressed as sailors, while the third was a local sec man.

"Keep your hands away from those flints," the

sec man ordered, "and mebbe you live for a while longer."

His flintlocks on the table, Ryan placed his hands in his lap and eased the safety off the SIG-Sauer hidden under his shirt. Unfortunately, the new arrivals' weapons were already drawn. He needed a diversion to get a bead on them.

Without warning, Mildred jerked her arm while Jak flipped his hand. The plate from under the bowl skimmed through the air and smashed into the face of a sailor, and the sec man staggered backward to the wall with a knife in his throat. The attack startled the last man for only a second, but before he could react, Doc lunged forward and buried his blade into the man's throat, slicing vocal cords and the jugular.

By then Ryan had his piece out and finished them off with a whispering round to the head. The lifeless bodies collapsed to the floor, as Mitchum appeared from the kitchen with a primed flintlock in both hands.

"Run! They know!" the man shouted, then stopped, taking in the scene. "Shitfire, they beat me here."

Ryan swung his 9 mm pistol toward the man and the two stayed motionless until Mitchum slowly lowered his blasters.

"You have to leave immediately," Mitchum stated urgently. "I was with the new sec man picking up his things from the dock when a fleet of peteys arrived. Some big caliber named Glassman told us that you're all wanted by Lord Baron Kinnison, dead or alive. Baron Thayer is closing the ville like screwing the lid on a jar, and wants you trapped in here.''

Mitchum gestured at the corpses. "Those fools must have decided to try and capture you themselves and not share the reward.''

"Has he sealed off the front gate yet?'' Ryan asked, his blaster still pointing at the sec chief.

"Blocked solid. You'd never get out that way now.''

"Any other exits?'' Krysty demanded, pulling on her backpack.

Mitchum made a sour face and looked away before speaking. "Just one,'' he growled, as if there were a bad taste in his mouth. "There's a secret escape tunnel for the baron. Only Thayer and myself know about it.''

"And them,'' J.B. said, gesturing over his shoulder at the sailors in the corner.

With a grim expression, Mitchum suddenly noted the sailors and fired his blasters. The two men slammed into the pink walls, the double booms of the muzzle-loaders rattling the bowls on the tables, and the framed pictures on the walls, making a couple fall to the floor and smash.

"Hated to do that,'' the colonel said sadly. "I

knew them, good men both. But there was no other way.''

''Is the kitchen staff alive?'' Krysty asked.

''They ran away when I walked in with my blaster out.''

''Good.''

''Come with us,'' Mildred said, putting the bulky flintlock and ammo pouch on the table, then drawing her .38 ZKR target pistol.

Mitchum sadly shook his head. ''Can't. Thayer will chill my brother and his wife if I'm caught helping you.''

LeMat and sword at the ready, Doc went to the front door and checked outside. The ville was still, no reaction yet to the sounds of battle. Strange, it was almost as if the bookstore was soundproof.

''So, where is the exit?'' Ryan demanded, getting rid of his own excess weapons. Then he holstered the SIG-Sauer and unwrapped the Steyr from his bedroll.

''Go to the baron's home. There's a locked latrine on the south side. That's a fake. Ladder inside leads down to a tunnel. That's the only way out, aside from the front gate.''

''Any traps?'' J.B. demanded, working the bolt on the Uzi.

''None that I know of.''

''Thank you,'' Krysty said in earnest.

''Just paying his debt,'' Ryan said, working the

bolt on the longblaster to chamber a round, then sliding it over a shoulder. Drawing the SIG-Sauer, he pointed it at Mitchum. ''Where do you want it?'' he asked brusquely.

''Leg,'' the colonel replied tightening his jaw, then added, ''And this makes us even! The slate is clean. We meet again, I'll ace your ass like any other invader threatening my ville.''

''Fair enough,'' Ryan said, then shot the sec men in the outermost part of the thigh, well away from the bone or major arteries.

As Mitchum fell, slapping a hand on the wound to staunch the flow of blood, Ryan shot him again in the upper arm.

''You bastard,'' Mitchum groaned, raw hatred contorting his handsome features, both hands busy putting pressure on his wounds.

''Now nobody will doubt any story you tell them,'' the one-eyed man replied, and moved out the door into the night. The ville was quiet, the darkness lying over the trailers like a thick blanket.

Few people were moving about on the streets, and the companions stayed in the shadows as much as possible. They backtracked out of the moonlight when a squad of armed troopers ran by, heading for the front gate. The men were armed with flint-lock pistols, crossbows and nets. An unnerving sight those. It meant they wanted to capture the companions alive.

"Looks like he was telling the truth," Dean muttered.

"Could be," his father replied tersely. "But he betrayed his own baron to repay us, so who's to say he didn't do the same thing to us for some other reason? Trust nobody."

"Not even the dead," Dean said, finishing the old saying. "I remember."

"Gaia, watch over us this night," Krysty said to the sky, and distant thunder seemed to rumble in reply. But whether that was an agreement or denial, there was no way to know.

There were bright lights and drunken singing coming from the gaudy house, and as they passed by a window opened, somebody relieving himself into the street.

"Ah, civilization," Doc mumbled under his breath.

Easily avoiding some people hurrying to their trailers, Ryan led them on a circular path to finally reach the baron's home from the other side. Crouching, they hid in some bushes while a contingent of guards and sailors marched past, longblasters cradled in their arms. Baron Thayer was in the squad, as was a stranger in the livery of the lord baron. Ryan frowned. So that was Glassman, their new hunter. The Deathlands warrior didn't know what happened to Brandon, but he hoped it was painful and lasting. They would have been long gone if not for the sec man's interference.

"I do not see the latrine," Doc rumbled, squinting into the darkness.

"Me neither," Krysty said, her eyes held open wide, taking in the night around them.

Ryan was forced to agree. Even with the pale moonlight coming through the clouds, he still couldn't see much of anything. However, the ville was becoming well lighted, torches burning on every corner. Oddly, the palace was still masked by the night. To lure them there? Could be.

Just then a couple of sec men walked slowly by, speaking softly, longblasters resting on their shoulders.

"Let's ask for directions," Ryan whispered, drawing the panga.

Jak pulled out a leaf-bladed knife, and the men moved, sliding up behind the sec men. Ryan placed the curved blade of the panga around the throat of one, the touch of the cold steel making the man freeze motionless. Jak thrust his blade into the head of the second man, just to the right of the spine where it joined the skull. The man stopped moving instantly, then the teenager twisted the blade and the sec man exhaled once, sliding to the dirt as if his bones had turned into water.

"Cry out, and you're chilled," Ryan whispered in the sec man's ear. "Now drop it."

The blaster fell to the grass.

"Okay, where is the baron's private latrine?"

"The what?" the guards whispered, acting confused.

Jak stabbed the man in the upper arm, then grabbed the fresh wound and squeezed. The sec man inhaled sharply, tears coming to his eyes before the teen finally let go.

"You bastards," the guard panted, his face ashen white.

"Not what I want to know," Ryan said in a dangerous voice, and Jak tightened his grip again, blood welling between his strong fingers.

The sec men broke into a sweat. "Okay, okay! No more! It's past the horse corral, behind the woodpile."

Ryan maintained his position while Jak disappeared into the darkness to return a few minutes later and showed a thumb.

"You get to live," Ryan said, when the guard unexpectedly broke free and spun with a blade in his palm. He slashed for Ryan's belly, but the man swayed out of the way and Jak buried his blade into the guard's left kidney. Caught in the middle of a shout, the sec man could only gasp from the pain, and Ryan kicked the doubled-over man directly in the face. Bones audibly crunching from the strike, the guard fell sprawling, a hand clawing madly for his dropped blaster.

Silver flashed in the moonlight as Doc lunged forward, spearing the man through the heart with his sword. The sec men jerked at the strike, then went still. Placing a boot on his chest, Doc yanked the blade out and wiped it clean on the dead man's shirt.

Following Jak across the grounds, the friends easily found the latrine just past the horse corral. The small wooden hut was surrounded by weeds, and placed strategically behind the tall pile of cut wood so that nobody could see who was entering or leaving.

Footsteps on the gravel made everybody pause, and they waited for discovery as the horses were released from the stable, and a dozen troopers rode off.

"Looking for us," Krysty guessed. "Better hurry."

Going to opposite ends of the woodpile, Ryan and Jak kept silent watch for more sec men while Mildred used her flashlight to illuminate the padlock on the door. Removing some tools from his munitions bag, J.B. got busy with picks and probes, the lock yielding in under a minute.

"Piece of junk," he commented, sliding the chain through the loops and placing it gently in the weeds. "Could have kicked it open except for the noise."

Easing open the old splintery door, Ryan found

there was no floor, only a knotted rope hanging into the darkness. Fireblast, it was the cannie ville all over again. Hopefully, this time there wouldn't be an ambush waiting for them.

Reaching into a pocket, Ryan pulled out a gren and made sure the pin was firmly in place, the tape tight around the priming handle. Going to the hole, he dropped the gren down the hole and listened. Three seconds later there was a thump of it landing, and then silence, no reaction to its arrival.

"It's clear," he announced, starting down the rope.

After a couple of yards, Ryan dropped the last few feet and landed with his blaster out, sweeping for targets. He was in a brick tunnel that extended into the distance in both directions. There was a diffuse light coming from bulbs inside wire cages along the ceiling. The electricity was probably coming from nuke batteries buried in the walls, and even those predark powerhouses were slowly dying over the long centuries.

The gren had rolled a few feet down the tunnel, and he reclaimed the explosive charge, double-checking to make sure the pin and handle were in place. Just then, the rope jiggled and Dean dropped to the concrete floor, blaster in one hand, bowie knife in the other.

"We're alone," Ryan said, tugging the rope

three times to signal it was okay for the others to come down.

Soon, the companions were gathered together, and Jak put his lighter to the rope, the old hemp slowly igniting and starting to burn upward out of sight.

"Wet rope top with canteen," he said, pocketing the lighter. "So no burn latrine."

"Well, it'll certainly slow down any pursuit," Mildred said, watching the fire crackling up the access way. It was concrete pipe with rusty holes along the side where iron rungs had been set for easy access. Only rust stains marked where they had once been inserted into the resilient material.

"Indeed, madam, that is, until they find another rope," Doc rumbled anxiously. "My dear Ryan, I really cannot voice my sincere wish to vacate this untoward locale quite strenuously enough."

"Yeah, we've got to blow this pesthole," Ryan agreed, stabbing his knife through the wire cage to break the bulb and plunge that section of the tunnel into darkness. Give the baron something else to worry about if he made it down here.

"Which way leads to the sea?" he asked, sheathing the blade.

Tilting back his fedora, J.B. checked his pocket compass. "That way goes inland, toward the jungle," he said, pointing. "The other heads to the ocean."

Could be a wag hidden in the trees, or a boat on the beach. A boat was what they needed, so they might as well head for the water.

"I'm on point," Ryan said, switching to the Steyr. "J.B. covers the rear. Three-foot spread."

Walking on the toes of their boots to try to hold down the echoes, the companions soon saw a flickering silvery light from ahead and rushed forward to find the end of the brick tunnel blocked by a wall of falling water. Doc tested the depths with his sword and pronounced it safe. Shielding his blaster with his body, Ryan dashed through and found himself on the sandy shore of a small lagoon. A waterfall rushing from overhead completely masked the entrance of the tunnel, where the freshwater fed into a small pool filled with tropical fish. The shore was edged with tall mango trees festooned with fishing nets laced with green leaves. In the background he could hear the gentle sounds of waves cresting on the sand. But it was impossible to see anything on the other side of the disguising barrier. Thayer had done a good job here. Then Ryan noticed something large and covered with canvas moored on the nearby beach. There was their boat.

Going to the waterfall, he stuck a hand through and gestured for the others to join him. In short order the rest of the companions exited the tunnel and marveled at the beautiful hidden grotto and its pristine golden beach.

"That our boat?" Mildred asked, squeezing some of the excess water from her beaded locks.

"Hope so," Ryan said, and, grabbing a fistful of canvas he yanked hard. The material easily slid off, exposing a wag underneath, not an oceangoing vessel of any kind.

It was a predark school bus, covered in splotches of green and brown, jungle camou. The glass windows along both sides had been replaced with thick sheet-metal tack welded into place, and the front windshield was protected by a heavy iron grid, the bar studded with knife blades gleaming with oil. The rear window in the exit door had the same. Triangular spikes with barbed tips jutted from the rims of the wheels, and double tires were bolted to each axle, giving the wag tremendous traction. Blasters were everywhere, but there were no attached weapons that they could spot. With all the weight of the armor, Ryan doubted the wag made much speed, but it looked ready to travel.

Jimmying open the door, J.B. climbed inside and saw that the back of the wag was stacked high with crates and barrels of supplies, poorly lettered wording showing what each contained: led, blakpoder, dri fesh, watr, chyen and such. Crates of longblasters filled the rear seats, and a crossbow hung from the ceiling along with quivers of bolts.

"Enough supplies to start a new ville," Mildred said over his shoulder.

"I think that was the idea," Doc noted wryly. "How fortunate for us."

"Well, this clunker isn't War Wag One or the Leviathan," J.B. said, taking a seat by the front door. "But it'll do for today."

Jak went straight to the rear door and checked its status, while Dean took a spot in the middle. Closing the double doors, Ryan dropped his backpack and sat just behind the driver's seat. Krysty slid behind the wheel and turned the ignition switch one click to check the gauges and controls. Ryan knew that she had the best night vision, so it made sense for her to drive the wag. Headlights would only have made them a moving target for the flintlocks of the ville sec men. Or worse, any cannon the ville might have mounted for wall defenses.

Dim lights brightened on the dashboard, and Krysty tapped the fuel gauge with a finger to make sure it was a true reading.

"Okay, we have plenty of battery power and full tanks of juice," she reported, strapping herself into the seat.

"Head for the docks," Ryan directed. "Glassman has PT boats there. If we strike fast, we might be able steal one and use its Firebirds to blow the others apart."

"Sounds good. Buckle in. Here we go!" Krysty

clicked the ignition switch all the way, and the engine turned over but didn't start. Then she saw the choke on the dashboard, set that to the middle position, pumped the gas and tried again. This time the engines caught with a sputtering cough, rattling and backfiring before roaring into life, black smoke blowing out the tailpipes. Startled birds flew out of the trees screaming, as the bus backfired again, sounding louder than a shotgun.

"Unless they're deaf, the sec men will know where we are now," Ryan grumped. "Hit the gas, and let's move!"

Shifting gears, Krysty hit the clutch and rocked the bus back and forth a few times to escape the sand, then rolled forward, building speed, and plowed through the camou netting to emerge on a rocky beach. The log wall of Ratak ville stood on a gentle swell to their right, the docks straight ahead. A four-masted schooner was moored in the deep water, six of the deadly PT boats tied at the wooden pier. An oil lantern draped with cloth hung from a post, giving off a peculiar green glow. A seasoned traveler on ships, Doc had no idea what that could possibly mean.

Keeping the headlights off, using only the muted moonlight, Krysty rumbled along the sandy beach, the ocean spray misting the windows on the left side. Quickly, the companions got ready to board and storm the first petey. But the bus got only halfway there, when brilliant electric lights crashed on to sweep the beach and captured them in a deadly wash of clear illumination.

Ryan fired the Steyr out a blasterport at the searchlights, and one winked out. Instantly, the .50-caliber blasters from the PT boats began to hammer away, the heavy-duty combat rounds chewing a path of destruction along the sand toward the war wag. Then another petey added its firepower to the assault, and another.

"Gaia!" Krysty shouted, hitting the gas and twisting the steering wheel to get away from the withering crossfire.

But she was too slow, and a brief flurry of lead rattled the wag, punching a neat line of holes through the sheet metal covering the windows. Then there was a flash from the schooner, and a cannon roared, the beach exploding exactly where they had just been.

"It's a trap!" J.B. shouted, firing the Uzi out a blasterport at the crews of the PT boats. Several of the men toppled over, but more took their places, and the incoming barrage of lead didn't even pause.

"Hold on!" Krysty called, and slammed into a higher gear, the engine revving with power.

Sand kicked up from impacting bullets, and several more hit the bus to musically ricochet into the darkness.

"Head for the ville!" Ryan shouted, firing steadily.

"What?" she demanded, glancing at him in the rearview mirror.

Ryan dropped a fresh mag into the breech of the Steyr. "Got to make a firewall!" he replied.

"Gotcha!"

A group of sec men carrying Firebirds crashed through a stand of trees directly in front of them. Pushing for more speed, Krysty felt the steering wheel jar as the wag rolled over the screaming men.

Now heading for the ville, Krysty saw flintlocks fire along the top of the wall as she steered right for the small front door. As she got near, the door swung wide and a sec man on horseback rode into view. She plowed directly into them, the man and animal mashed into bloody pulp as the bus hurtled their mangled bodies into the doorway. Hitting the brakes, she swung the rear of the vehicle around until it was pointing at the entrance. Jak kicked open the aft door and pushed out a barrel of fuel, then slammed the door shut.

Krysty hit the gas again and roared off as the companions poured blasterfire onto the fifty-five-gallon drum.

They were near the edge of the clearing when a spark from the bullets hitting the barrel finally ignited the fuel and a tremendous fireball blossomed in front of the only exit, the splashed juice dribbling fire along the wooden walls of the ville.

Working the clutch, Krysty shifted gears and broached the side road, really building speed now that the wag was on smooth ground. The trees flashed by in a blur until the friends reached a field and turned off the road to cut across the grassland heading for the savanna on the horizon.

Behind them, alarms bells rang as blasterfire shook the trees searching for the escaping outlanders.

Chapter Twelve

His food supply exhausted days earlier, Baron Kinnison was nestled in the corner of the cell, standing on the bunk, slowly chewing a warm piece of rat when there came the sounds of boots in the outside corridor.

Swallowing the morsel of food, the baron wiped his mouth on a sleeve, then drew his blaster and knife. Unfortunately, the blade wasn't as sharp as it had once been. Hampered by the darkness, Kinnison had missed stabbing the scurrying rats several times, damaging the needle tip of the stiletto on the granite floor. In desperation, he lit his only candle and killed as many as he could before the rodents understood what was happening and fled for their lives. Skinning and eating the raw flesh, the baron then stuffed the corpses into cracks in the walls. With those blocked, no more rats could get into the cell, and Kinnison could sleep for quite a while, recharging his body and clearing his mind.

But as time passed, he had been forced to clear the cracks and smear some blood on the floor to entice the rodents back and maintain a steady food supply.

The footsteps in the corridor stopped in front of his cell. Kinnison assumed his old position and put both hands into the air, trying to appear as if he were still shackled to the ceiling. Just let the fools get close enough, and he would be out of the stinking prison in a heartbeat.

There was a clanging of keys and squealing of the rusty lock, then the door swung open and a grinning sec man walked inside.

"Ah, he's asleep."

"So wake him up," another said, chortling.

Kinnison tried not to move as a bucket of seawater splashed on him. The salt sizzled in his open sores, the pain beyond description, but Baron Kinnison moved from an instinct of raw will and slashed open the throat of the first guard even as the man reached for his blaster. He stumbled away, spraying his life onto the dirty stone walls.

With a curse, the second guard tried to shove the door closed and Kinnison fired the revolver three times, the big-bore .45 punching into the door and driving it back, cracking the wrist of the sec man holding the latch. The guard could only stare in shock at the bones jutting from his skin when Kinnison charged. He hit the portal at a run, his five hundred pounds forcing it open all the way and crushing the guard between the door and wall.

Pinned helpless, barely able to breathe, the guard tried to draw his blaster and fire a shot to summon help. But Kinnison savagely sliced along the length of the exposed arm, from wrist to elbow, severing tendons and arteries. The guard cried out in pain, dropping the weapon, and the baron kicked it away for later. Now the urge for revenge filled Kinnison with blind rage, and he pulled the door away, only to slam it on the man several more times, bones cracking and blood gushing until he was fully satisfied the traitor was aced. Then he dragged the corpse into the cell and looted both guards for more shot, powder and extra knives.

Pausing in the corridor, Kinnison brushed back his wet hair and listened for any response to the fight. There was nothing to hear but the excited murmurs of the other prisoners. They knew something unusual had just occurred and were terrified it would happen to them next.

Lifting the dead guard's oil lantern, Kinnison went to the nearest door and turned up the wick to let the prisoner inside clearly see his bandaged face.

"B-baron?" the woman gasped through the tangles of her long gray hair. She backed into the corner and began to whimper.

"Hello, dear sister," he said, unlocking the door. "There has been a revolt and I have been deposed.

But fight with me to reclaim the throne, and you will be set free. Free!''

But there was no response as the man undid the shackles around her wrists. Still shaking, the Lady Dana Kinnison simply stood there rubbing the thick calluses on her wrists.

Kinnison handed her the ring of keys and a bloody knife. ''Free the rest, sister, and head for the armory. Together, we'll fight to the dock and get off this hellhole.''

Lady Kinnison stood confused, her arms still partially raised from the years of confinement, the endless rapes and beatings having stolen the will to act from her weakened mind.

''Well?'' he insisted. ''Decide, woman!''

The woman looked at him with the dull eyes of an animal, and Kinnison sighed in disappointment, then slit her throat with a backhand slash. Reclaiming the items from her scrawny body, he went to the next cell and made a similar offer to a cousin. The baron went to every cell, family and friends, continuing down both sides of the dank corridor until he had an army of thirty, and ten more corpses.

''Give me a blaster,'' one of the men demanded, his face hidden by twenty years of hair. ''You got three.''

Kinnison knew this was a turning point, so he placed the loaded flintlock into the prisoner's bony hands, then helped the weak man to place the barrel against his own throat. The man's eyes went wide in shock, then gleamed in bestial pleasure.

"This is your chance," the baron said, pushing back the hammer until it clicked into place. "Pull the trigger and everything done to you will be avenged.

"Or," he added quickly, "you can use that powder on the next sec man you see and earn yourself a place in the council once more." Kinnison almost choked on the next words, but he got them out and tried to sound sincere. "I was a fool to mistrust loyal men and have paid the price. Join me in my fight and command troops once more. Or fire that blaster and warn the guards. They may even let you live and go back to your cell. Twenty more years of chains and torture—isn't that worth the single moment of satisfaction you would get chilling me?"

Murmuring among themselves, the crowd shuffled its feet, anxiously waiting for the matter to be settled. Breathing heavily, the prisoner stared at the blaster, then at Kinnison, the internal battle clearly visible on his haggard features. Finally, he released the trigger and lowered the blaster.

"A high seat on the council," he growled in correction.

"Done," Kinnison said, releasing the revolver in his pocket to pass out the other flintlocks. Damn feeb took so long the baron almost believed that he would rather live forever as a prisoner, if only he could ace the baron who put him there. He was a fool and would have to be executed immediately once Kinnison was back in power.

Leading his pack of rats up the stairs, Kinnison unlocked the door at the landing and eased it open only a crack, then started mumbling about a woman's breasts.

As expected, a sec man came to the door and peeked there. "What you got there?" he asked eagerly. "A new prisoner for us to ride?"

Kinnison stabbed the stiletto into the man's left eye, the blade penetrating deep into his brain. Already dead, the body fell to the floor and the prisoners swarmed over the warm corpse, taking his clothes and weapons. Then a woman noticed some food on the table and the starved people tore the bread apart, swallowing the chunks intact, almost gagging on the first wholesome meal any of them had eaten in months.

While they licked the crumbs off the floor, Kinnison went to a blaster rack and unlocked the chain, passing out pistols and longblasters, along with heavy pouches of ammo.

"Everybody know where the armory is?" he asked.

They nodded eagerly, fondling the weapons.

"I'll distract the guards," Kinnison lied, making

a mark on a burning candle with his thumbnail. "When the wax burns down to here, you come charging out with blasters firing. Chill anybody you see. I'll meet you at the armory, and we'll make our stand. By noon tomorrow, the mansion will be ours, then the ville and finally the entire island. Nothing can stop us now. Victory or death!"

"Vict'ry," a man cackled, and the rest took up the cry, their hoarse whispers raised in a determined chant, broken by ragged coughing.

Kinnison hid his repulsion. It was pitiful. Then the baron saw that several of them were giggling like children. The wild, feverish looks on some of their faces made Kinnison think many thought this was merely a wonderful dream and wasn't actually happening. How could it? But that was fine. Their madness would make them dangerous and draw lots of attention from the sec men, giving him the few minutes necessary to reclaim his ville.

Exiting the dungeon, Kinnison hesitated to listen for the sounds of marching guards coming this way, but this wing of the mansion was quiet. His heart pounding, the baron walked barefoot along the cold stones, pausing only to snatch a pillow from a chair set close to a window. There was some kiwi fruit in a bowl, and he gobbled it down without peeling it first, the tangy juices running down his swaddled chin. It tasted better than sex, and the baron won-

dered how he could have ever thought the fruits
were too tart to eat. Simply wonderful.

Soft singing could be heard from outside, the
words drifting through the windows as he proceeded along a hallway. Celebrating his demise,
were they? Somebody would pay for that.

Reaching the main corridor, Kinnison slipped behind some tapestries and bypassed a group of visiting barons chatting with the ville quartermaster.
Selling them Firebirds, eh? More fools to chill
when he got the chance.

Darting around a corner, he surprised a maid and
he stabbed her in the heart, leaving the blade in
place to hold down the bleeding until he dragged
her into a closet.

Exiting the closet, Kinnison saw that the corridor
was clear, a lone armed guard standing before the
closed doors of the throne room. That shotgun was
real trouble, but he had no choice. Summoning his
courage, Kinnison sheathed the blade, then with
blaster and pillow ready, he made his run toward
the sec man, moving as fast and as quietly as he
could. When the baron was only a yard away, the
sec man spun, reaching for his alley-sweeper, then
balked in surprise.

"Baron Kinnison!" the sec man cried out.

Shoving the pillow against the sec man's chest,
Kinnison shot him directly in the heart, the cushion
muffling the shot. The man sagged, and Kinnison

hauled him to a chair, propping up his head with
the reverse side of the pillow, and placed the shotgun across his lap. Ah, quite lifelike.

Kinnison felt troubled about the death, but it
would have been unwise to waste a moment learn-
ing if the man was glad to see him, or ready to
shout a warning. The baron consoled himself with
the fact that every throne in history was built on
the dead. Such was the way of the world.

Going to a suit of armor standing in a nearby
wall niche, Kinnison lifted the visor and fumbled
about inside until finding the switch. He lost a fingernail forcing the mechanism to operate. Been too
long since it had last been oiled.

As the pedestal disengaged, he pushed it into the
wall and squeezed his bulk into the cramped passageway beyond. Bandages and skin were scraped
off painfully until he was deep enough into the passage before he could swing the secret door closed
again. Obviously, the baron had been much thinner
when he last used it.

Lighting the candle he had been saving from the
stash in his cell, the baron forced himself along the
passageway, the rough bricks tearing the scabs off
his sores, the salty damp clothing burning like red-
hot coals against his diseased flesh. It was becoming difficult to breathe in the cramped quarters, but
Kinnison forced himself onward. Victory or death.

Reaching a flight of stairs formed by the back

side of stone lintels, Kinnison froze as the sound of marching could be clearly heard from the hallway underneath, closely followed by blasterfire and wild shouting. Nuke those feebs! His army was attacking early. Now racing against the clock, Kinnison maneuvered faster through the narrow crevice until reaching a small storage room hidden inside the thick walls of the predark post office. Panting from the exertion, he fumbled with a wooden chest, breaking the wax seal along the edges, and extracted a bundle of oiled cloth. Lovingly, he unwrapped the machine pistol and quickly thumbed an empty clip full of fat greasy bullets from a plastic sandwich box. One of the most important lessons his father had ever taught the young baron was to never leave a rapidfire loaded for long periods. The spring in the clip would get weak over time, making the blaster jam exactly when you would need it the most. Vital data, indeed.

Going to a spyhole, Kinnison worked the bolt on the MAC-10 and peeked out at the roof of the mansion. A squad of sec men was smoking seaweed cigars and casually talking as they milled about. The news of the mass escape hadn't reached up here yet, but it would soon. He had to move.

Carefully, the baron counted their numbers until he was sure all of them were in sight at the same time. Then putting the barrel of the MAC-10 machine pistol to the hole, he cut loose at their shins,

blowing away clothing and flesh until the screaming men were lying on the roof, and he emptied the
clip into their faces.

Pushing open the panel, Kinnison now heard the
alarm bell and knew he had won the race by only
a heartbeat. Going to the Firebird launch pod at the
edge of the roof, Kinnison looked down upon his
domain, savoring the sight. Then he turned and,
lifting a Firebird from the pod, hugged it close until
his fat arms warmed the missile and he felt a stirring of the pilot within. Leaning close, Kinnison
whispered the words of command to the tiny mutie
and slid the Firebird back into place. Then he lit
the fuse with the lantern that was always present
and watched it sizzle steadily. Ten minutes to go.
All was ready.

Waddling to the doorway, he slid the external
bolts home, sealing off the roof from anybody who
might alter his settings. Then returning to the secret
passageway, Kinnison worked his way to the
ground floor, leaving streaks on the walls from his
forced travels. His shirt and pants were in rags,
most of his bandages flapping loose, exposing his
horrible mottled flesh beneath. The oozing sores
still stung from the bath of salt water from the jail-
ers, and Kinnison was ashamed to admit losing a
finger in the passageway.

At the suit of armor, Kinnison looked through a
spyhole into the corridor to make sure it was safe

to leave, but saw two more armed sec men staring aghast at the dead man in the chair. The tall private shook the corpse, and the shotgun clattered to the floor, the body slumping sideways to expose bloody clothing.

"Nukeshit, this guy is aced!" he cried, backing away.

As the other guard stuffed two fingers in his mouth to whistle for more sec men, Kinnison rammed the MAC-10 into the opening and fired off a sweeping burst. Removing the blaster, he checked the results and was pleased to see the guards prone on the floor, bleeding profusely.

But even with the rapidfire behind the stone-block wall, the noise was bound to bring help. Leaving the passageway, Kinnison walked to the double doors on the throne room and peeked through the keyhole. Sure enough, Griffin the usurper was holding court with the new leaders of the island, discussing the unexpected revolt.

"How did they get out?" Baron Griffin demanded, banging a fist on the arm of the throne. "And what happened to the guards?"

An officer saluted. "We have no idea, my lord. The doors weren't battered down or the locks shot off. It's as if they were opened with the proper keys."

"Kinnison," the new baron growled. "I don't

know how, but somehow that fat bag of pus is behind this.

"Colonel, take a squad and find out if the former baron is still in his cell," Griffin demanded, worrying a fingernail.

"We have, my lord," another replied. "But he's long gone. Probably hidden deep in the jungle somewhere."

"Not yet," Kinnison growled as he entered the room, the chattering MAC-10 mowing down the front line of sec men and barons. The rest dived for cover behind their chairs and the food-laden buffet table.

"You!" Griffin shouted, drawing a blaster.

Swinging around the chattering machine pistol, Kinnison peppered the chancellor on the throne, tearing out gouts of wood from the arms of the chair, throwing off Griffin's aim. His blaster barked twice, hitting nothing. Then Kinnison rode the bucking rapidfire into a tighter grouping and tore Griffin apart, blowing away his fingers, shattering an elbow, breaking his knees and removing his manhood in a barrage of hot lead. The 9 mm rounds stitched a zigzagging path across his body, the spent brass arching through the air to land tinkling on the floor.

Bleeding from a dozen locations, the mutilated man tried to rise, but instead he fell to the stone floor, twitching and choking, drowning in his own blood.

Putting a burst into the ceiling to capture everyone's attention, Baron Kinnison slapped in his last clip and walked boldly into the room, covering the crowd with his smoking weapon. Many of the sec men had weapons out, but none dared to fire, unsure if the baron was alone or if squads of soldiers were en route to the throne room to back his play. Exactly what Kinnison had been counting on—their fear of betrayal. Like the thief frantic with worry that others would rob his stolen treasure, the traitors expected treachery from others.

"I'm the baron of this ville," Kinnison stated loudly, glaring at them from within his swaddling bandages. "And if I don't rule here, then nobody does. Surrender, or the island will be destroyed."

"Can't chill us all with only one blaster," a captain stated grimly, his hand yanking back the hammer on his mammoth handcannon.

"Don't need to," Kinnison replied. "In a few minutes every Firebird on this island will launch, streak high into the sky and then curve back to blow this mansion and the ville below to pieces. The powder mills, the armory, all have been targeted. Maturo Island will burn, and nothing can stop them but my word."

Incredibly, the fat man then tossed the blaster

aside and casually walked across the room to sit in the throne.

"Swear an oath of loyalty and obedience to me," he said, flipping over a hand, "or die. Your choice."

"It's a bluff," a lieutenant said, licking dry lips.

Suddenly, there was a roar as a Firebird launched from overhead.

"That was from the roof!" a sergeant exclaimed.

"The first of hundreds," Kinnison said slowly, trying to heighten the tension. Their fear was the only tool he had to regain the throne. This trick either worked, or he died. It was that simple. All or nothing. Victory or death.

Holstering his piece, a young corporal went to one knee. "We are yours to command, Lord Baron," he said.

Kinnison spent precious moments studying the sec man. He had to be a new recruit as the face was unknown. Clean shaved and bald, the sec man moved with the grace of a jungle cat, only small scars marking his face. His gun belt was woven canvas, not the usual black leather, and the handles of his handcannons were heavily carved. Some sort of a tattoo peeked out from under a sleeve, and a gold earring hung from a lobe. A former sailor. How interesting.

"What's your name?" the baron ordered, fighting off a stomach spasm. His need for more jolt was making itself known again.

"Rochar Langford, my lord," the young man answered calmly.

Kinnison was impressed; the man wasn't afraid. Amazing, and potentially useful. The baron grandly gestured. "Your oath is accepted. Rise, Chancellor Rochar Langford."

"Ch-chancellor?" Langford gasped, then collected himself and gave a salute. "Sir, yes, sir!"

Realizing the untenable position of indecision, the rest of the people in attendance also knelt and swore to obey the baron. The pledges of fidelity were strong, and well delivered. But Kinnison coldly remembered when they had given the exact same oath many years ago, before the revolt. His grandfather used to say that promises were like pie crusts, made to be broken.

"My lord, what about the Firebirds?" a major asked anxiously, glancing at the ceiling as if he could see the missiles streaking through the air.

"They have been neutralized," Kinnison stated, and waited. There was a long dramatic pause, and the baron feared he had timed the blast wrong when a powerful explosion sounded from outside.

Surreptitiously, the sec men exchanged glances, wondering how the hell the fat man could control the Firebirds without speaking directly to them. Settling into his throne, Kinnison was pleased to see the fear of his unknown abilities fill their faces. Excellent. It would be quite a while before he was challenged again.

"Chancellor!" Baron Kinnison snapped.

Directing some servants to drag away the body of Griffin, Langford turned. "My lord?"

"Send a squad of sec men to collect the escaped prisoners and chain them in the powder mill. We will need their cells. Soon enough the dungeon will be packed with traitors waiting for execution."

The crowd of barons and officers didn't take that news well, and several began to quietly slip out of the throne room.

"I'll handle it personally, sir," Langford replied, watching the door close behind the officers. "Sergeant, take a squad and follow those men. Don't let them leave the island without my direct authorization."

"Yes, sir," the sec man said, saluting.

Kinnison smiled. Competent help, at last. "Good man. Then release the carrier falcons to our peteys and sailing ships. They are to stop hunting pirates and muties to concentrate on locating the outlander Ryan and his group. I want a recce of every ville within a five-day sail."

"Sir!"

"And increase the reward to weapons, powder and slaves."

"It will be done."

A lieutenant cleared his throat. "My lord, Griffin ordered their immediate deaths. Should we now have the troops try to capture them alive?"

"No! Chill them all on sight," Baron Kinnison declared with a frown. "Except for the two women. Break their arms to keep them from escaping and bring them to Maturo Island."

"Yes, my lord!"

As the guard raced away with the orders, Kinnison smiled to himself. Yes, the outlander sluts were perfect. Under torture they might tell many important things. And if they knew nothing useful, well, he needed new wives to start trying again for a son. Maybe several this time. Fresh meat should do the job nicely.

That was, for as long as they lived.

Chapter Thirteen

"Try it again!" Ryan shouted, putting his weight behind the tree branch and shoving the end deeper into the mud under the stuck tire. Getting ready, the rest of the companions put their shoulders to the mired bus and dug in their boots.

"Third time is the charm," Doc muttered.

"Shut up, you old coot," Mildred growled, squeezed tight between J.B. and Dean.

"Here we go!" Krysty shouted out the side window, and started the engine, blue exhaust pouring from the tailpipes. Then pumping the gas pedal, the woman shifted gears and stomped on the clutch, rocking the long wag back and forth.

The companions pushed as the back tires began to spin freely in the slick mud, sending out a spray of muck until smoke rose from the hot rubber. The wag started to inch forward, then Ryan cried out as the tree branch broke from his grip and sailed off into the nearby trees.

"Kill the engine!" Ryan spit, flexing his stinging hands. "Save the juice!"

As the engine dieseled off, the wag promptly set-

tled into the mud once more. Fireblast! After all
they had been through, to be stopped by something
like this. Krysty had carefully avoided the roads
and cut across barren fields, pausing only to let
Ryan set fire to the savanna to hide their trail. Going miles out of the way, J.B. blew up a bridge and
tried to make it seem they had crossed to the other
side first. Then they drove off with tree branches
tied to the bumper to erase the tire marks. Jak took
a turn behind the wheel, driving the wag down the
bed of a shallow river, so the water would wash
away any marks, then started into the mountains
and drove back out over the wag's tracks to lay a
fake trail. Reaching the grasslands, the companions
were confident of not being followed. Then they
encountered the mud.

"Mebbe we should empty the bus," Dean suggested, rubbing his shoulder where it had been
pressed against the wag. "Make it lighter."

"Wouldn't help," J.B. stated, shifting his stance
in the mucky soil. "Not when we're already this
deep."

"Acing mud." Jak scowled in annoyance, sliding off his jacket to toss it through the open back
door of the wag. His shirt was sleeveless, and the
hard rippling muscles in his pale arms were clearly
defined. As were countless scars.

Using a strip of cloth to bind her beaded hair,

Mildred said, "This is more like quicksand than mud."

"A rose by any other name," Doc rumbled, brushing some speckles off the frills of his shirt. He was getting filthy, and thought that he'd have to ask Emily to soak it as soon as he got back to keep the material from permanently staining.

"Hey, any block and tackle in the wag?" Dean asked, cracking his knuckles, exactly as his father often did. "Mebbe we can hitch the axle to a tree and pull the bus free."

"Sounds good. Go check," Ryan said, trying to shove the branch deeper under the left tire. "Everybody else get some more branches. We need to chock every tire firmly."

"Can't hurt," Mildred agreed.

Straightening his fedora, J.B. swung the Uzi to his front and stood guard while the others trundled out of the soggy ground and headed into the trees for fresh supplies of wood.

Slogging around the bus, Dean climbed inside and scraped the soles of his boots clean on the metal step before going to the rear of the wag and rummaging through the stacks of boxes. He found a tremendous amount of smoked food, but little in the way of tools. Could they have missed a stash back at the lagoon?

"Any luck?" Ryan shouted through the rear door.

"Nothing yet!" Removing a wicker basket of blankets, the boy uncovered a long narrow crate. Unlike the other containers, this one was tied securely shut. Using his bowie knife, Dean cut the ropes holding it closed and flipped over the hinged top.

"Hot pipe!" he cried out, lifting a fat tube into view. "Firebirds!"

"Let me see," J.B. said, opening the rear door.

Stepping over some boxes, Dean passed him a tube, and the Armorer studied the weapon. Just a simple bamboo tube lacquered with tree resin until it was fireproof, with carved wooden grips so the gunner could hold the weapon steady. Jammed inside was a black-powder rocket with a crude fuse hanging from the side. That was it. Yet the crude weapons had created Kinnison an empire of villes unlike anything in the history of the Deathlands.

"Love to take this apart and find out how a black-powder rocket can change course to hunt down a target," J.B. muttered, testing its balance and weight. Very nice.

"Comps," Jak said as if that settled the matter.

Turning in her seat, Krysty snorted. "The lord baron is barely able to make black powder. No way he can build chips to guide rockets."

"Then how make go left right?" Jak demanded.

Krysty shrugged in reply, and J.B. gave a start as the tube in his hands trembled slightly at the words. Had the rocket responded to the spoken directions? Dark night, what the hell were these things?

"Here's six more," Dean added, shoving aside the loose collection of wood chips in the crate. "Nope, there's eight!"

"Put this away and leave them be." J.B. handed back the weapon and watched the boy repack the Firebird and close the crate. There was something unnerving about the rockets that made him want nothing to do with them.

Continuing his search, Dean soon had checked every box without success.

"No tackle," he reported out the rear door. "Not even a wrench."

"Okay, we try something else," Ryan said resolutely.

Leading the way, Mildred and the others returned with more branches from the nearby woods. Ryan began snapping off the smaller branches, then used the panga to sharpen their tips.

"Find a rock and drive these stakes into the mud behind the larger branches under the tires," he directed, using his bare hands to do the job. Standing, he inspected the work. "Mebbe that'll hold them in place long enough to give us some traction. Only need a minute or two."

"Consider it done," Doc rumbled, and got busy with the other side.

Ryan turned to the doorway. "Krysty! This time rev the engine high as she'll go before slipping it into gear."

"Could bust the tranny, lover," Krysty said.

"No other way. We've got to chance it. If Glassman arrives and finds us trapped, it's going to be bad."

"Do my best."

Resuming their positions, the companions braced their heels against additional branches stomped into the mud. It was Jak's idea to give them more stability. Every little bit helped. Ryan joined them, putting his back to the bumper, his knees slightly bent. Mildred was at the other side of the wag in the same position, but he knew it was for different reasons. The healer had to protect her hands.

"Get ready!" Krysty answered and started the engine, bluish-gray fumes spewing from the tailpipes. Slowly, she gunned the predark engine, building its rpm higher and higher, until the wag was shaking from the barely restrained power of the roaring diesel. On the rusty dashboard, the woman noticed the fuel gauge dropping steadily.

"Now!" Ryan shouted, shoving against the wag with all of his strength, tendons rising into view on his hands and neck.

Spraying out mud, the rear wheels spun freely in the slick material until touching the buried branches. Those shot backward to hit the restraining stakes, which immediately began to lean over. But the trembling branches held in place for a moment, and briefly the tires spun on the anchored green wood, the bus creeping forward a scant inch. Muscles surged as the engine roared. Then the wag lurched ahead another inch and triumphantly rolled out of the depressions to keep going.

"Gaia, we did it!" Krysty shouted, and started to slow down.

"Keep moving!" Ryan shouted, waving both arms. "Don't stop or you'll get stuck again!"

A hand waved from the driver's window in acknowledgment, and Krysty swung the bus in an easy circle, going back for the companions. Wary of the edged spikes sticking out of the wheels, Mildred jumped on board at the side door, and Jak used the rear. It took a few more circles before everybody was on board and the wag moved sluggishly through the sticky field for the distant horizon once more.

Dropping into their seats, the companions sparingly used some of the water from their canteens to wash hands and faces clean. Boots and clothes would wait until the mud dried and could be simply scraped off.

"Too bad we can't use the road," Krysty said, turning on the windshield wipers. The spray of muddy droplets from the front wheels was speckling the glass and making it difficult to see clearly.

Unfortunately, the old blades merely smeared the stuff, making it worse. Locating a puddle of water, Krysty drove straight through, and the resulting splash washed the windshield clean for a moment.

"Roads are too dangerous," Ryan said, belting on his blaster again. The semi and automatic weapons had stayed in the bus to keep them out of the mud; only the people with revolvers had kept on their blasters while working outside. "Mud like this will smooth out after a while and erase our path."

"Also faster," J.B. said, cleaning his glasses. He held them to the light, then rubbed some more. "The road follows the shoreline. This cuts through the middle of the island and saves us miles."

"If we don't get stuck again," Krysty muttered, fighting the wheel. Driving across the field was becoming progressively difficult. If she slowed too much, the bus would get trapped again, but too fast and the wheels started to hydroplane on the slick layer of water that hid the tacky mud below. Almost like quicksand and dirt combined. That was an ugly thought. Better watch for smooth areas with no plants growing and avoid those.

Concentrating on the driving, Krysty didn't hear the warning until the second time Ryan spoke.

"Watch for the stickie!" he repeated, pointing with his blaster.

Krysty glanced to the right and there it was,

charging at the wag. Trying to avoid a collision, she twisted the steering wheel, but the distance was too short. The wag slammed into the humanoid creature, the spiked fender tearing open its belly, guts and blood gushing out. Dropping from sight, the bus thumped over the body and kept moving.

"Damn thing just stood there," Krysty said, glancing at the rearview mirror. There was a pool of blood in their wake, nothing more. The body was driven underground by the weight of the bus. "I didn't have a chance to swerve."

"Probably never saw a wag before," J.B. commented, pulling his hat over his eyes and slumping in his seat. With Ryan standing guard with the Steyr, it was safe to catch a quick nap.

"Never will again," Doc added in wry humor, starting to run a whetstone along the edge of his sword. The blade had gotten a few nicks in the last fight, and this was his first opportunity to sharpen the steel.

"Most likely it was attracted to the sound of the engine," Mildred said, releasing her hair and shaking it back into shape. Almost mindless, stickies always rushed at loud noises and bright lights such as explosions and campfires. The muties weren't all that easy to chill with blasters. Ugly bastards, too, with their octopus-like suckers on their hands and feet, weird eyes and almost nonexistent mouths.

Mildred had no idea how the creatures ate enough to stay alive.

WISPY CURLS of smoke rose from the blackened ashes at the front of Ratak ville. The fire had raged out of control for more than a day, and the log wall now sported a charred hole large enough to sail a petey through. A mutie Hunter had already tried to get inside, the thing driven off only by the combined blasters of the ville sec men and those from the petey fleet. One against a hundred, and the Hunter still managed to chill four guards and escape alive. Damn the jungle muties to Davey; they were harder to ace than the Lord Bastard himself.

Standing in the cold morning air, Captain Glassman watched the work crews and sipped at a hot mug of coconut milk laced with shine, feeling the warmth seep into his bones. Out at sea, his crew had spotted dirty clouds on the horizon and the mornings were getting chilly. Which meant that the rains would be coming soon. More bad news.

Now ville sec men stood guard over the gap in the wall, while his own troopers walked the parapets, armed with Firebirds. Using only their bare hands, heavily shackled slaves sifted through the embers trying to locate the irreplaceable metal hinges for the heavy door. From the nearby jungle came the sound of axes, a work crew already felling trees to replace those destroyed by the flames.

Raising his mug, Glassman used the last sip to toast the slaves' good luck in finding the hinges. If those were lost, or severely damaged, then the ville was in real trouble.

Marching boots and the clatter of weaponry heralded the arrival of Baron Thayer and his personal cadre of guards. They looked well-rested and freshly scrubbed, clothes clean and boots polished, unlike the grimy sec men who stood guard during the night and fought off the Hunter as it came roaring through the wall of fire. Glassman narrowed his eyes at the sight. Sleeping while the ville was attacked.

"Good morning, Captain," Baron Thayer hailed, walking over to join the man. "How goes the work?"

Smiling, Glassman pulled his blaster and slapped the man across the face with the iron barrel. Twisting, Thayer stumbled and fell to the ground. His bodyguards reached for their weapons, then stopped as a Firebird streaked over the ville to detonate in the sky. With hands only inches from their weapons, the ville sec men glared at the petey sailors on top of the wall, pointing a dozen of the long black tubes in their direction. Slowly, the sec men moved their hands and backed away from the baron. Never wavering, the sailors tracked their movements with the Firebirds.

"Idiot! Feeb! Incompetent ass!" Glassman

shouted, cocking back the hammer and pointing the blaster at the prone baron. "Ryan and his people were here. In your ville. Eating their dinner. Right here! You had them in the palm of your mutie-loving hand and let them escape? How is that possible?"

"You dare to strike me," Thayer growled, touching his aching cheek. There was the coppery taste of blood in his mouth, and a tooth felt loose. "I'm the baron of this ville! Within these walls, I rule supreme!"

In response, Glassman tightened his finger on the trigger. The hammer fell, flint scraped steel, throwing off a spray of sparks that ignited the black powder in the primer pan, which set off the main charge in the barrel. The actions took a second to happen, and Thayer could only cringe before the flintlock thundered in the morning air. The baron's face exploded from the crushing arrival of the .75 mini-ball, his teeth and eyes flying in different directions as his skull burst apart, brains and hair blowing across the ground.

"The baron," Glassman muttered, handing the smoking blaster to a waiting sailor. "Not anymore, dolt."

The sailor immediately passed the captain a fresh blaster and began to reload the spent weapon.

Staring at the still body, Glassman was surprised to discover that he didn't feel any shame or remorse. There was no shock or revulsion at the sight of chilling like before. In fact, deep inside, the former healer had to admit that he liked it, the taking of a life by force. He had used his healing skills to avoid fighting, to make himself far too valuable to ever risk in combat. And whichever side won would always need the services of a healer. He had tried to be beyond violence, not from the love of life, but from the fear of losing his own. Since childhood, Glassman had been terrified of being hurt. Just a sniveling coward, yellow to his bones. But on this mission for Kinnison, he found that new doors were opening inside his mind, and the rush of a chill was becoming a delight, only equaled by the release of sex. Something deep inside the man rose to fight off the growing madness, tried and failed. Glassman felt its departure and stood very alone in the middle of the ville, knowing that with this death he had crossed a line and would never be the same again.

"Colonel Mitchum!" he bellowed, still staring at the ground.

Hobbling through the crowd of busy slaves, the sec chief stopped a few yards away from the captain. He glanced once at his aced baron, then didn't give the headless corpse another thought.

"Yes, sir," Mitchum said, resting awkwardly on his crutch. The colonel was unshaved, having stood watch with his men through the long night. His clothes were filthy, a leg and an arm stiffly wrapped in bloody bandages. The gun belt from around his waist was slung across his chest in the manner of a bandolier, the holstered flintlock in easy reach of his good arm.

"Ryan gave you those wounds," Glassman stated.

"Yes, sir, he did," Mitchum growled, and felt the rush of hatred warm his face.

A slave cried out in triumph, lifting a hinge from the hot ashes and waving it about. An overseer snatched away the object and whipped the woman back to work.

"Find Ryan before he leaves this island and he is yours to punish for a day," Glassman stated. "Execute the others on the spot. Understand me? No rape, no games, just put lead in their head."

The words "or else" weren't said aloud, but Mitchum clearly heard them spoken anyway.

"Then I'm baron here," Mitchum said bluntly, standing a little taller.

There was a momentary pause. "If you find Ryan, yes. Until then, I'm in charge."

"Deal. Give me his revolver," Mitchum said eagerly, jerking his chin at the dead man.

Glassman gestured and one of the local sec men removed the gun belt from the body and gave it to Mitchum. The cracked leather was speckled with gray and red, but the colonel didn't care. He was going to be the baron here! Mitchum draped the gun belt over his other shoulder, the two different blasters crisscrossing his chest.

"They have the Juggernaut, and if they drove over the grasslands, they could be anywhere on the island by now," Mitchum said, checking the draw on the S&W .22 revolver. "Ryan had mentioned wanting a boat, and there's only three villes on the island to steal one. Cargo ville burned their boats because of the plague—Ryan and his people told us about it. Ours are too well guarded, which leaves Cascade."

Teams of men began to drag the first of the felled trees into the ville.

"Never heard of the place," Glassman said suspiciously.

Mitchum grinned. "Little ville to the south, mostly predark ruins built on top of a waterfall. Bitch to see from the ocean. The mist from the fall sort of hides it from sight."

Glassman wasn't overly disturbed by the news. Kinnison knew about the dozens of villes scattered throughout the Thousand Islands that remained hidden to avoid paying tribute to him. None was very big, or of any military importance. Aside from the armed dockyard of the pirate fleet.

"How far away is it?" he asked.

"Five days on horseback. Two by sea. You have to arc far around our island if going south to avoid the reefs. Can't take the northern route at all, unless you're willing to pay the toll.''

"Pirates?" Glassman asked, feeling a rush of excitement over the prospect of battle.

Scratching at his stubble, Mitchum frowned. "Wish it was. Those we could handle. An old deeper lives off the north shore. It might be safe. He sleeps a lot, but when he wakes up hungry…''

"Fair enough. Get your men ready. We leave in an hour."

The taste of ashes filling his mouth from the smoke, Mitchum hawked and spit. "South it is."

"For us," Captain Glassman stated. "But where that wag can roll, horses can run. You're to take troops straight across the island, while we steam around. Then we'll crush them between us in a two-sided attack at Cascade."

"Should work," Mitchum said thoughtfully, then added, "if you give us some Firebirds."

The captain turned his head sideways, as if looking away from the sec man, but his eyes never left Mitchum. "You want more," he said stiffly. "And yet the records I was given by the lord baron say this ville owns eight already."

"Not anymore," Mitchum said hatefully, both hands clenched into hard fists. "They've sort of been stolen."

Chapter Fourteen

As the miles rolled by, the companions ate a cold meal from MRE packs, their blasters close at hand. On a couple of occasions, they saw more of the muties staggering about in the soggy fields, then a pack of them ripping apart a drowned opossum. At the first hint of the noisy wag's badly tuned engine, the stickies swarmed after the vehicle, but were easily outdistanced. Keeping a careful watch on the dashboard, Krysty balanced the rising engine temperature against getting away from the stickies. She took a life only when necessary, and would rather bypass the muties than brutally run them over.

After a few hours, Jak took Krysty's place behind the wheel, and later on in the day, Ryan replaced him. Each shift was kept short, as steering through the thick mud was exhausting work. Half-blind from the dirty windshield, each driver had to stay alert for buried logs and rocks, holding on to the steering wheel with both hands to keep from losing control.

"How are we doing?" Mildred asked, grabbing the luggage rack bolted to the ceiling and walking to the front of the school bus. An experienced car driver before being frozen, she was worried about the old engine. It had probably been quite a while since the wag had been driven anywhere, and a trip like this would be hard on a well-maintained vehicle.

"Engine is running hot, and the oil pressure is low, but we already knew there was a leak somewhere. You can see blue in the exhaust," Ryan said, darting a glance at the dashboard. "Aside from that, the wag is okay. But we better start looking for a place to stop and refuel. The tank is almost dry."

"Need bushes, too," Dean admitted in a husky voice, his legs tightly crossed. "Some things can't be done out the window of a moving wag."

"Yes, they can," J.B. said, from under his hat. "It just ain't very comfortable."

Suddenly, the bus dipped slightly and the sound of the engine rose in pitch as it revved higher, struggling to compensate. Grinding gears, Ryan pumped the gas pedal and fought to keep the engine operating. But their speed dropped to a mere crawl, and the engine temperature gauge rose alarmingly.

"What's wrong, damage from that stickie we hit?" J.B. asked, coming fully awake in an instant.

"Fucking mud again," he cursed, revving the engine and shifting to a higher gear. The bus sluggishly waddled along, then backfired from the rush of fuel. "It's different, thicker or something. Can't seem to get any speed."

Appearing from a clump of bushes, a stickie holding the bedraggled body of a rat watched the long wag roll by and started after it hooting in delight.

"Sinking?" Jak demanded, grabbing his backpack and jacket.

"Not mud this time," Mildred said. "It's quicksand."

Ryan muttered a curse. A tree branch wasn't going to work on that crap. If they halted to refuel, the wag would get jammed like a misfire in the ejector port. They couldn't stop for any reason.

"Get that scope up here," he barked. "We need to find dry land, and I mean now."

Quickly, Mildred got out of the way, and the Armorer went to the front of the wag, the Navy longeyes already in his grip. Fully extending the antique, J.B. scanned the landscape ahead of the struggling wag.

"Don't go to the left. I think that's a lake," he reported. "More mud straight ahead on your twelve, but I see trees to the right. Not sure the bus can drive between the trunks they're so close, but that has to be solid ground."

"Where?" Ryan asked, adjusting the clutch as the wag backfired again, even louder than before.

"Mile, mebbe two. On your three."

"See them."

"Incoming," Dean said calmly, jacking the slide on his Browning. "We got a stickie on our tail."

"Don't shoot it," Ryan ordered. "It may be able to reach us because we're moving so slow, but it can't get in. Too well armored."

The boy nodded and put his blaster to a blaster-port and tracked the approach of the humanoid creature. It caught the mired bus easily and began to hit the outside armor plating with its suckered hands, desperately trying to find a way in.

"Heading for the rear door," Dean announced, the barrel of his Browning semiautomatic pistol never wavering. Just then, the handle jiggled and an inhuman face appeared in the grille-covered panel of the exit.

"Shitfire. I need that window clear to see behind us," Ryan growled, fighting to alter the course of the vehicle toward the trees. "Ace it."

The Browning barked once, and a hot brass casing kicked from the side of the blaster and hit the floor to roll away under the rows of seats.

"He's gone," Dean stated.

Ryan could only grunt in reply, both of his hands white-knuckle tight on the steering wheel. Ahead, he could see it was a real forest, just what they wanted. But a mob of stickies was forming between the trees and the companions, almost as if they understood what was happening.

Checking over his LeMat, Doc looked in that same direction and blanched. There was an army coming their way, thirty, maybe forty of the muties.

"Can we go around them, maybe refuel from inside?" Mildred asked, pulling a box of cartridges from her backpack and stuffing them into a pocket. "Rip up the floorboards or something."

"That would only make us sink for sure," J.B. grumbled, thumbing rounds into the S&W M-4000 shotgun and laying it aside.

"Gaia, look at them," Krysty said, staring out the dirty window. "The engine noise must be pulling in every stickie for miles. Mebbe the whole valley."

"Could live here," Jak said, opening his Colt Python to check the rounds. Satisfied, he closed the cylinder with a gentle pressure so as not to damage the catch. "Wait for prey, like hellflowers and trapdoor spiders."

"Lord, I hope not," Mildred replied, checking the load in her own weapon. "Because that would mean it works, and they eat regularly."

Doc began to mutter in that strange singsong manner that meant he was quoting somebody from the past. "'Lieutenant Broadhead, I'm only an engineer. Here to build a bridge,'" the old man whispered hoarsely. "'What do I know about Zulu warriors?'"

Finally pointed straight for the forest, Ryan

scowled as he saw the stickies stop and just stand there, waiting for the bus to come to them. Was it possible that these swamp stickies were smarter than the ones in the Deathlands? They would find out any minute now.

"Here they come," Ryan said, arms shaking as he controlled the bus.

As the vehicle sloshed into the mob, the stickies parted and didn't attack as expected, but started to climb onto the wag, as if trying to drag it down by their sheer weight. Worst of all, it was working. The bus slowed even more, the engine temperature drastically rose and the wag sank deeper into the muck. The engine backfired again, then again, from the buildup of back pressure as the tailpipes became blocked by the quicksand.

To the people inside, the noise sounded exactly like gunshots. The stickies went crazy, hooting loudly and beating the wag with their sucker-covered hands. In a matter of seconds, the bus was coated with them, a busty female hanging off the iron grid covering the front windshield, several walking on the roof, dozens of hands beating on the sheet steel blocking the side windows, making a rumbling noise like thunder. Two muties were tugging on the right-front access door, and several more rode the back bumper, hitting the grid-covered windows and exit door. Then the glass in a window shattered, and arms were thrust into the wag, eagerly searching for prey. But the jagged shards of glass ringing the frame sliced the limbs apart, fingers and suckers raining to the floor, and the stickies fought one another to pull themselves loose, which only worsened the damage.

But with the glass gone, their calls became even louder. Mixed with the banging on the sheet metal it was deafening, and the companions couldn't talk to one another. As if sensing defeat of some kind, the muties redoubled the attack, smashing a headlight, ripping off the wiper blades and radio antenna, and bits of decorating molding went flying away.

"They're testing our defenses," J.B. said, swinging the Uzi to point in every direction. The noise and the hooting masked their numbers, making the thirty sound like a hundred.

"Smart," Doc rumbled, thumbing back the hammer on his piece.

"Simple animal instinct," Mildred retorted. "Often, baboons do this sort of thing at zoos to tease the tourists."

Ryan glared hatefully at the stickie clinging to the glass of his tiny ventilation window. Unable to shoot the thing on the windshield, Ryan hit the horn. The startled female dangling from the windshield dropped off and was run over by the wag. But then a furious male leaped upon the windshield to attack the man and was instantly impaled on the array of knives welded to the iron grid. The slick blades piercing every limb, the dying creature pumped out its life onto the dirty glass, effectively blocking Ryan's vision of the trees ahead. The one-eyed warrior knew that a crash was imminent, but there was no way he was going to slow.

Savagely twisting the wheel back and forth, he sent the bus rocking side to side, the spikes on the tires slashing the legs of the muties running along, the crippled creatures falling, clutching at the damaged limbs. Several tumbled from the roof and landed on their brethren, or fell under the deadly wheels.

But the smell of their own blood fed the madness of the muties, and the beating on the wag increased until there was a screech of tortured metal, and the sheet steel covering a side window was bent away. Multiple hands and faces moved over the predark glass searching for an opening. Now there was nothing between the humans and the mutants but a pane of safety glass more than a century old.

"Blades first," Jak growled, a knife in each hand.

"Indeed," Doc rumbled, holstering the LeMat and pulling the length of Spanish steel from its ebony sheath.

As the safety glass shattered in a spray of tiny squares, Jak jerked both hands forward. Hooting in pain, two stickies beat at the knives sticking out of their faces and dropped away. Another tried to take their place, and Doc lunged at it, the sword slicing open its throat with surgical precision. Gushing blood, the invader dropped into the crowd. But more took its place, and other sections of sheet metal started bending away under the pressure of the enraged muties.

Briefly, Dean looked at the case of Firebirds. If he could just get outside, the missiles would fly away and explode in the distance, drawing the mob away. But if he was stupe enough to launch a rocket from inside the bus, the back-blast of exhaust would fill the wag and burn them alive. They had enough armament to stop a tank, and it was useless against some mud-covered stickies.

Ryan could see the trees were close and tried to spot a path or something to use, but blood and flopping limbs of the aced mutie were making that nearly impossible. Once more, he tried for his blaster to blow off its head and get an unobstructed view. But the moment he let go, the bus veered to the side, and he was forced to use both hands to steer.

By now, the stickies were all over the wag, their suction-cupped fingers playing with the windows and tugging on the doors. The companions stabbed at anything that came through the broken windows, the interior of the wag getting brighter with the removal of every panel of steel. Krysty tracked the ones on top with her blaster, but withheld firing. She wouldn't waste ammo on a guess.

"Dumb ass bastard welder, couldn't weld for shit!" J.B. cursed, his hands tight on the grip of the Uzi.

There was a crash from the rear of the bus, and the back door unexpectedly swung open. A young stickie was halfway through the small window, triumphantly holding the latch. It hooted in victory, and Dean blew it away. Then an adult swung in from the side and tried to climb over the stack of crates. From the far end of the wag, Doc fired the LeMat, the strident discharge of the hogleg seeming even louder in the confines of the bus. The stickie literally flew backward out the open doorway, its head a crushed mess.

Scrambling through the supplies, Jak reached the door just as another mutie climbed inside. Spinning sideways, the teenager buried his combat boot into the mutie's stomach, driving it outside. Then grabbing the handle, Jak hauled the door shut and forced the locking bolt into place.

"Too close," he grunted, flinching as a gob of quicksand was flung through the hole to splatter on the wall. Were the muties throwing that to blind the teenager? Just how smart were these things?

"How the hell can they run through quicksand?" Dean demanded, ducking another gob sailing in through the busted side window.

"Check the deader on the windshield," Krysty snapped. "It's got webbed feet, like snowshoes."

Looking at the corpse, Mildred was amazed at the evolution of such a useful appendage.

Once more the stickies tried for the broken windows, and the companions hacked away at the hairless limbs, fingers and mouthing suckers falling to the floor. Again and again, Doc thrust deeply with his sword, going for throats and bellies. Then a stickie grabbed the blade and wrestled it from his grip with surprising strength. The creature tried to escape with its prize, but Jak grabbed the arm and pinned it to a seat, while Doc tried to force open the stubby fingers to get back his blade. But the stubborn creature refused to relinquish the weapon, so Doc was forced to hack off the fingers with his belt knife to reclaim the sword. Shrieking, the creature tumbled off the bus, cradling its destroyed hand.

Holding on to the luggage rack, J.B. went to the front of the wag. "Go faster," he urged.

"Can't. Bastard engine is at the red line now," Ryan shot back. The gauges on the dashboard flashed in warning, and the wag was barely traveling twenty miles per hour. "I push any harder, it'll blow."

"Then we start shooting," the Armorer said, and sent a burst through the access door. The muties fumbling with the portal were blown off in a shower of glass, blood going everywhere.

In response, windows smashed on every side, and dozens of arms reached through to grab for the companions. A sucker-covered hand touched Mildred's med kit on a seat and pulled it to a window. The straps caught on the iron grid, and Mildred emptied her blaster outside until the stickie let go and the med kit dropped to the floor. She snatched it away and tossed it onto the luggage rack out of reach.

But the deadly hands were everywhere, clawing for anything edible. In the rear, a Firebird was hauled away, and the plastic cover of a seat was ripped off, springs and foam padding bursting free from their tight confines. A canteen was taken, then an empty MRE envelope. The mutie attack was mindless, but unrelenting, and the companions raked the windows with blasterfire, hot lead tearing off chunks of the swamp dwellers. Mutie fingers and suckers rolling around loosely with the spent brass made walking tricky on the blood-streaked floor. A stickie got Krysty by the hair, and the woman cried out in agony as the creature tried to pull her along by the living filaments. Doc placed the LeMat on the thing's wrist and blew its hand off. Weakly, Krysty dropped to a seat, violently trembling, then slowly stood and began to fire again without regard for conserving ammo.

Opening the side vent, Ryan blew the knee off one trying to crawl onto the hood. The mutie fell, thick blood streaking the polished metal. Reaching through the angled vent, Ryan tried to push off the deader on the grid and only managed to cut his arm in the process.

Crouching, Ryan saw the trees were only yards away, and then he noticed a breach in the woods, a pathway that led into the cool greenery. He didn't give a damn where it went, as long as it was away from this nightmarish hellzone.

A steady hammering could be heard above the blasterfire. Suddenly, the back door flew open and a stickie climbed into the bus. It tried to crawl over the stacks of supplies and failed, then began tossing the boxes of food and ammo outside to clear a path for the others right behind. Krysty fired twice, winging the creature in the shoulder, then Mildred triggered the shotgun, blowing the mutie to pieces and destroying several of the boxes in the process.

"Close that door!" she bellowed, racking the slide.

"Can't. It's gone," Dean replied, firing at a leg that creeped into view on the bumper. There was an answering hoot, and the wounded limb was withdrawn for the moment.

"What mean, gone?" Jak demanded, thumbing fresh shells into his exhausted weapon. A stickie reached for the teen from behind, and J.B. put a burst from the Uzi into its face.

"They tore it off!" he replied, dropping a clip to slap in a fresh magazine. "The door's a hundred feet away and sinking."

"How many more are there?" Mildred asked urgently. "Anybody keeping count of the dead?"

"Fifteen aced," Jak replied. "About ten more."

"Mebbe twelve," J.B. added grimly.

Pursing her lips, the physician used a word that her father the Baptist preacher used to pretend didn't even exist.

"Can't let them whittle us down," Krysty said, her hair coiled tightly to her head to prevent further grabs. "Okay, we form a firing line, right here." Kneeling on the slaughterhouse floor, the woman pointed her weapon at the rear door. The others joined her in a cluster and waited, panting for breath.

"On my command," Krysty said sternly.

A stickie reached into the bus and paused, expecting to be attacked. When nothing happened, it dared to dart inside and paused, staring at the motionless humans. Then hooting loudly, it began to climb over the stacks of crates as more stickies swarmed into the vehicle. As the creatures got past the boxes, they charged up the aisle for the motionless people.

"Eight," Krysty said, as the muties rushed closer, arms extended. "Nine, ten of them inside!"

"That's the lot. Chill the fuckers!" J.B. shouted, cutting loose with the Uzi on full-auto, the compact machine pistol chattering on and on as he emptied a full clip into the massed targets.

Doc and Jak threw thunder from their big-bore handcannons, misshapen heads exploding from every hit. Krysty and Dean maintained a steady discharge into the crowd with their blasters, as J.B. reloaded and rode the Uzi into a tight grouping. Holstering her .38, Mildred stood and used the shotgun, the fléchette rounds tearing the muties into screaming hamburger, intestines slithering out of broken bodies, blood washing over the rubber mats in a tide of death.

Pausing to reload, the companions stared into the swirling mists of acrid gunsmoke, waiting for the next wave of muties. But as the smoke cleared from the winds pouring in through the smashed windows, they saw only twitching bodies piled on the floor and seats. A motion under the seats caught Dean's attention, and, walking over, he knelt in the blood and fired a round into the head of the stickie trying to crawl away. It jerked once, then went still.

"Two more on the roof," Ryan said, trying to switch on the defroster and drain some heat from the boiling engine.

"Mine," Jak said, angrily scowling at the ceiling.

Then the bus violently shook as it hit something under the bog, and started bumping along as if rolling over railroad tracks. Their speed increasing, the front end lifted clear and the vehicle drove out of the quicksand and onto solid ground.

"We're out!" Ryan announced, slightly easing his hunched position behind the wheel.

"Thank God," Mildred said, slumping into a chair.

Dodging saplings and rocks, Ryan headed for the path, the off-balance tires shuddering from every irregularity in the ground. Stickies could be heard moving about and hooting loudly on the roof.

"There's a road!" Krysty said, standing alongside the man, trying to look over the aced mutie. "Jog left!"

Downshifting, Ryan twisted the steering wheel, and the rough vibrations smoothed. Predark pavement? Ryan hit the gas and the bus rapidly built speed as it raced along the cracked strip of old asphalt. Far behind, a couple of stickies ran out of the quicksand, but were quickly left behind in the dust.

Muffled footsteps could be heard on the roof, and Jak tracked their progress with his weapon. "Still got them," he growled menacingly.

"We're far enough away," J.B. said, holding on

to the luggage rack to stay erect. "Might as well, slow down and refuel."

"After we get rid of our uninvited guests," Doc said, shifting the fire selector pin of the handcannon to the shotgun round.

"Especially this bastard," Ryan complained, bobbing his head to try to see around the bedraggled corpse on the windshield. Blood was still trickling from the multiple knife-blade wounds, and it was becoming impossible to see clearly. The wiper blades were long gone, causalities of the stickie attack.

"I'll get him," Krysty offered and went to stand by the access door, a slim hand holding on to the chrome-plated pole, as she waited for the wag to stop.

Just as Ryan started to downshift, he saw the fallen tree lying across the road ahead of them, a massive decaying log that a walking man could easily step over. But for the wag it was an impassable palisade. Chunks of rubble lined the predark road on both sides, giving him nowhere to turn, and with the tree trunk only yards away there was virtually no time to slow. Only one choice then.

"Roadblock!" he yelled, standing on the brakes and throwing the gears into reverse. "Brace yourselves!"

Instantly, the wag bucked as if hitting an invisible wall. Every loose item in the vehicle was thrown to the front, a deluge of bodies and boxes burying the companions. A pair of hooting muties flew off the roof and smashed into a tree, the bodies wrapping bonelessly around stout branches.

Brakes squealing, engine roaring, the wag decelerated from fifty to thirty miles per hour in only seconds. Then the screeching transmission exploded from the strain of the reversal, the spinning gears tearing themselves apart and shotgunning out of the floor. Ryan fought the wheel as the speed dropped further, but it wasn't enough, and the wag slammed into the old tree, plowing through in an explosion of rotten wood. The collision sent the vehicle airborne for a few yards, then dropped to slam onto the asphalt in a resounding crash of crumpling metal and smashing glass. The radiator erupted into a geyser of steam, the axles broke apart and the spinning tires shot away.

Still in motion from sheer inertia, the wreck threw off a spray of sparks from the chassis scraping along the rough surface of the roadway. Shuddering, jerking, clanging, the destroyed wag noisily ground to a halt a good fifty paces farther down the road.

Only the steady ticking of hot metal slowly cooling broke the profound silence of the roadway.

Chapter Fifteen

Crouching sec men armed with knives and flint-locks stole toward the smoking ruins of the school bus.

A trapped bubble of air rose from the quicksand lake to burst on the surface, sounding very much like a human cough. Condors flew high in the stormy sky above, and tropical birds twittered in the oak and birch trees of the nearby forest, waiting for the night when they could hunt. Darting from stone to weed, a rat scurried along the ground with an ear held triumphantly in its jaw. The tattered bodies of the fallen stickies were strewed along two miles of mud and quicksand, ending in the crumpled remains of the wrecked school bus. A column of smoke rose from the quietly burning engine, and the rear door was gone, showing piles of crates and more corpses inside.

A short distance away, a dozen more soldiers sat on their horses with longblasters pressed to their shoulders, shiny new flint in every weapon and tense fingers on the triggers.

"If there's a God still in heaven, hear my plea,"

a corporal whispered hoarsely. "Let the outlanders still live, so I may avenge my brother."

Mitchum leaned over in his saddle and pressed the point of his knife to the sec man's throat. A drop of blood rose from the skin and flowed easily along the razor-sharp blade.

"Don't speak again without my permission," Mitchum whispered, applying more pressure. The sec man inhaled sharply, craning back his head to keep from being cut. "Or I will wear you as boots. I learned many things as a prisoner of the cannies. Skinning a fool was only the beginning."

"They killed my brother," the corporal said without moving his jaw. He could feel the warm blood flow down his throat. "Shot him in the back in cold blood. Want them bad."

Mitchum studied the rage in the man's eyes and returned the blade to its sheath. "The man who died in the mountains with us," he said slowly. "Trying to outdraw the white-skinned man."

"That was Cob, my older bro," the sec man grunted. "I'm Whyte."

"Fair fight. I was there," the officer said out of the side of his mouth, now watching the troopers creep inside the bus. The men with longblasters got tense, leaning forward in anticipation to the brutal recoil of their black-powder weapons.

"Don't care," Whyte snarled, looking up at the

mounted officer, reaching for his own knife. "I want them!"

Smoothly, Mitchum drew his blaster and slapped the corporal on the back of the neck just below the swell of the skull. Whyte didn't even gasp as he limply dropped to the ground. His hands dug at the pavement for a moment, then stopped, but his back rose and fell in the rhythm of life.

"Anybody else speaks out of turn," Mitchum said softly, cocking back the hammer of his piece, "and he dies on the spot. Now drag this feeb away and remove the corporal stripes from his shirt. He's a private now."

A private saluted the officer and hauled the unconscious trooper away just as a sec man appeared at the rear of the bus. He splayed an empty hand, closed it, then cut the air with a flat palm.

"Scorch!" Mitchum spit angrily, and thumped his heels on the horse's rump to get it moving. Reaching the wreck, he slid off the animal and tethered the reins to a broken sapling. There were lots of them about, forming an orderly path that zigzagged to the vehicle. The driver had to have been dying or blind to hit so many.

"Any sign they had been inside?" Mitchum demanded of the waiting sec men.

The leader of the recce saluted. "Yes, sir. Lots of blood and spent brass is everywhere."

"Must of been a hell of a fight," another man

agreed. "There be bullet holes in the windows and roof."

"A gangbang," the colonel stated gruffly. The swamp stickies had been doing a lot of that lately. Attacking in larger and larger groups to ace passing norms. Blasters weren't stopping them anymore.

"Mebbe they are aced, sir," a corporal suggested, peeking in through a busted window frame. "And something dragged the bodies away. Lots of things will eat norm flesh that's black with rot, but never touch a fresh mutie corpse."

"That's true," the sergeant agreed, kicking at some debris on the cracked pavement.

Yes, it was possible, even likely, but Mitchum didn't trust such an easy answer. He wouldn't believe Ryan was dead until he saw the body and cut out its heart.

"What about their possessions?" Mitchum demanded, walking around the twisted shell of the broken wag. "Are their backpacks or the rapidfires still inside?"

"No, sir," a private answered. "We looked, but those are gone."

"They're alive!" Mitchum growled, slamming a fist into the side of the bus, denting the weakened metal. Ryan and his people were alive and had escaped again. Animals might have dragged away the bodies, but not the blasters.

"What a heap of dreck," a sergeant snorted in

disgust. "Must of hit that log and gone flying. Shit-fire, both axles are busted to pieces, and the engine block is cracked. Look at that oil spill! There's no way I could fix this wag. It was in better shape when we dug it out of those ruins."

"Might be able to find a few parts that work," a private suggested, lifting a wheel-bearing assembly from one of the axles. It was slightly bent, but still should work. He tucked it into a pocket.

"Stop that," Mitchum directed, going for his horse. "We'll scav for anything usable on the return. But first we find those rad-sucking outlanders and send them to Davey in pieces."

Mounting his horse, he walked it to the middle of the roadway, watching the trees for snipers. Nothing was stirring, but he didn't relax. Something was terribly wrong here; he just didn't know what it was.

"I want a recce of the whole area," Mitchum directed. "If they walked away, there'll be tracks. Sergeant, form three teams of five men. The outlanders are still alive, and we will find them!"

"Yes, sir!" the sergeant replied with a smart salute.

Then a voice shouted from inside the wag. "Hey, there's a pile of flintlocks in here, and they ain't even scratched!"

"Any ammo?" another asked, walking closer.

"Sure! Lots!"

Battle instincts flared, and Mitchum spun in the saddle.

"Don't touch those!" he bellowed. "It's a trap!"

But the warning was too late. A sec man cried out as something inside the bus burst into a sizzling chem spray. There followed a small explosion, then a roaring whoosh as flames filled the bus, stretching out the windows and doorways to completely engulf the vehicle in a rapidly expanding fireball.

"They boobied the fuel!" a man shrieked as a burning wave of shine blew him out the door, clothes and hair instantly bursting into flames.

Desperately covering his face, Mitchum dropped behind his horse for protection as the hellstorm washed over the group of startled sec men, igniting them like greasy torches.

The conflagration consumed the entire area, the growing flames reaching to the trees, and the screams of the dying men seemed to last forever.

PUSHING THEIR WAY through the dense greenery, Ryan stopped as Krysty whirled to look behind them.

"Trouble?" he asked, grabbing his blaster.

"They found the booby," she said. "I pity them."

"Fuck 'em," Jak snarled, limping along. A tree branch had been cut into a crude crutch, and the teenager was stiffly hobbling along, his face a mask of barely contained fury.

Hoisting her med kit, Mildred didn't blame him for being angry. A barrel of shine had fallen on his leg in the crash, giving the teenager a sprained ankle. She had wrapped it tight with wet strips of cloth that would tighten as they dried. Not much, but it was the best she could do. The sprain had to be very painful, but the teenager didn't complain. Mildred had two aspirins she was holding in reserve until nightfall to help him get to sleep. But the more he walked, the worse it would feel.

"Hated to use all of my plas in one shot," J.B. said, removing his hat to wipe off the sweatband with a handkerchief. Then he set the fedora back in place. "But once the wag was broke, that aced the plan of trading it for a ship at Cascade."

"Hope it got them all," Dean said grimly, rubbing his sore ribs. Nothing was broken, but he had a lot of painful bruises.

"I think we can count on some of the sec men surviving," Ryan said, "and that soon these hills will be crawling with troops."

"Can stop reporting back," Jak said, dragging a thumb dramatically across his throat.

"Ace that. We want them to report to the local baron," Ryan explained. "He'll send out troops to hunt for us, and we'll sneak into the ville tonight and steal a boat."

"Dangerous," Krysty said, taking out her canteen and drinking deeply. "But it should work. Surprise will be on our side."

"No other options," Ryan said grimly. They were strangers in enemy territory, with every hand turned against them. Back in the Deathlands, rapidfires offered a man some degree of protection; here they were a death warrant.

"Needs drive where the devil must," Doc rumbled cryptically. "We didn't start this conflict, but by God we shall finish it!"

"I just want to leave," Ryan said, checking the clip in his handblaster. "Not interested in starting a war. Too many of them, and we're low on ammo. I have twelve rounds for the SIG-Sauer. Two mags of five for the Steyr."

"Four," Jak said, patting the blaster on his hip. "And lost knife stickie fell out window."

"Three rounds," Krysty said. "And one is a black-powder reload that might not work."

"Two," Mildred said.

"Nine," Dean announced proudly. "Full clip."

"Uzi is out," J.B. stated. "Six rounds for the scattergun."

Fireblast! They wasted a ton of precious ammo in the fight with the stickies. At least they still had most of their food and water. "How much farther to the ville?"

Pulling out a sextant, J.B. shot the sun and did

some quick calculations. The he carefully unfolded a map. Found in a redoubt, it was old and faded, the plastic coating worn thin in spots, but the priceless antique was still readable.

"Dark night, I have no idea where we are," he complained, looking upward to scowl at the sun partially hidden by storm clouds. "According to my map, we're half a mile in the ocean."

"Nuke quakes must have moved the island," Krysty said.

"So we're lost," Mildred stated with a frown.

"Pretty much," he said, tucking the sextant inside his shirt. "We know the ville is somewhere close, and to the south. That's it."

Pulling out his compass, J.B. checked the direction. "And south should be that way," he pointed. "Toward those big trees with the flower— Hey!"

Everybody waited expectantly while J.B. stared at his compass. "There it is again," he muttered.

"What?" Dean asked, craning his neck to see.

He showed the boy. "Every couple of seconds, the compass needle flicks to the west. Something electrical that way," J.B. stated, looking at the dense greenery to their right. "Something big and still in operation."

"A pulsating magnetic field," Mildred said thoughtfully. "If Cascade had an airport before, it could be the ILM beacons for the landing field."

"Not south, west," Jak said, leaning against a

tree and massaging his armpit where the crutch had been rubbing.

Listening to the sounds of the forest, Ryan slowly said, "It's got to be close. The atmosphere is so fucked up with rads that mag fields can't reach very far. A mile or so, at the most."

"Beacon is a sort of radio?" Dean asked.

Still studying the compass, J.B. nodded. "Yes."

"Very close, then," Krysty agreed, her hair fanning outward. "And the landing field should be far away from the buildings. The ville may not even know it's there."

"Could be a good place to rest," Mildred added.

Jak shot her an angry look, then relented and shrugged. He was a crip at the moment. Only a stupe would deny it.

"Sounds good. Dean, think you can climb one of these," Ryan asked, thumping the trunk of a mutated oak, "and get us a recce?"

The boy studied the tree closely. "Sure," he stated, and dropped his backpack to the ground. Tightening his belt, the boy started shimmying up the thick trunk and disappeared into the foliage.

"Anything?" his father shouted.

"Nothing yet!" came back the answer. "Wait a minute."

The companions drew closer to the tree, hands on their weapons in case of trouble. A minute passed, then several, their expressions began to turn worried.

"Dean?" Krysty called gently through cupped hands.

But only the rustle of leaves responded, a few colorful birds taking flight from the dense overhang of greenery.

"I'm going after him," Ryan declared, passing the Steyr to the redhead. Dropping his backpack, the man grabbed a low limb and chinned himself off the ground just as Dean dropped through the leaves to land sprawling in the bushes.

"Plane," the boy said standing, his face bright with excitement. "Think I found a plane!"

"In the air?" Mildred asked in concern, scanning the sky through the holes in the sylvan canopy. It was one of her biggest worries. Even worse than a runaway plague. Anybody who got a powered airplane into the sky could seize absolute control of the Deathlands. There were few enough weapons working these days, and nothing that would challenge a skyfighter. Even an old box kite like the Wright brothers made for the U.S. government to use in World War I and some black-powder bombs would be enough. Just the threat of death from above would make most villes surrender automatically. The destruction of the world from the sky bombs had burned a very real fear of aerial attacks into the very souls of the human survivors.

Dean shook his head. "No, just caught in the branches. About a mile away. Big one. Looks intact."

"Useless," Krysty said. "If it's visible, it's been looted."

The boy shook his head. "No way you could find it from the ground. Got to be high to see it."

There was a pause. "I think," he added honestly.

"Even crumbling walls can offer shelter," Doc offered as comment.

"An airplane," Ryan muttered, rubbing his chin. "Same direction as the pulse?"

"Yes, Dad."

"Remember what the Trader taught us about crashed planes," J.B. said, patting his empty Uzi machine pistol.

"Just what I was thinking," the Deathlands warrior said, almost grinning. Shelter or not, there could be salvage. Blasters, ammo, food, hidden sagely away where nobody would ever find them. Lots of things they needed.

"Let's check it out," Ryan said, and started pushing a path through the tangled growth.

GROANING SOFTLY, Whyte awoke to a pounding headache and the stink of burning flesh. Almost immediately, there was a violent explosion, and something fell alongside the sec man with a thump. As his vision cleared, Whyte saw it was a dead stickie with a gaping hole in its bleeding chest. The mutie worked its suckers a few times as if fighting for life, then went still.

Hastily scrambling away, the sec man drew his own blaster and scanned the area for more of the muties. There were none, but he gasped upon seeing the smoking remains of a huge explosion.

The bus was spread wide open, resembling a metal flower that had been set on fire. Thick black smoke from the chassis was curling high into the overcast sky. The charred remains of norms and horses lay strewed across the asphalt, many of the bodies in pieces as if torn apart by wild animals.

After a moment, he realized it had to be from their ammo pouches detonating when the men were set on fire from the explosion. Cooked alive, then blown in two. Black dust, what a bad way to get aced. Wasn't even quick.

"A bastard trap," Whyte growled angrily. "Triple damn the outlanders. I'll make them pay."

"Over here!" a voice called.

Spinning, Whyte cocked back the hammer on his big flintlock. But only the dead were in sight, skins burned black, hair gone and clothing reduced to a layer of ash over the charred remains. Then he noticed a smoking blaster being waved from behind the sprawled body of a cooked horse. Approaching carefully, the sec man went around the chilled animal to discover Colonel Mitchum on the ground, his legs pinned under the beast from the knees down.

"Get this off me!" Mitchum ordered brusquely, wriggling.

"Yes, sir," Whyte replied, and grabbed the reins. But as he pulled they broke apart, the leather straps severely weakened from the firestorm.

"Get a longblaster," the colonel directed. "Shove it underneath and I can drag myself out. Hurry! My legs went numb an hour ago."

"Gotcha," Whyte said, rummaging around until he found a flintlock rifle that hadn't been blown apart when its ammo cooked off from the heat. Carefully shoving the barrel under the limp beast, Whyte shoved hard upward and the half ton of deadweight slowly lifted off the ground.

Grunting from the exertion, Mitchum wriggled free, leaving his boots trapped under the beast, and rolled away. Whyte released the rifle and let the carcass drop.

"It was you," the sec man said awkwardly. "You shot that stickie coming for me."

"Of course," Mitchum growled, massaging his legs and bare feet. With the return of circulation, pins and needles were making his legs tingle painfully and he rode out the return of feeling, not daring to move an inch.

"You saved my life," Whyte said, feeling angry and confused at the same time.

"Had to," Mitchum said, trying to stand and surprised to find that he could. His legs were throbbing like drums, but strength was returning faster than expected. Excellent. First good thing that had happened on this accursed island in months.

"You saved my life 'cause we're fellow sec men," Whyte said in an unaccustomed rush of pride. "Sir, I...I..."

"I shot the mutie because I needed you to move the fucking horse," the colonel snapped, pulling the Colt Woodsman .22 from his belt. "Thanks, feeb."

As Whyte gasped, Mitchum emptied the tiny revolver into the sec man. The small slugs drove the trooper backward, but he was still standing when they stopped coming. Blood soaking his shirt and pants, Whyte fought for breath as he tried to draw his own blaster, but the weapon dropped from nerveless fingers.

"Also needed your boots," Mitchum said as he calmly picked up the fallen weapon and finished the job.

Shoving the massive .75 flintlock into his belt, the colonel then tossed away the useless predark revolver. Five rounds and the man had still been standing. What kind of a shitty weapon was that?

Stripping the warm corpse of footwear, blaster and ammo, the colonel got dressed and reloaded the hot blaster. Then he proceeded to search among the dead for what supplies and additional weapons he could find. When he was finished, the sec chief had a little food and no water, but a good knife, two handcannons, a single longblaster, plus plenty of shot and lead. More than enough.

"Now it's your turn, Ryan," Mitchum muttered as he stumbled into the forest, searching the ground for the tracks of the hated outlanders.

Don't miss

SHADOW FORTRESS,

the exciting conclusion of
THE SKYDARK CHRONICLES.

James Axler

OUTLANDERS®

SARGASSO PLUNDER

An enforcer turned renegade, Kane and his group learn of a mother lode of tech hidden deep within the ocean of the western territories, a place once known as Seattle. The booty is luring tech traders and gangs, but Kane and Grant dare to infiltrate the salvage operation, knowing that getting in is a life-and-death risk....

In the Outlands, the shocking truth
is humanity's last hope.